HEARTLESS FOE

EVA CHASE

SHADOWBLOOD SOULS - BOOK 4

Heartless Foe

Book 4 in the Shadowblood Souls series

First Digital Edition, 2023

Copyright © 2023 Eva Chase

Cover design: Sanja Balan (Sanja's Covers)

Ebook ISBN: 978-1-998752-23-2

Paperback ISBN: 978-1-998752-24-9

ONE

Riva

I wake up with a jolt of my nerves. A tremor ripples through my throat, as if I've just finished shouting out a name.

Dominic!

My pulse is thundering. I shove myself upright and then sway with a rush of dizziness.

Aches run down my back and arms. The stretch of a scab over a partly healed cut on my shoulder throbs.

I blink, struggling to clear my glazed vision. I'm sitting up on a bed—a large bed, heaped with layers of sheets and a blanket.

Whitewashed walls surround me. A vanity stands in one corner; a deep red rug covers most of the open floor.

It doesn't look like a prison. But I didn't ask to be here, and I've been wrenched away from my men, *again*.

My claws shoot from my fingertips to dig into the soft sheets, and my muscles tense to spring into action. But at the same moment, an overwhelming sensation rolls over me, pinning me in place like a boulder.

We fought so hard. I went so far to carve our way to freedom.

Do the guardians have their own claws so deep in us that we can never totally break free from them?

The overwhelming sense of doom squeezes my lungs.

I clench my jaw against it. Anger sparks beneath the suffocating fog, burning away the thickest patches.

Whoever attacked us this time, they hurt all of us. They sent the truck and van crashing to the side of the road.

The man who loomed over me when I lay bleeding on the roadside and claimed we'd *helped* him—he told the woman with him to shoot Dominic.

What have they done to Dom? What have they done with all of my guys?

The fresh zap of panic breaks through the rest of the fog. I scramble off the bed, my gaze darting around me, cataloguing every inch of the room that might hold a clue to escape.

Around the edges of the rug, worn stone tiles show, giving the impression they've been walked on for decades, if not centuries. Thin beams crisscross the ceiling. Most of it is white like the walls, but delicate designs in pastel colors decorate some of the spaces between the beams.

The curved headboard and the vanity gleam with rich brown wood and old-fashioned bronze detailing. Embroidered pillows lie on a window seat beneath a tall, arched pane that's framed by gauzy red curtains to match the rug.

None of this *looks* like a prison. It's possibly the fanciest room I'd ever been in.

What the fuck is going on? Are King Arthur and his knights going to show up next?

I shake myself out of my daze of confusion enough to take better stock of my body. My upper arm and shoulder are bandaged, as is my side beneath the unfamiliar pastel-blue T-shirt I have on. Bruises mottle my lower arms and my calves when I tug up the legs on my equally new khakis.

They're already fading, but given my shadowblood tendency toward quick healing, that doesn't tell me much.

More disturbing are the metal bands wrapped around my wrists. I could believe they're simply silver bangles if their thick, flat surface didn't suggest a deeper layer of tech inside.

Like the tracking anklets Clancy had us wear. Although these could at least pass for regular jewelry to someone who doesn't know better.

I tug at the bands experimentally and find them unyielding. I suspect even my full supernatural strength couldn't snap them off.

Maybe if I could hit them with a heavy tool… but it's probably better not to test that until I discover exactly what they do. What the consequences would be.

The glint of silver prompts my hand to my chest. But my fingers feel nothing beneath the fabric of my shirt.

My necklace—the cat-and-yarn charm Griffin gave me so many years ago. It's gone.

Did I lose it in the crash, or did our new captors take it from me?

Through the pang of loss, a rosy, citrusy scent tickles my nose. I duck my head lower and realize it's coming from *me*.

When I sniff my arm, the faint perfume winds into my lungs. My stomach knots.

Whoever brought me here, they washed me up as well as bandaged me. Stripped me down and then dressed me up like a doll.

They even rebraided my hair. I trail my fingers over the silver and darker gray strands and feel how smooth the woven locks are, with none of the grit or straggling flyaways from our battle with the terrorists Clancy sent us up against.

As more of the haze in my head clears, I rest my hand against my collarbone. My necklace might be gone, but the three splotches like thumb-sized bruises remain, connecting me to the three men I've confirmed my love for in the most concrete bodily way.

Through our connection, I can sense their location and occasionally flickers of intense emotion. Right now, none of the latter is echoing into me, but I can tell that Andreas, Dominic, and Jacob are nearby. Probably in the same building.

If I can sense Dominic, does that mean he must still be alive? I have no idea how our strange bond would react if one of us died.

Clinging on to a shred of hope, I stalk to the window. As I clamber onto the cushions and brace my hands against the ledge, the scenery beyond the pane steals my breath.

Right below the window, which appears to be on the

second floor of the building, lies a small stretch of tiled patio dotted with neatly trimmed shrubs and bright bursts of potted flowers. A low stone wall forms a border on the far side of the patio.

And past that wall… sweeping mountain ranges of pale brown stone and mottled greenery stretch out as far as my eyes can see, undulating waves of rock draped in warm sunlight. As if I've found myself lost in the middle of a stormy ocean solidified in mid-churn.

I spot what looks like a church tower on a distant hill and maybe a cluster of rooftops even farther abroad, but no human habitation close enough for me to distinguish actual people.

We've definitely come a long way from the tropical island where Clancy and his guardians held us. There's an actual autumn here—some of the trees on the slopes have lost their foliage, leaving them with a vaguely fuzzy appearance. When I press my hand to the glass, a trace of a chill seeps through.

What month is it now? On the guardians' island with its constant summery weather, I lost all sense of the time passing.

I pull myself away from the window to yank open the drawers on the vanity. They're empty, but the closet in the corner holds an assortment of slacks and jeans, tees and sweatshirts, and even a few casual dresses on hangers.

I waver and then tug on a hoodie that makes me feel a little less like a preppy catalogue model. It'd be good to have additional pockets in case I get the chance to stash anything in them.

Then I move to the room's main door. I grip the

handle, preparing to evaluate the resistance the lock gives me.

But the door isn't locked. The knob turns easily in my hand.

My heart stutters with shock. I nudge the door open and find myself staring out into a high-ceilinged hallway lined with more arched doorways and lit by elaborate sconces holding electric candles.

What crazy dream have I stumbled into? I shake my head and am considering outright slapping myself to make sure I'm not hallucinating when one of the other doors squeaks open.

Zian edges into the hallway, looking as dazed as I feel. As a rush of relief washes over me at seeing him alive and well, he swipes his hand through his short black hair and swings his brawny frame toward me.

I can't throw myself at him with a massive hug the way I itch to, because getting too up close and personal with Zee could trigger the traumatic memories he doesn't know how to control. I settle for hurrying over to him with an anxious smile.

Zian's dark brown eyes light up with matching relief. His arms rise and then stiffen, locking before he can offer an embrace.

I stop a couple of feet away from him, and with deliberate care, he rests his hands on my shoulders. His gaze searches mine. "You're okay?"

His rumbly voice is strung with worry beneath the typical gruffness. I nod, glancing over him in turn.

Our new captors have dressed him similarly to me, in khakis and a plain T-shirt—and with the same metal bracelets at his wrists. The edge of a bandage pokes from beneath the neckline of his tee, and bruises like mine darken the peachy-brown skin of his arms. Another shows on his jaw.

"You?" I ask, just to be sure.

His mouth twists. "As much as I can be. Where the hell are we? What happened?"

His hands slip from my shoulders as he turns to take in the hall again. Before I can tell him that I don't have any more clue than he does, more doors start to open up and down the hall.

Nadia slips out first, her steps a little wobbly and her black pixie cut slicked to the side around a bandage on her temple. Her uneasy gaze meets mine, and she dashes over.

I catch her in the hug I couldn't give Zian, hoping it gives a little reassurance to the teenaged shadowblood girl who's become something like a friend. Her statuesque frame is several inches taller than mine, but she clings to me like she needs me to hold her steady.

My gut twists. Nadia has always seemed like one of the most resilient of the younger shadowbloods.

I'm not sure how well I can help her regain her footing when I'm so shaken myself.

As I ease back from her, a face as dark as midnight pokes from another doorway. Ajax, the younger teen who can pick up fragments of people's thoughts, creeps out slowly.

"This is crazy," Nadia says in a rough voice, her head swiveling to take in the hall. "Do you—"

She cuts off her own question when a tall guy with rumpled blond hair emerges farther down. A smile flashes across her face brighter than the supernatural glow she can emit at will. "Booker!"

Nadia flings her arms around the guy who I think has become more than a friend to her over the past few weeks. The awed grin that stretches across his face, giving him the surfer dude impression he has at more relaxed times, seems to confirm my suspicion.

The need to find the rest of the men *I* love hums through me. I spin around and hustle down the hall, sensing that both Andreas and Jacob are in that direction.

As if drawn by my approach, they push their doors open before I've even reached their rooms, Drey just a couple of seconds ahead of Jake.

Andreas takes advantage of his small lead to sweep me up in his lean brown arms and press a giddy kiss to my mouth. I grip the back of his neck and stroke my fingers over his tight curls, clinging to this one moment of joy.

A hand comes to rest on my back, and Drey releases me. Jacob wastes no time pulling me into his own embrace.

He leaves my feet on the floor, gathering me against his muscular frame with his chin tucked over the top of my head. His warmth and the steel-solid feel of his body surround me.

Jake said he'd be my armor when I needed it. He feels like armor now, holding firm against whatever this place is going to throw at us.

"Wildcat," he murmurs, the two syllables of the old nickname managing to contain relief, anguish, and devotion all twined together.

I nestle closer against him, absorbing as much of the

strength and determination radiating off him as I can. Knowing that whatever respite we're getting now is temporary.

He might act as *my* armor, but the other shadowbloods, especially the kids, need me to fight for them. The powers the younger ones can wield are much weaker than ours—the original six, the ones they call Firsts.

A gentle but hesitant voice reaches my ears. "Jake— Riva. We're all... Where's Dominic?"

I ease back from Jacob to see that his twin has joined us. Griffin's softer but otherwise identical sky-blue gaze considers the hallway from beneath the sweep of his slightly longer golden hair.

He looks more alert than he did the last time I encountered him in an unfamiliar building—the first time any of us had spoken to him after four years of believing he was dead. Four years in which the guardians tortured his own emotions out of him, a loss he's only just started to recover from.

I'd take more reassurance from the fact that he hasn't reverted back to his previous robotic state if it wasn't for the question he asked. When I look down the hall again, I spot a couple more of the younger shadowbloods: Sully, a stout older teen who can work illusions, and Lindsay, the mousy-haired kid with an affinity for earth.

But no sign of Dominic.

I close my eyes, focusing on the mark that connects me to our quiet, thoughtful healer. "I think he's... downstairs, somewhere."

Jacob frowns. "Why would they separate Dom from the rest of us?"

Uneasiness twists through my gut. I can't think of any reasons that are *good*. We don't even know who "they" are yet.

Before I can say as much, one more figure steps into view at the far end of the hall—but not a welcome one. My stance goes rigid at the sight of the tall, wiry woman I last saw aiming a gun at Dominic.

She clasps her tan hands loosely in front of her, her dark eyes studying us intently, framed by a sleek bob of similarly dark hair. "You will accompany me to the drawing room," she says in a mild, even voice, and turns on her heel without waiting for our response.

We all glance around at each other.

Jacob's jaw clenches, but I grasp his hand. "We should get a better sense of what the hell is going on here before we make any moves."

He grudgingly nods. We both know I won't hesitate to join him in leaping to the attack when the time is right.

Just minutes before we were re-captured, I slit our previous captor's throat with my claws. The only upside of the washing our new keepers gave us is that I'm no longer splattered with Clancy's blood.

We Firsts trail behind the strange woman warily. The younger shadowbloods follow our lead with nervous expressions.

Zian holds up his arm and flexes his wrist around the bracelet. "We've all got these. Have yours done anything?"

As the others shake their heads, I turn my arm, studying one of mine. "Not so far."

Andreas lets out a halting chuckle. "Somehow I think we're going to find out what they're for soon."

The woman leads us down a curving staircase with an elaborate wrought-iron banister and through a hall wide enough to be a room itself. The doorframes on either side are carved with floral motifs, and the floor glints with a geometric mosaic of tiny tiles.

But I don't give a shit about the decor once she's ushered us into a room full of elegant armchairs and antique wooden side tables. Because against the opposite wall stands an enclosed hospital-style bed that holds Dominic's limp form.

Two

Riva

With a lurch of my heart, I hurtle straight to Dominic's side. My hands thump against the transparent plastic shell covering the bed harder than I meant to, but Dom doesn't so much as twitch.

He's lying on his back, his light brown skin washed out to a sickly tone, his dark auburn hair loose from its usual short ponytail and strewn across the thin pillow. His two thin, orange-brown tentacles jut from beneath the hospital gown he's wearing to rest equally limp on either side of his slim frame.

Several medical electrodes cling to his body: a couple on his forehead, others on his neck and shoulders, and more wires snake from beneath the gown. They lead through a small slot in the plastic shell to a boxy machine nearly as tall as I am that's poised next to the head of the bed, dappled with blinking lights that mean nothing to me.

Tubes wind through the slot as well, reaching to his nose and mouth and a spot on his forearm. Delivering oxygen or medication or I don't know what else.

My lungs constrict. For a second, horror grips me so tightly I forget how to breathe.

Then I catch the rise and fall of Dominic's chest—subtle but visible beneath the gown.

He's definitely still alive. Of course he's alive, or all the medical equipment wouldn't be necessary.

If he's alive, then his body will gradually be healing, no matter what he's been through. Right?

My other men have gathered around me, staring at Dominic with equal dismay.

Jacob's head jerks around to seek out our guide. "What the fuck happened to him? What are we even doing here?"

To punctuate the sharpness of his tone, a sconce snaps off the wall overhead and careens into the ceiling before clattering to the floor. Jake doesn't have the best control over his telekinetic ability when he's upset.

The woman who escorted us here dips her head without any sign of concern and motions to the other end of the room. "My employer will explain that to you."

For the first time, I really take in the space beyond Dominic's bed.

Delicate paintings of leafy saplings and lightly clouded skies cover some of the walls beneath the high, beamed ceiling; the rest of the aged surface shines pale yellow. More small tiles like in the hallway stretch across the floor in a pattern of spirals. A huge glass chandelier dangles overhead, sparkling with the sunlight spilling through the arched windows.

Several of the many armchairs stand in a circle around a broad, boxy wooden table that looks oddly modern compared to the rest of the furnishings. The top of that table is lifting up with a soft mechanical whir to reveal a widescreen TV.

The moment the screen is fully upright, it flickers on. A man appears, sitting behind an elegant but sturdy wooden desk against a wall painted similarly to the ones around us.

A man who's familiar for the same reason our escort is. He's the one who stood over me when I lay aching next to the rolled truck.

The one who told the woman to shoot Dominic.

As my hands ball automatically, he leans his burly body forward with his elbows braced on top of the desk. It's hard to judge his size with nothing to use for a clear comparison, but he might be as big as Zian. He's built like a linebacker—a linebacker who's been squeezed into a slick, slate-gray suit.

His athletic bulk combines with the rest of his features to make me think of a lion. A mane of thick hair, mostly gray but shot through with lingering streaks of tawny brown, drifts to just above his broad shoulders.

And his peering eyes… There's a feral energy to their intensity that raises the hairs on the back of my arms even though he's only present digitally.

His voice does nothing to dispel the impression, rolling from his lips in a throaty baritone. "Greetings, my shadowbloods. Welcome to your new home."

My hackles rise automatically at the "my." I don't have the patience for small talk.

I step closer to the screen. "We didn't ask to be stuck in someone else's idea of a 'home.' Who the hell are you?"

The leonine man offers a smile with a flash of white teeth. "You can simply call me Balthazar. Mr. Balthazar, if you want to be polite about it. I've taken over control of the shadowblood project from the guardians who never got past silly diversions. You belong to me now."

Andreas has tensed at the introduction. The name niggles at my memory in the brief moment before he speaks.

"You were part of the Guardianship, weren't you?" he says. "Or you used to be—one of the founding families? They said you'd disappeared."

Balthazar shows no reaction other than the slightest twitch of his gaze. "I have no current association with those fools. Don't worry. I'll make sure you fulfill your purpose to the most impressive possible extent."

His mouth stretches in a wider grin. A shiver passes over my skin.

He's talking as if he thinks we'll be happy to fulfill whatever he thinks our impressive purpose is.

Clancy, the former leader of the guardians, had big dreams too, but he always couched them in practical terms. Even at his most horrible, he maintained an air of military discipline and feigned compassion.

I'm getting the sense that the man in front of us now is utterly insane. Would that be better or worse?

The alarm bells blaring through my nerves are inclined to say worse.

Griffin is eyeing the screen, his mouth slanted at an uncertain angle. "What about Dominic? Is he recovering?"

"Why do you have him set up in the fucking living room?" Jacob demands, jumping in.

Balthazar waves a thick-fingered hand dismissively. "He is receiving the necessary treatment to maintain his current state."

I can't stop the words from bursting from my throat. "His *current* state? He looks like he's in a coma!"

Balthazar's slow blink only adds to the predatory vibe he's giving off. "Indeed. And he'll remain there, where you can check on him, to help motivate you. As long as you follow your orders, you can ensure the systems supporting him stay on."

A chill sweeps through me. There's no need to read between the lines—he's outright saying that he'll kill Dom if we don't behave.

Zian stares at the screen. "You can't just leave him like — We *need* him."

He breaks off his protest with an anguished growl. My other men and the younger shadowblood stir restlessly around me.

But what *can* we do? We have no leverage here.

Yet.

This psychopath might think he owns us, but he's more than insane if he thinks I'll let him get away with his machinations for a second longer than I absolutely have to.

Unfortunately, Balthazar is already taking very obvious precautions. My pain-seeking banshee scream won't do anything to an image on a screen, and neither will Jacob's talents. Zee can't unleash his wolf-man brutality on a man we can't even reach.

Balthazar remains unmoved by Zian's plea. "You can learn to function without him. His talents are not directly relevant to my interests, so he's more useful as he is."

My teeth grit, but I force my voice to come out even. "What about the other shadowbloods? There were three other kids with us when you found us—and you've obviously been to the island too." We left Nadia and Ajax behind there when we left on Clancy's last mission for us.

"You don't need to worry about them either," Balthazar says in the same nonchalant tone. "I've taken all of the living shadowbloods into my custody, but it's suited my plans to keep the majority of them at other locations. Most of you here have shown initiative and proven the usefulness of your talents, so you've earned my direct attention."

I resist the urge to hug myself. His attention hardly feels like a reward. My fingers itch for my missing necklace, for the comfort of its rhythmic clicking when I snapped the charm open and shut, but I don't want to ask this unknown enemy about it.

I don't want him to realize how much it bothers me that he's taken it away.

Griffin cocks his head. "*Most* of us have earned it?" he repeats for clarification.

Balthazar smiles again, looking even more the carnivore. "I needed a couple extra bodies to serve as a demonstration. I assume you've wondered about the bracelets you're wearing."

I reach for the metal band on my left wrist, adjusting

it where it clings to my skin. "And you're going to tell us what they're for, or leave it as a surprise?"

He chuckles softly. "I'm going to show you. For a less severe infraction, you'll find yourself injected with a sedative that will knock you out almost instantly. Like so."

The final syllable has only just left his lips when Nadia stumbles into me from behind. As I spin around, a choked sound spills from her mouth.

She falls to her knees, her shoulders already slumping. Booker cries out, leaping to her side—just in time to catch her sagging body before it crumples to the floor.

I crouch down with him and pat her face, my pulse racing. Her eyelids don't so much as flutter.

My throat tight, I glance up at the others. "She's out cold."

"The sedative will wear off in a few hours," Balthazar says from the screen. "If you breach the boundaries of this villa's grounds, it will trigger automatically. Trusted members of my staff and I can also implement it at our will as well."

I help Booker lower Nadia to the floor in as comfortable-looking a position as we can manage. As I push myself to my feet, holding back a quiver of rage, Jacob glowers at his own bracelets.

I can practically see the wheels turning in his mind as he imagines how he'll use his talent to pry them off.

He's shaken an entire mountain before. If anyone could do it, he could.

But Balthazar is clearly aware of our strengths—and our tendency to rebel. He smooths his hands across his desk. "If you attempt to remove the bracelets, you'll set off the same effect—or provoke harsher consequences. This is what you can expect if you launch an attack on me or my people."

That's all the warning he gives us. The ominously vague threat has barely landed when a hissing sound cuts through the air.

We all flinch—and Lindsay shrieks.

Blood and the dark smoke of our shadowkind essence spurt from her forearms. Some mechanism in the bracelets has severed her flesh from her wrists to her elbows.

With a yelp, I throw myself at her. She's already swaying as more blood gushes from her gaping arteries. Panicked pheromones flood my nose.

I clamp my fingers around one wrist, but it's been gouged nearly in half as well. Her hand flops limply against my hold.

There's no way I can hold the full incision shut. Blood drenches the mosaic tiles while shadowy essence clouds the air.

The other shadowbloods are shouting around me. I have no idea what to do other than keep holding on to Lindsay while she cries out.

Words tumble out of me—frantic attempts at reassuring her, as if there's any way this situation can be okay. Zian grabs her other arm, but he can't seal the wound any more than I can.

The only one of us who could save her is lying unconscious on the hospital bed by the wall.

Lindsay's knees give. Her head droops, her face waxy pale.

Suddenly, I'm shouting too. "Stop it! You made your point. Help her!"

On the TV screen, our captor remains silent. The woman who brought us to the room stands beside the table, motionless.

"What the fuck is wrong with you?" Jacob snarls at her. "Do something!"

His arm jerks up as if he's going to yank her right over with his talent—but before he's given her so much as a tug, he staggers on his feet. His eyes roll up as a potent dose of Balthazar's sedative washes out his mind, and he slumps over on the ground.

My throat stings, raw and aching. I want to scream, but what would that accomplish? I'd end up sprawled unconscious on the floor with Jacob and Nadia, leaving Balthazar totally untouched.

Lindsay has crumpled too, her body slackening as it sinks into the pool of blood that coats the floor around her. Her eyes stare blankly at me, her lips parted as if she's on the verge of asking me a question she'll now never speak.

I swallow a sob, unable to convince my fingers to release her arm, as if I might still be able to pull her back.

That prick who thinks we belong to him decided her abilities weren't useful enough? She was just a kid—she couldn't have been more than fourteen.

And he cut off her life without so much as a blink, as if nothing mattered more than his sick demonstration.

Griffin has knelt next to Jacob, checking his pulse. A hand grips my shoulder, and I glance up in a daze to find Andreas leaning over me, his face tight with horror.

Balthazar's voice carries from the screen as calmly as if this was a standard job orientation meeting. "You see that I have the means to easily keep you in line if necessary. For the time being, you have free run of most of this property, but you *will* obey any requests made by myself or my primary staff, Toni and Matteo."

I glance over at the screen, fury searing through my chest.

Our captor is gazing at us with that fucking smile curving his cruel mouth. "What we're doing here is far from a game, and I trust that you understand now that I'm not playing around."

THREE

Riva

Zian stares down at the drop beyond the stone wall for several beats before straightening up with a hopeless expression. "We're not getting anywhere that way."

My fingers curl around the edge of the wall, my claws scratching the limestone blocks. We've been exploring Balthazar's expansive "villa" and grounds for the better part of the afternoon, and nothing we've seen has given me any basis to argue with Zee.

The stately mansion is built on a narrow hilltop amid the churning sea of rock I saw from my bedroom window. The plateau that holds it and its patios and gardens drops away into a nearly sheer cliff on all sides.

There is a gate at one end, beyond a row of nearly manicured hedges, with a narrow bridge that connects the plateau to a lower one with a gentler slope. But it was built with a drawbridge in the middle. A drawbridge that's currently raised.

Even I couldn't hope to jump the entire thirty-foot gap beneath it.

Sweet smells fill the air from the flowers and waxy-leaved trees still vibrant in the cool autumn air, but I can't take any enjoyment from the atmosphere. My stomach is knotted too tight.

I dig my hands into the pockets of my hoodie and turn to face the others. The mountain breeze tugs at the strands of hair it's worked free from my braid.

"He picked a location even more secure than the island," I say with a humorless smile.

Nadia rubs one of her bracelets. "And trapped us with these awful things too. They're not *bracelets*—they're... they're manacles, without even needing chains attached."

Her brown face is still a little grayed after her dose of the sedative, but she makes the declaration in a typical dry tone. We're all nervous about how our captor might be monitoring our conversations, but I have to think he knows we'll discuss our predicament.

If he's listening in, he'll probably enjoy hearing us despair.

The only thing we have to be careful about is if we *do* stumble on an opportunity to get the fuck out of this nightmare.

She has a point about the bracelets—or manacles, as I can't help thinking of them when I look at them now. I can practically see the metaphorical chains tying us to the villa behind us and the madman who brought us here.

"It's a nice place for a prison," Booker says, attempting

an easy-going attitude but offering a smile as pained as mine. "Fancy old house, free run of it—even a pool."

I glance toward the rectangle of turquoise water in the middle of the nearby patio. I dipped my fingers into it during our survey and discovered it's heated to make it appealing despite the cooling weather.

I take to swimming about as well as the average cat, but water has been useful to us before. We disguised our conversations when we were conspiring against Clancy using the warble of the island's waterfalls.

If Balthazar is following our voices through the bracelets, I suspect they wouldn't pick up much when submerged.

Not that I have anything to say right now that would make it worth taking a dip.

I lift my chin with all the defiance I can summon. "We have to make the best of it while we're here."

I'm not sure if I manage to sound confident enough to be reassuring. Seeing Nadia's shakiness after she came to, Booker's concern for her, and everyone's anguish over Lindsay's death has left me feeling even more overwhelmed than before.

How am I supposed to help the younger shadowbloods hold it together when I've got a deluge of my own frustration and grief washing over me?

But it's because of me that they're here. Balthazar took advantage of the escape attempt I planned, of the fact that I'd gotten rid of Clancy.

He made it sound like he'd have taken control eventually anyway, but who knows whether he'd have succeeded.

My thoughts dart to Dominic's slack form within his plastic shell, and my heart wrenches as if pulled toward him.

Andreas peers up at the house. The two-story building forms a vast C around a central courtyard. We've determined that our bedrooms are all in the eastern wing, with an elaborate kitchen, dining room, and other common areas including the drawing room that holds Dominic's hospital bed beneath us.

In our search, we've come across a few doors that remained locked to us. We haven't been able to venture into most of the west wing so far.

Drey speaks in a low voice, almost lost to the wind. "Are we figuring that Balthazar is actually *here*? That room he sent the recording from—it's somewhere in the western wing?"

"Yes," Griffin says immediately, equally quiet. When our gazes all flick to him, he offers a subtle shrug. "I don't know him well enough to identify him just by feel. But someone over there was feeling things that matched how he presented himself in the video while he was talking to us."

Jacob is still a bit sallow from his own sedation, but at his twin's remark, his eyes light up with vicious enthusiasm. "Could you tell exactly what room he's in?"

Griffin shakes his head, frowning his apology. "I only have a vague sense of direction—and even that only because there aren't many people other than us and him in the area."

We start wandering across the tiled patio toward the front of the house. Zian's mouth pulls into a grimace. "It's a shitty trick, keeping Dominic messed up like that. If they let him wake up, he could heal himself."

"We don't know if he *can* wake up," I say, even though the words hurt coming out.

Andreas kicks at a pebble and sends it rattling across the stones into a planter. "Dominic was always worried that he didn't pitch in enough, only hanging around to act as backup. But we needed him so much. We couldn't have gotten away with half the stuff we've been through if he hadn't been there to patch us up after the injuries we took."

It's true. I want Dominic back with us for his own sake, to have his pensively sweet presence beside me. But I also never fully realized how many gambles we made in part because we knew we could afford to take injuries that otherwise would have killed us.

Oh, Dom…

I bite my lip and reach out to squeeze Nadia's shoulder, meeting her eyes and then the other younger shadowbloods—Booker, Sully, and Ajax. "We only just got here. We haven't had much time to figure things out. But we have each other. That's already better than the island."

Under Clancy's rule, we only saw each other in random shifts, confined to our solitary rooms in between.

A hint of a smile touches Booker's lips. He slings his arm around Nadia's waist and gives her a little squeeze. "That's right. No getting rid of me now."

She manages to snort even as she leans into his embrace. "Looking on the bright side. I should be good at that, huh?"

My attempt at a pep talk hasn't soothed all of the kids.

Sully shudders, gazing toward the gate and the truncated bridge beyond.

"It's fucking crazy," he bursts out abruptly, his face flushing. "That asshole is totally fucking psycho. He's going to end up slaughtering us all like animals, like he did to Lindsay—"

He cuts off his own rant with a snap of his mouth and bolts toward the gate.

"Sully!" My pulse hiccups, and I launch myself after him.

Over a distance, I could outrun any of the younger shadowbloods—and most of my guys as well. But my initial shocked hesitation and Sully's desperation give him all the head start he needs.

As I dash after him with other footsteps thumping after me, he's already throwing himself at the shoulder-height gate. He flings himself up and over the bars.

I reach him in time to snatch at him, but I only catch his sleeve before he's wrenching away.

Wrenching away… and taking just a couple faltering steps farther before he teeters. He sprawls forward at the edge of the bridge.

His name rasps from my throat. "Sully."

There's no point in yelling it now. He couldn't respond even if he wanted to.

Within the span of a few heartbeats, he's slumped on the dusty pavement, unconscious.

Nadia sucks in a sharp breath. I turn abruptly to look at the others—especially the kids.

"Balthazar *told* us that if we go past the walls, the

sedative will automatically kick in. It doesn't do us any good testing it."

There aren't even any guards posted by the bridge. We don't see any of the villa's staff until we draw back into the garden with an anxious air, trying to figure out what to do about Sully, and a couple of men in trim blue uniforms come trotting out with a stretcher to collect him.

"Where are you taking him?" Booker calls out to them as they carry Sully back to the house.

They keep walking as if they haven't even heard him.

I feel as if my entire stomach has solidified into a chunk of stone like the blocks surrounding us. Andreas glances at me and tucks his arm around my shoulder, but the warmth of his embrace barely penetrates my skin.

The sense I had when Balthazar spoke to us this morning stabs even deeper through me.

This isn't like any of the other times. He isn't like a regular guardian.

How the hell are we ever going to get out of here?

Fuck, how can we even *think* of getting out of here when Dominic can't leave his enclosed bed?

Those are the thoughts traveling through my mind when another man emerges from the villa's main doors.

This one is dressed in regular clothes: a black mock-turtleneck and dark gray slacks that hang a little loose on his gaunt body. Every movement highlights the sharp angles of his joints. You'd almost think he was a robot constructed out of giant toothpicks.

He strides over to us with an air of brisk authority, the breeze ruffling his salt-and-pepper hair. A tuft of a pure white beard points down from his chin.

He stops about ten feet away and snaps his fingers at us. At *me*, it becomes clear a moment later.

"Riva. Come."

Like I'm a dog he's bringing to heel. My posture goes rigid, another flare of the anger that's feeling increasingly futile searing through my chest.

"What for?" I ask. "I haven't done anything wrong."

Jacob and Zian are already stepping in front of me like bodyguards. I can tell from their stances that they'd pummel the guy to pieces if I gave the slightest indication it was necessary.

The man regards them with what might be a spark of amusement in his pale eyes before motioning to me again. "It's not a punishment. You'll be the first to extend your powers. The procedure is totally painless."

He has a softly rounded accent, his dictation just slightly halting in a way that suggests English isn't his first language.

Zian frowns. "You have a procedure to increase our powers?"

"It should accomplish that." The man rubs his hands together, and his gaze takes on a flintier cast. "It will be better for you and for Mr. Balthazar if it does. I believe he told you that you should follow my instructions—I'm Matteo, or Matt if you would rather. Let us go."

My primary staff, Toni and Matteo. We've already determined that the coolly taciturn woman who led us to the drawing room is Toni.

My mouth goes dry. For a split-second, I'm back in that room, Lindsay's blood drenching my hands,

Balthazar's voice ringing through the air. *I'm not playing around.*

If it were just me, I'd say no and face whatever shit these villains would throw at me. Balthazar doesn't want me dead any more than Clancy did.

I'm too useful to him, whatever he's after.

But I suspect he'd happily torment any of my guys to punish me. And not just that.

He's already made it clear that he considers Dominic expendable other than as a point of leverage. And Nadia is here to use as an example rather than because he values her skill.

It isn't even really a choice, is it? I'm not gambling anyone else's life for a pointless act of rebellion.

I square my shoulders and ease past Jacob and Zian, ignoring Jake's grunt of protest. "I'm coming."

Matteo walks ahead of me, his loafers rapping out a staccato rhythm on the tiled floor as he leads me through the house. He unlocks a door with a swipe of his thumb in a swift pattern I can't follow.

We pass through a small fore room into one that's about the size of my bedroom here. Unlike the rest of the house I've seen, though, this area has been given a modern style, the walls and ceiling blank white with no carvings or decorative paintings, the chair in the middle of the room pure steel. The still air holds a crisp lemony scent.

A thick transparent pane sections off one end of the room, behind which lies a small desk with a stack of computer equipment. Two cameras peer down over the space from opposite corners.

Matteo nudges me to sit in the chair. "We will be

focusing on your vocal talent today," he tells me calmly, clicking clamps into place around my wrists just below the manacle bracelets. "No physical strength."

My stomach sinks even farther. My "vocal talent" is for inflicting torment and death with a shriek.

It's already more powerful than I'm comfortable with. Balthazar wants to make me even deadlier?

I try to relax into the chair, pretending I'm complying. I don't *have* to stretch my abilities.

We played this game at our original facility all the time. Holding back our strength, acting as if we were pushing ourselves to our limits while hiding our full capabilities.

A steel cabinet stands behind the chair. Matteo opens it and shuffles through its contents, but I can't see what he's doing.

When he comes up to the side of the chair, I glance up at him, but he grasps my jaw. In the second when I waver between resistance and caution, a sting radiates through my neck.

He holds up the syringe he just used to inject something into me, his lips curved in a thin smile. "My own creation, in consultation with Mr. Balthazar and the records of your 'guardians.' We will see how much it frees your full potential. Some adjustments may be necessary as we experiment."

We, he says, as if I'm a willing participant in his research. I start to grit my teeth…

And my jaw loosens of its own accord. A warm melting sensation is spreading through my body, easing the tension that was wound through it.

My pulse hitches—and then it slows too, settling into a steady thump.

I should be panicking. I should be fighting this.

But the defiance I was clutching on to crumbles into ashes.

As I grapple with my body's betrayal, Matteo steps into the paneled section of the room. He retrieves a cage from under the desk and returns to set it on a small table in front of the chair.

A bird cage. Three bright green parakeets ruffle their feathers behind the bars, peering at me with beady eyes.

Matteo returns to the paneled section. The pane hisses over to fully seal him in. Understanding clicks in my head that it must be soundproofed.

He speaks into a microphone on the other side, his voice projecting into my side. "You will kill them, finding the fatal point quickly rather than lingering on the pain. And you'll work on using as soft a sound as possible."

I should fake my way through this, act as if I simply can't follow his instructions.

My lips part of their own accord. A vibration creeps up my throat, training my attention on the humming nerves of the feathered creatures a few feet away.

I know what flesh I'd need to sever to end their lives immediately, even if the hunger inside me craves a longer stream of pain.

A silent wail of refusal fills my mind—and a whisper of a shriek spills from my lips, cutting the first bird down.

Four

Andreas

I drift from one end of the sitting room to the other, absorbing the scene around me. Letting the impressions settle in my mind in the hopes I'll understand the itch niggling at me, insisting that something's out of place.

A thin gray light seeps over the antique wood and ornate upholstery of the room's furnishings. Silence reigns through the vast villa, nothing reaching my ears but the occasional chirp of a bird outside and the soft rhythm of my own breath.

In the first couple of days after our introduction to Balthazar's home, I've found myself waking up just before dawn and meandering through the rooms. Searching for any clue I can find about the mansion's owner and associates while I don't feel quite so monitored.

Of course, for all I know, he's got hidden cameras covering every inch of this space. He could be watching me right now from his protected office, wondering what I'm up to.

My skin creeps, and I rub my arms. Frustration winds through my chest with a deepening squeeze.

We've ended up trapped yet again. Treated like objects for this sick bastard to toy with.

He might say it's not a game, but he sure seems to enjoy toying with our emotions.

There has to be something I can learn from his chosen residence, though. I can't believe he set up the whole house just for us to occupy it.

It has a lived-in feel to it, with little traces of human occupation that wouldn't have been left by someone staging the house for sale. Patches of wear show on the thick rug by the fireplace. Scuffs mark on the floor beneath chair legs that have scraped at the varnish.

And also…

I stop by one corner and take in the room again, trying to avoid any assumptions. Just letting every aspect of it seep into my consciousness.

The niggling sensation expands, and my gaze narrows in on specific objects. That side table between two of the chairs… it has a style that doesn't quite fit with the others in the room. A little bulkier and clunkier-looking.

A floor lamp in another corner gives me a similar impression—that it's more modern and industrial than the main vibe of the furnishings. Kind of like the house was mainly decorated by one party, but someone else insisted on adding their own, different touch here and there.

If that's true, who would Balthazar have let share the responsibility?

I glance around again and sigh. The revelation—if I'm even right—doesn't get me very far. It could easily simply be the mark of an interior designer handling most of the décor with Balthazar sticking a few of his own purchases into the mix.

But it's possible he has a collaborator he treats as more of an equal than an underling. Someone he shared responsibility over the décor with.

I have no idea whether that would be a good thing for us or a bigger problem than we're already facing.

As I've done in the other rooms I've examined, I move to the sideboards and cabinets along the walls, opening them up to poke around inside.

Here, I find some dusty leatherbound books behind a glass door, a sheaf of blank linen paper in a drawer next to a baggie of faded potpourri… and on the shelves beneath it, a record player with a small stack of records.

My heart skips a beat at the final treasure. I have no idea if the device works, but amid the memories I've gleaned from so many minds over the years, I have a visual of how to work the thing.

Riva has gone without music since we arrived here— and I doubt she had much chance to enjoy it on the island either. Once she's awake, I'll bring the player to her room and set it up for her.

It won't make that much of a difference to our situation, but when you've got next to nothing, you have to hold on to the little things.

With the small victory warming me, I pad over to the door. Just as I rest my hand on it to ease it open, the faint whisper of footsteps reaches my ears.

I nudge the door ajar just a crack. Peeking through the thin gap, I make out Toni's tall, slimly toned form striding past me down the hall.

She has no idea I'm here. It's a perfect opportunity to peek inside the mind of the woman who appears to be one of Balthazar's most trusted associates.

I train my gaze on her, grateful when she momentarily slows to peer through the doorway of one of the rooms down the hall. There's no need to narrow my search this first time; I want my first glimpse of her past to be totally unedited.

You never know what might turn up in a person's head.

A tingle shoots through my eyes, and I careen into a memory.

Riding a bike—a glance down at childishly skinny knees pumping away—adrenaline rushing through her body—hair whipping back from her face as she veers around a turn in the sloping road—

I jerk my attention away to latch on to some other target.

A classroom, university from the look of the students —a professor droning on while pointing to a projected map at the front of the room—Toni's pen hissing diligently over the page in her notebook—

On to the next.

A darkened room, fancy furnishings like the villa but with a more modern feel—picking her way through a mess on the floor that's a mix of broken glass, puddles of what looks and smells like wine, and torn strips of fabric that might have once been clothing

—stance tensed as she tilts her head, listening... for what?

I hold my focus there, intrigued and unnerved. What the hell happened there? What does it have to do with the woman Balthazar trusts?

Does it have anything to do with the man himself or her reasons for working for him?

The past Toni I'm inhabiting edges farther forward, and a ragged wail splits the air from somewhere deeper in the building, beyond her view. She straightens up and—

The memory shatters. I sway forward, blinking hard to reorient myself to the pale morning light and the peacefulness of the just-waking villa.

Toni has marched out of sight. As soon as I lost my view of her head, I fell right out of her mind.

I grimace. There's no guarantee I'll ever find my way back to that specific memory.

Then again, there's no guarantee it's anything at all useful to us anyway.

With no further reason to stay hidden in the sitting room, I slip out into the hall and make my way toward the spiral staircase of the eastern wing that'll take me back to the bedrooms. The sun has brightened outside, so the others will be up soon if they're not already.

I hesitate as I come up on the drawing room where we spoke to Balthazar—our one and only meeting with the man so far, if you can even call it a meeting when he never entered the room. The quiet beep of the medical machines draws me inside.

Dominic lies as still as ever beneath the plastic case that contains him on the hospital bed. As still as death.

A shiver passes down my spine at the thought. I walk over to him and stand there for a moment, gazing down at him in silent vigil.

I'm aware of stories of miraculous recoveries, stolen from memories of people I passed by or lifted from books and newspaper articles I absorbed. They feel about as useful as a handful of ash.

No story is going to restore our friend to us. I've got nothing that would heal him.

As I stand vigil over him, my gut burns with that knowledge. *We're going to get you out of there*, I promise in my head, with no idea how I'm going to fulfill the vow. *We're going to get you better. Somehow.*

When I turn back to the doorway, I have to suppress a startled flinch at the sight of a figure on the threshold.

But it isn't anyone I'm upset to see. Ajax treads into the room and comes over to join me.

He looks at Dominic too, with the solemn expression that seems to fall naturally over his dark face. I can't stop myself from asking, "Can you pick up any thoughts from him?"

Is Dom's mind still working within his cage of a body? It's possible the guy I grew up with is already gone, and the figure before us is only a shell, a trick being held over our heads.

I don't want to believe that.

Ajax adjusts his slender frame as he considers Dominic. He turns to me with an anxious swipe of his hand over the stubble of hair on his scalp. "Not right now. But that doesn't mean he's not in there. I'm no good at making the thoughts come."

That's fair, even if I can't suppress a pang of disappointment. "I get it."

The younger guy opens his mouth and then closes it again as if unsure of what he wants to say. The pang in my chest congeals into guilt.

He can't be more than fifteen years old. I shouldn't have put even a little of my hope on his shoulders.

But when he does speak, it has nothing to do with Dominic. His deep brown gaze holds mine intently. "*Your talent—you can reach into memories whenever you want, right?*"

I nod. "Yeah. Why?"

Ajax hesitates again and then pitches his voice lower. "I think I saw Balthazar before. A long time ago, when I was really little, back at the old facility."

My eyebrows leap up. "Really?"

He shrugs awkwardly. "I'm not totally sure. The details are fuzzy. But he gives me the same kind of feeling that man did. Do you think… if you looked in my head, would it be less fuzzy for you? It might be good to know a little more about him."

A weird rush of gratitude sweeps through me. Ajax might only be partway through his teens, but this isn't the first time he's approached me offering something of himself that we could use.

It doesn't matter how young they are—all of the kids here know what stakes we're dealing with.

"I might," I say. "When I go into a memory, it's always fairly clear. But older or shakier ones are sometimes fragmented and difficult to totally piece together. It's worth a try. Do you want me to take a look now?"

He draws his chin up as if in preparation—as if he thinks he needs to brace himself. Really, he won't feel anything at all. "Go ahead."

So, for the second time that morning, I fix my gaze on someone's head and let myself tumble in.

Unlike with Toni, I have a clear target in mind. I can focus on a specific person and dredge up only the memories connected to that figure.

Balthazar, Balthazar, Balthazar.

The first images that rise up are from two days ago in the drawing room. I shove those away as soon as I recognize them, not wanting to relive the unnerving confrontation.

I swerve straight into a memory of a brightly lit gymnasium. Ajax is sitting on an athletic mat, the tiny, childish hands of his younger self fiddling with a sliding puzzle.

A broad, burly man has just ambled over to a couple of helmeted guardians who were watching over the kids nearby.

Ajax glances up, adjusting my view through his eyes. The newcomer has his profile to us, and the thick waves that frame his face are all golden-brown with just a few tiny streaks of silver, but I recognize our current captor in an instant.

He's too far away from Ajax to overhear their spoken conversation. After a brief discussion, Balthazar strolls through the room, veering toward Ajax first.

He says nothing to the boy, just peers down at him for a few seconds before moving onward. But one thought resonates from his mind into Ajax's, audible as if it were spoken.

What would Peter make of that one?

Nothing else slips from Balthazar to my temporary host. The man prowls on through the room, regarding the other kids in their training—and then one of the guardians marches over to escort Ajax away.

With the dwindling of the memory, I pull myself out, more purposefully than I was able to with Toni. The Ajax of the present peers at me with a mix of apprehension and curiosity.

I offer him a crooked smile. "Thank you. It was him. I'm not sure we can do much with what I saw, though."

How much is it safe to say about what I've learned, when the man himself could be listening in now? He might have worked with someone named Peter—someone whose opinions mattered to him.

It's probably better if Balthazar doesn't know what clues I might have gained.

It's a piece of a puzzle. Who knows when we might find others that would pull it into an enlightening picture?

Ajax smiles back, his posture relaxing. He pauses again before speaking, this time sounding a bit sheepish. "I— You can project memories too, can't you? Your own. I was wondering…"

He ducks his head and then meets my eyes again, the previous solemnity returning like a shadow falling over his face. "No one will tell me if Devon is okay. I know you don't know either, but I think it'd make me feel a little better to see him again, even if it's from before. If you don't mind."

Oh, the poor kid. He told me right from the start, when he offered to help us escape from the island, that there was someone he cared about, someone he'd been forced apart from.

During the chaotic couple of days when we were hacking our way through the jungle, it became obvious that he and the other boy were a lot more than friends to each other. That hectic time was probably the only chance they'd ever had to show their affection without worrying about the guardians intervening.

And then our freedom was torn away from us again. Now none of us has any idea where Balthazar has even stashed the other kids.

I can't imagine how I'd feel if he'd torn Riva away from me. No, actually, I do have some idea—because that did happen four years ago, after us Firsts made our original escape attempt and the guardians took her away.

It was total fucking agony.

"Sure," I say. "I'd be happy to. Why don't you sit down —it's pretty disorienting."

As we move to the armchairs in the center of the room, I sort through my memories from our escape from the island for the moments when I saw Ajax and Devon together—laughing, holding hands, leaning on each other.

Will seeing the past really do Ajax that much good? I'm not sure.

But he asked for it, and I can give it.

It isn't anywhere near enough. What we really need is a new future.

FIVE

Riva

I peer into the fridge for several seconds before stirring myself into action. Sliced ham, cheese, mayonnaise. That'll make a decent sandwich.

Balthazar's villa might be fancy to look at, but we had better meal service on the island. Here, he's simply left us with a bunch of groceries, and it's up to us to put them together into breakfast, lunch, and dinner.

I guess he didn't want any more staff than necessary who could become potential targets of our talents. But what do he and the staff who *are* here eat?

Maybe there's a whole second kitchen in the western wing, and they're dining like kings over there.

I will admit the fresh loaves of bread that appear every morning are pretty nice, as bread goes.

Zian steps up to the cutting board as I turn, so close the warmth of his body tingles over my skin even though he's carefully not touching me. He holds out his hand, his tone light. "Pass it over, Shrimp. I can slice it."

The intensity in his dark eyes suggests the offer means a lot more to him than saving me a few seconds of work. Zee is always trying to show how much he wants to be here for me in all the ways he feels he safely can.

So I give him a soft smile in return and hand over the loaf.

While Zian hacks off a few slices, I open up the packages of ham and cheese and get out a butter knife to spread the mayo. We assemble our sandwiches with swift movements that are almost synchronized.

I'm just raising mine to my lips when Booker's voice carries down the hall outside with an urgent tremor. "Riva?"

My hands jerk to a halt in mid-air, and Zian freezes next to me. I was just outside with Booker and Nadia—I told them I was coming in to grab some food.

What could have happened in the few minutes I was gone?

I drop the sandwich onto the plate and hustle into the hall with Zian right behind me. Booker hurries over, his gaze twitching nervously toward the rooms around us.

"What happened?" I ask as he reaches me, pitching my voice low with the instinctive sense that if he's this upset, it's probably something we don't want to be obvious about discussing.

He rakes his hand through his shaggy hair and motions toward the end of the hall. "We saw something… Nadia and I found a loose tile behind one of the planters and were crouched down checking under it—it was nothing but dirt. But we were ducked low enough that he probably didn't see *us*... I'd think I'm crazy if Nadia hadn't noticed it too."

I raise my eyebrows at him. "*What?*"

Booker takes a deep breath as if to steady himself. "There was a man—short and kind of round—shorter than you even, I think. I glanced over the planter and saw him standing on the patio, looking out over the mountains. And then after a moment, he started to turn around and just *vanished*. Disappeared in thin air."

My pulse stutters, and Zian and I exchange a look. We've seen people do that before—well, they weren't exactly people.

I motion for Booker to head down the hall with me. "He could have been a shadowkind. They can disappear into the shadows if they want to. Show us where you saw him."

The description he gave doesn't sound like any of the shadowkind I've met, but Rollick—the demon who gave us the most help while we were on the run—had tons of beings he worked with. Could he have figured out where we are and sent someone with a message or an offer of aid?

Cautious hope sets my heart thumping faster.

Zian and I follow Booker out into the grounds. I cross my arms over my chest as the chill of the air seeps through my long-sleeved tee.

Nadia is standing by the planter where I assume Booker left her. He motions to a clear area between a few potted shrubs near the wall at the back of the house.

"He was standing right there, just a few feet from the wall. Then he turned toward the house."

I walk across the tiles there, glancing around. From what I understand, shadowkind can still watch and listen when they merge into the shadows.

If this one came looking for me and my friends, he could still be here. Maybe he'll show himself at my arrival.

Zian prowls after me, casting his gaze around. I catch a ruddy glint as his X-ray vision activates.

No one emerges. Booker frowns, shifting his weight restlessly.

"He might not want to show himself again out in the open like this," I suggest after a minute. "Why don't we wait where you were hidden before and see if he makes an appearance then?"

As we crouch down by the planter, Nadia scoots closer to me. "It was so creepy. Booker told you how he just blinked away like he was nothing?"

I nod. "All shadowkind have that power."

"If it really was a shadowkind," Zian puts in. "You're sure he was older than any of us? Maybe Balthazar brought in a new shadowblood who can turn invisible—Andreas might not be the only one with that ability."

Booker shakes his head. "I'd have thought he was at *least* thirty."

"What do you think he'd have wanted?" Nadia asks me and Zian.

I frown, peering around us and then back toward the section of patio Booker indicated. "I have no idea."

As the last word leaves my lips, a plump figure just as Booker described him wavers into view—right at the wall this time, fleshy hands resting on the upper stones, head tipped to the breeze that whips up the cliffside. The wind ruffles his hair, which is chestnut with an odd purple sheen, and tugs at the forest-green suit that covers his portly body.

He's got to be a shadowkind. I've seen several of them materialize from the shadows just like that.

He still doesn't seem aware of our presence. Is he waiting for someone to approach *him*?

I take a gamble and push myself upright.

"Hey," I say tentatively as I step around the planter. "Do you—"

That's all I've gotten out by the time the shadowkind man whirls toward me, drops his jaw in surprise, and wisps away into the shadows again.

My voice dies in my throat. I scan the patio. "I wasn't going to accuse you of anything. I just wanted to talk. I know you can still hear me."

I pause and then try again. "Would you please just—"

The clearing of a throat cuts me off. I spin around to find Toni stalking across the patio toward me.

She jerks her hand in a beckoning gesture. "Leave that alone. Balthazar wants to see you."

I stare at her. "What—you *knew* there was a shadowkind here?"

Toni gazes back at me with her usual implacable expression, not a strand on her sleek black bob out of place. "I said to leave the monster alone. Are you coming?"

My stomach sinks. She doesn't look remotely concerned about the potential intrusion, even though she called him a monster. She's more worried about protecting the shadowkind man from *my* questions.

What the hell is going on?

Zian steps forward, his shoulders flexing. "If Riva's going, then I am too."

He's massive enough that he looms half a foot over her substantial height, but Toni shows no sign of being intimidated. "He only asked to speak to Riva. You can stay here awake, or we can sedate you. It's your choice."

Zian's posture stiffens. I set a careful hand on his arm in the briefest of reassuring gestures. "It's okay. I can handle talking to him."

I'm not going to admit how much I'd rather have Zee by my side while I did, not in front of Balthazar's lackey.

When Toni gestures toward the house again, impatiently now, I shoot Booker and Nadia an apologetic glance and follow her. Maybe Balthazar will have more answers for me than his employee was willing to offer.

She leads me back to the drawing room where Dominic lies in his eerily still slumber. My feet drag for a moment on the mosaic floor while my gaze lingers on him, my stomach twisting tighter.

Toni nudges me on toward the table that's already lifted to reveal the TV screen. She must make some signal I can't see, or maybe Balthazar is watching from a camera, because the moment I've come to a stop in front of the TV, his image blinks onto it.

"Riva," he says without preamble, fixing his predatory gaze on me. "I have a few questions for you."

My skin twitches with discomfort. "I have a few for

you too. Why is there a shadowkind man hanging out around your house? Or a monster, if you call him that?"

Balthazar's expression turns baleful. "I see no reason to justify the type of people I employ to you. But it is—"

"It matters," I break in, glowering at him. "I thought the guardians wanted to slaughter all the 'monsters.' Isn't that the whole reason you made us?"

For a moment, Balthazar simply blinks at me—slowly, as if sizing me up for dinner. "I've told you already, I have no current association with the Guardianship. But I want to hear about one of their founders. You and your friends broke into Ursula Engel's house."

My hands ball at my sides, but it's obvious he isn't going to say more about the shadowkind man. He did confirm that he considers him an employee, though.

It doesn't make any sense.

I keep my answer short, because he obviously already knows and *I* see no reason to give him unnecessary details. "We did."

"I believe you left her home with at least a few items that belonged to her."

I gaze steadily back at him, unspeaking. If he wants an answer from me, he can ask a fucking question.

Balthazar shakes back his graying mane without breaking eye contact. "What happened to Engel's computer?"

Her laptop? My mind darts automatically through the memories of the first few days after the bloodbath at her house—the first time my guys saw my full powers in action.

We never found anything all that interesting on the

computer. Hints about the later generations of shadowbloods, yes, but few definite facts.

Of course, a lot of the data was transcribed in a code none of us knew how to break.

"I don't know," I say honestly.

Balthazar's mouth tenses with a scowl. "Did you dispose of it somewhere?"

"No." Inspiration sparks in my chest, and I jump on the chance before thinking it through. Before taking long enough that our captor might realize it's a strategy rather than an answer. "We carried it with us the whole time. Until Clancy's people caught us again."

"You brought it into the facility with you when you attempted to break out the shadowbloods there?"

This time, I hesitate on purpose. I want him to think I'm avoiding telling him the truth.

Balthazar narrows his eyes at me. "Riva, you know the consequences of defying me."

I do. I swallow thickly and glance toward Dominic, only partly for show.

When I answer, I keep my voice quiet, as if I'd rather not say it at all. "No. Our packs were in the vehicles we came in."

"The vehicles the monsters you worked with brought you in."

"Yes," I bite out, noting as I do that whether he employs the shadowkind or not, he does still call them monsters like the rest of the guardians do.

He rubs his chin. "Then it stands to reason that they'd still have it."

I shrug. "If *they* didn't throw it out. Maybe Rollick took it back to his stupid hotel."

The second after I've spoken, I clamp my lips together as if upset I revealed that much.

Balthazar eyes me for a moment. "A hotel, hmm. And where was that?"

When I keep my mouth shut, his gaze flicks toward Dominic's bed. I tense my shoulders.

"Miami," I say flatly. "So take it up with him if it's so important to you."

If he sends people out to Rollick's hotel looking for the laptop and they're caught at it, Rollick will realize they've got something to do with us. They might give him a trail back here.

If the demon cares at all about getting us free. Which isn't a given. But it's the closest thing to a way of reaching out to him that we've gotten so far.

I don't think the man on the other side of this screen has any hope of coming out on top against the ancient being whose true form could make my knees wobble just with the power emanating off him. At least not on Rollick's home turf.

"Did he know why the computer was important?" Balthazar asks.

I can answer that question honestly too. "I can't remember how much we told him about it. But he could probably figure out that we wouldn't have been lugging around the thing if it was just dead weight."

Our captor hums to himself—almost a leonine purr. Then he tips his head to me. "That's all I need at the moment. I'll have a job for you soon."

With that, the screen goes black. I stare at it for a few seconds longer as if he might reappear.

A job? What kind of job is this psychopath going to send me on?

I realize abruptly that Toni has left. I'm alone in the drawing room—other than Dominic.

I should mention to the others what Balthazar was asking about. The more information we all have about his interests, the more easily we can find a weak spot.

As I step out into the hall, Nadia eases to a halt just beyond the doorway. She was heading over to see if I was done with Balthazar, from the looks of things.

Her mouth is tight, her Amazonian stature diminished by the hunching of her shoulders. The sight wrenches at me.

I step closer, not sure what would help. "Are you all right?"

The girl ducks her head. "Yeah. I guess. They took Booker—for that whole ability-enhancing procedure they're doing."

A shiver runs through her body with a waft of anxious pheromones. She lifts her gaze again. "Does it hurt?"

At least I can reassure her on that point. "No. Not at all."

Not that I enjoyed what I was made to do while under the influence of Matteo's drug.

"Okay." Nadia doesn't sound all that comforted. She hugs herself, still deflated.

I grope for the right words. "Is anything else bothering you? I mean, other than the general suckiness of this entire situation?"

I'm aiming for a dry tone to match her usual attitude, but the corner of her mouth only twitches slightly. "I just… It's going to sound stupid. *You* can handle anything…"

"Hey." I push myself forward and rest a hand on her shoulder. When Nadia leans toward me, I tuck my arm right around her, wishing she wasn't so much taller than me so the gesture would feel more big-sisterly. "I get scared too. If you need to get it out, I'd want you to tell me."

She exhales raggedly. "Ever since we got here… Ever since he talked to us, and made me faint… He doesn't even think I'd be useful. I'm just here so he can threaten the rest of you."

I swallow thickly. I can't deny anything she just said.

Nadia goes on, her voice turning ragged. "Any moment if he gets upset, he could knock me out again. Or blast out my wrists like he did to Lindsay. I might not even know it's coming."

I grope for words, but nothing I could say feels adequate. I have no idea what it must be like to have that fatal uncertainty hanging over her.

I pull her into a full hug. "I'm sorry. None of us wants to risk you—or anyone else—getting hurt. We're not going to take any unnecessary chances. I promise we'll do everything we can to make sure we all get through this mess like the ones we have before."

Nadia hugs me back. "I know. It isn't your fault."

But it is. Before she met me, the teenage girl I'm trying to console was all wry smiles and flippant remarks, highlighting her presence with neon shirts. After all the trouble I've dragged her into, she's really just a shadow of herself.

My fingers curl toward my palms where they're braced behind her back, a prick of my claws digging into my palms.

I have to make sure all this agony is worth it.

Six

Riva

The limo grinds to a halt outside the grand façade of a towering hotel, which is lit up against the night. I gaze up at the looming stone face through the vehicle's back window.

I've always been aware that I'm on the petite side, but on this rare occasion, I feel particularly small.

Which might be silly, because my slim body is wrapped in a dress with so many ripples of satin I might as well have expanded by half. The dainty heels I found waiting on my bed alongside it will give me a couple of extra inches in height as well.

An ostentatious necklace dripping with gems encircles my neck. It only makes me miss my cat-and-yarn charm more.

On the seat across from me, Sully gives the hotel an anxious glance of his own and tugs at the bowtie of his tux. He looks like he's ready to puke.

Jacob reaches over from his spot at my side and folds his firm hand around mine. With his blond hair perfectly slicked back and his muscular frame filling out a tuxedo of his own, he'd set my heart racing for much more enjoyable reasons if I wasn't focused on the brutal purpose of our visit.

When I look over at him, he catches my gaze and holds it with his usual unshakable intensity. "You've got this, Wildcat. We'll watch for any problems and make sure they're taken care of before you even have to think about them. And if anyone hassles you, they'll regret it."

He flashes a grin that's tense but determined. I've seen what happens to people who try to hurt me in Jake's presence.

One time it ended with a heap of severed hands poured onto my bed.

I squeeze his fingers in return, mindful of the manacles still hugging our wrists—under the sleeves of the guys' tuxes, under the satin gloves I'm wearing. But I don't think I'm going to say anything our captor doesn't already know, if he's listening.

My voice comes out in a murmur. "I don't want to do this."

Jacob lifts his other hand to my cheek, his gaze searing into mine. "I know. We keep having to pick between a whole lot of shitty options. But I'm with you, no matter what."

I don't doubt that—it's hard to imagine now that there was a time when his declaration of loyalty would have made me snort in disbelief. We've picked our way out of a lot of the shit we were already mired in.

It would be nice if for once we could clamber out into something other than an even bigger heap of crap.

A solid partition separates us from the driver, but his voice filters through a speaker. "You should proceed inside now."

Yes, we wouldn't want to make Balthazar impatient. I grit my teeth and push open the door.

I don't know who our captor is in the wider world or how he might be associated with any of the people heading into the hotel around us, but no one questions us as we march up the steps and through the opulent lobby to the ballroom where a gala is being held. He's arranged for our acceptance here somehow.

Stepping into the vast room under a dozen twinkling chandeliers, I have to pause to catch my breath. There are people *everywhere*, all of them dressed as fancily as us, most of them at least twenty years our seniors.

It's a far cry from the elegant party Andreas set up for me back on Rollick's yacht, partly in apology for distrusting me before. Only five of us and two of Rollick's shadowkind allies attended that gathering, in a room that seems tiny in my memory compared to this one.

My gaze darts over the faces around us, both taking stock and searching for one in particular.

The one Balthazar has sent me here to murder.

The thought makes my claws prick at my fingertips. I hold them in and drift deeper into the ballroom with Jacob and Sully trailing behind me.

No one pays any attention to us, but I guess that makes sense when they're so busy paying attention to whoever the most prominent figures in the room are. Most of the attendees have gathered into clusters, several vying to chat with the people who've ended up at the center of those knots.

The scents my heightened senses pick up as I circulate through the room carry the tang of both excitement and tension. People have a lot of fraught expectations from this night.

I catch snippets of conversation as I pass—talk about bills and policies and programs. It's some kind of political event, but that's all I know about why they're here.

A waiter passes with a tray of champagne glasses. I snatch up one so I have something to occupy my hands and to help me blend in.

I raise the rim to my lips, pretending to sip as the rising bubbles tickle my nose. The bitter smell makes me want to grimace.

And then I spot him.

When he prepped us for this job, Balthazar showed me several photos over the screen in the drawing room. He didn't tell me the man's name, but knowing the shape of the face with its deep-set eyes and knob of a chin was more important anyway.

My target is one of the sought-after guests with his own cluster of devotees. As I watch from ten feet away, he lets out a chuckle and motions with his glass of wine.

Whatever comment he makes that I can't make out, it gets his colleagues twittering too. The man from the photos smiles warmly at them.

Nothing about him looks particularly villainous. For all I know, he's a perfectly decent human being.

Balthazar wouldn't tell me why he wanted the man

dead either. A far cry from Clancy, who made an extensive case for us putting our talents to use when he sent us out on a mission.

No, my motivation for going along with our new captor's orders is very simple. Either I kill this man, or Balthazar will kill one of the shadowbloods back home. Maybe more than one, if he's pissed off enough.

I could call his bluff. I mean, there'd have to be a point when he ran out of leverage.

But then where would I be? Standing in a deluge of blood, knowing it was my fault?

What would be the point of defiance if all I get in return is Nadia's death, Dominic's, who knows who else's?

I have no idea exactly how many of us Balthazar might decide are expendable after all.

So while I have nothing against the knob-chinned man I'm surreptitiously eyeing, my throat tingles with a contained shriek ready to be unleashed. A shriek every particle in my body wishes I could aim at the psychopath behind the screen back in the villa.

My target gradually circulates through the room, picking up new fawners and leaving some behind to pursue other objects of interest. He doesn't look particularly concerned, but I notice a couple of men keeping pace with him from a discreet distance, buff under their slightly less swanky suits.

Bodyguards? How important is this particular man?

No doubt that's why Balthazar sent me on this job. I won't be going at him with my claws and supernatural strength.

With my scream, I can kill him from across the room

without anyone having the slightest idea how to shield him.

And if anyone does realize something's off before I manage it, Jacob and Sully can distract them with their own talents.

Marble columns stand along the edges of the room, some of them hung with velvet drapery. I'll slip away into their shelter when I've decided to make my move.

Not yet. If Balthazar thinks I'm nothing but his tool, he's even more of a lunatic than he's demonstrated.

I ease closer to my target's cluster of conversation, wanting to get some idea what they're talking about. What he's all about.

Why our captor might want him dead.

At first, I only catch some comments about a dinner some of them recently attended and a concert they're looking forward to next week. Then one of the women close to my target leans in with an awed smile.

"You've done so much for fossil fuel interests in the face of all that pushback. People should look to you as a role model!"

The knob-chinned man laughs and waves off her compliment, and a bunch of his other colleagues heap on similar praise. Someone scoffs about "clean energy" as if it's a ridiculous idea—"As if there isn't always a price to pay somewhere."

My knowledge of current politics is incredibly limited, but I know what fossil fuels are. Does Balthazar object to oil and coal, or is he holding something else against the guy?

As I continue meandering after them, I pass a woman

who has the tip of a pen cap poking from her half-open purse. I brush closer and deftly retrieve the pen it's attached to.

Jackpot. Now I need something to write *on*.

I keep my ears pricked in the meantime, listening for other clues. My target gets into a discussion about funding and donations that I don't really follow.

Then a couple who appear to be together split off from the cluster to drift in another direction. The woman glances over her shoulder and shakes her head at her partner.

"They say he's got a good chance of making VP next term," her partner murmurs. "Rising up the ranks fast."

Is *that* why Balthazar wants him gone?

There's too much information, too many scattered pieces I don't know what to make of. Frustration coils in my gut.

I have to do something. Surely someone out of this mass of wealthy movers and shakers could stand up to the asshole who sent me here?

I eye a pamphlet left on one of the side tables and several crumpled napkins I know will only be dismissed as garbage before Jacob taps my arm.

He presses a thin cardboard edge against my palm. I peek down and see it's an index card, just a couple of words jotted on one side.

We didn't discuss the idea I came up with on the flight over here, but he must have noticed me stealing the pen. He can guess what I'm up to.

I pause at a side table as if examining more of the pamphlets and surreptitiously scrawl out my message.

Sadly, there isn't a whole lot I can say to whoever I deliver my plea to, but I do my best.

Investigate Mr. Balthazar, I scrawl on the back of the index card. I don't even know his full name. *There are kids being held captive in his villa.*

I fold the card once and look for a reasonable recipient, my stomach starting to churn. I settle on the man who told his wife that my target was rising up the ranks.

If he's interested in that man's career, then there's a decent chance he's at cross-purposes with Balthazar. I hope.

Gliding past him with as much grace as I can summon, I slip the card into the hip pocket of his tux. Not a single indication can have passed to my captor of what I've done, even if he's listening through my manacles.

The moment the card is out of my hand, the overwhelming urge to get out of the ballroom weighs down on me. I've done everything I can to save us.

Let's get the awful part over with and leave everything else behind.

I move toward the columns as I planned, ducking behind a swath of velvet close enough to my target that I'll still be able to see him. Jacob and Sully linger on the far side.

Standing at a gap between the fabric and the column, I fix my gaze on the knob-chinned man.

He might deserve this fate. It's just as likely he doesn't.

I know for sure that none of my fellow shadowbloods back at the villa deserve the punishment they'll receive if I don't go through with the job. I grip that certainty tightly, willing down the sear of guilt in my gut as well as I can.

My lips part. The vibration oscillates up my throat.

I was already learning how to pitch my shrieks quietly before Balthazar ever kidnapped us. I butchered an entire pen of sheep across a courtyard without alerting the terrorists I was building the power to slaughter.

My sessions with Matteo have honed my skills even further, faster than I'd have expected. Maybe because I've never let myself purposefully stretch the limits of my supernatural abilities before.

I was always too worried about how the guardians would exploit them. And yet here I am.

My hands ball at my sides. I drink in the air and think about Balthazar.

His arrogant smirk as he reminded me of the consequences of disobedience. His blasé tone when he talked about what Dominic was good for.

His stupid fucking face, so totally unperturbed, as Lindsay flailed and died in a pool of her own blood.

I will do this for him, but only because I have to. Only because I have to believe that eventually I can do it *to* him.

When I propel the pain-seeking scream from my mouth, it's the thinnest of whispers. No one would hear it unless they're standing right by my lips.

And because I've also been practicing adjusting how it hits my victims' bodies, I aim it right at my target's heart.

The thing inside me that revels in pain clamors for me to twist and torture. But I clamp down on those urges and give the hunger only the brief satisfaction of ripping the fleshy chambers in two.

The knob-chinned man jerks to a halt with a spasm. His hand flies to his chest; bloody spittle flecks his lips.

His adoring entourage lets out its own chorus of screams as he crumples to the floor.

And the three of us shadowbloods meld back into the crowd, heading for the lobby. A sour taste laces my mouth thanks to the dirty work I've just carried out.

SEVEN

Griffin

The pain is everywhere already, but somehow it keeps expanding. It creeps under my fingernails, claws up my spine, and pierces through my skull.

I ache from the roots of my teeth to the tips of my toes, and it just keeps coming. Building. Sharpening.

It goes on and on until it's impossible to be aware of anything but the physical sensations, until the wrenching scene projected in front of me blurs before my eyes and I have no room left in me to even start to care—

I jerk awake with a cry rasping from my lips.

The room around me is dark. It takes a few seconds for my mind to register the soft weight of the blanket over me, the broad mattress beneath me.

Nothing hurts except for the pang of horror resonating through my chest when I think back to the nightmare I just escaped.

I roll over on the lavish bed Balthazar gave me, as if he thinks a fancy headboard can make up for our enslavement, and press the side of my face into the feather pillow. My pulse thumps dully on.

It wasn't just a nightmare. It was a fragment of the past flashing back to me, haunting me.

The guardians wanted me to reject all of my emotions so thoroughly I wouldn't be remotely affected by a single feeling of my own. They inflicted every torment they could on me to achieve their goal.

I'm gradually getting better at tuning out the automatic jolts of pain that hit me in reaction to the emotions I've managed to let back in. But I have no defenses in my sleep.

In my sleep, I go through the whole treatment all over again.

After all the conditioning I went through, my body's instinctive reaction is to lock down. Shut away the slightest twinge of an emotional response. Shield myself against further physical agony.

I know I can't do that. When I'm numb, I might not experience any regret or sadness myself, but I deal out more than I can stomach to the people around me.

I let myself get duped into helping Clancy capture my brother, my only friends, and the woman I love. I lost their trust and maybe ruined our first escape attempt because I didn't even trust myself.

From now on, I'm going into every situation we face aware—both of what's going on around me and what's going on inside me. Everyone needs a conscience.

I sure wish Balthazar had more of one.

As I inhale and exhale slowly to relax my nerves, the static that's filled my head and my heart for so long ebbs. I focus on each flutter of emotion as I recognize it, giving my respect by labeling and acknowledging.

I'm afraid of what's going to happen to us here—and of what's already happened to us. I'm terrified that we've lost Dominic in every way that matters.

I'm lonely, here in this expansive bedroom by myself.

And I care—about Riva, about Jacob, about the friends I was torn apart from years ago and the kids who've become our new companions. I care so much that a conditioned wave of agony rises up on the heels of the sensation.

I clench my jaw against the physical pain and push myself out of the bed. There's one more emotion in me now—anger at the men and women who upended my entire physiology.

I don't know if I'm ever going to function like a normal feeling human being again, and that's their fault.

Some of the habits that've become ingrained in me provide comfort without sending me back into numbness. I start each day with a short shower and a brisk scrubbing, dress swiftly, and make my bed even though as far as I know no one else here is ever going to see it.

Then I get down to the little bit of work I can do that might help us survive.

I can't tell exactly where our captor lives in the house, but we have a decent idea based on what areas remain shut off to us. I head outside into the thin early morning light and meander through the fading gardens to the outside of the western wing.

The evergreen shrubs give off an invigorating piney scent. I drink more into my lungs as I come to a stop where my impressions become clearest.

Somewhere not far from here, a person is stewing. Frustration and impatience mingle with an unshakable sense of pride.

I've never met the man in person, only seen his digital image on a screen, but I can recognize Balthazar's presence now in an instant. I haven't met many—maybe *any*—others like him.

I don't know what he's thinking or doing, but it's possible that what I pick up on of his feelings will give us a clue about how to break free from his hold.

He's very self-assured. I can tell from comparing his emotional responses to the things he's said when he's talked to us that his frustrations are all aimed outward at whatever opponents he believes he faces, not inward at himself.

The impatience speaks of things he wants that he can't get without assistance, which he doesn't like at all. I get the impression that he's sure he could be accomplishing so much more if all the keys were already in his hands.

He has hopes, things that excite him. Every now and then, flickers of delight that's almost giddy reach me.

Unfortunately, I have no idea what provokes his happiness.

I might not figure much of anything else out until we start to push. Take action and observe how he reacts.

But any kind of action that's not within his orders is a risk. More blood could be spilled; more lives could be taken.

I want to be able to tell the others how we should handle him, but nothing I've felt from him has given me a solid answer. And I've made too many mistakes to want to gamble on my instincts now.

As I'm monitoring his inner state, Balthazar must do or receive something that works out well for him. His spirits lift with a mild but clear waft of satisfaction.

I putter around in the yard there for several minutes longer, pretending that I'm simply enjoying the scenery and the brisk autumn breeze. When no more significant shifts in our jailer's mood hit me and the pretense wears thin, I amble to the villa's rear door and make my way to the kitchen.

Andreas is already in there—his animated voice carries out into the hall, along with the sizzle of frying eggs. A low laugh that follows his words confirms that Riva's with him.

When I come in, Drey tips his head to me. They both smile in welcome—the tense smiles we've all been making since we figured out what our new prison entails.

"I made enough eggs for everyone if you want some, Griffin," Andreas says, scraping a bunch onto an already heaping plate. "But no pressure. I'm sure Zian will plow through everything the rest of us leave."

I'm about to say no, because I'm not particularly fond of scrambled eggs, but my newer mental habits kick in, honed by years of having only practicalities to guide my decisions.

Protein is an important aspect of any meal. We need our minds keen and bodies strong to get through this latest trial.

I smile back, sure my expression looks just as tight as theirs. "Thanks. I'll have just a little."

As I pop a couple of slices of bread into the toaster, Riva comes up beside me. She slips her arm around my waist, letting her hand tuck under the hem of my sweater to rest on the bare skin of my waist.

The contact sets off a flare of heat and a swell of affection through me in tandem—two emotional responses that my old conditioning can't touch. The guardians could never replicate what I'd feel when this woman is near me, so they never burned the feelings her touch stirs up out of me.

I want her, always, with a hunger that radiates through my veins. And I love her even more than I already did for the simple gesture she's just offered.

She knows that her embrace has done more to wake me up than anything else could come close to. It's automatic to her, to give me whatever she can of herself to help me return to the man I should be.

The man I owe it to her to be.

"Did you sleep all right?" she asks, leaning her temple against my shoulder.

I kiss the top of her head. "Not too bad."

I haven't told any of them about the nightmares. It's not as if they could do anything to stop them, after all.

Andreas has already gotten an assembly line of toast going. He leaves the frying pan to slather butter on the pieces, and Zian arrives as if on cue to add dollops of jam.

When the toaster dings with my additions, they slide both condiments my way. Riva lets go of me after one last squeeze and pours out glasses of orange juice for all of us.

It's become a sort of ritual, these joint breakfasts. A way of giving ourselves some semblance of normalcy in this horrible situation.

We carry all the trappings to the dining room on serving trays. Jacob has just finished setting the long table.

The six of us usually sit around one end while the younger shadowbloods gather at the other. Riva looks at the few empty chairs between us with a quiver of disappointment, but I think the kids need their allegiance to their own smaller group just as much as they need to belong with the rest of us. They know how to move over if they want to mingle.

It's a little easier to pretend this is somehow normal if they avoid the strategy discussions the six of us inevitably fall into while we dig into our meal.

As we sit down, Jacob gives my shoulder a swift pat that's almost a cuff. He's never been the most demonstrative guy, even when we were kids, but he's been offering that brief contact at least once a day since we got here.

I don't think he imagines he's helping me like Riva is. From the constant storm of emotion inside him—and the shudder of relief that runs through it at the gesture—I suspect he's reassuring himself that I really am still here.

A lump forms at the base of my throat. I'm grateful that my presence matters that much to my brother, after everything.

Picking up his fork, Zian glances over at me. "Anything interesting this morning?"

They all know about the most important new part of my morning routine. The trick is discussing it without potentially giving away to unknown listeners what I'm actually up to.

Reluctantly, I shake my head. "I saw a flower that made me happy, but I don't know what would make more grow."

Jake lets out a huff. "We could give 'you' plenty to feel something about."

Riva shoots a warning glance his way, and he clamps his mouth shut. He doesn't need my power to know she's worried about retaliation if he expresses too much of his hostility toward our captor.

But he doesn't know what else is churning inside our woman with her hair like moonbeams through the night. Only I can taste the fury simmering under her fear-driven caution.

She's in almost as much turmoil as Jacob. It barely shows in her movements, in the occasional brusqueness of her words, but she's got her own storm raging to be let out.

She found a way to get us free from our former jailers. *Twice.*

And yet here we are.

I don't have any words that could make her feel better about how badly our hopes have been upended. So I don't say anything about it.

I can't tell if she'd want me to try to comfort her anyway.

Zian compliments Andreas on the eggs—both the flavor and the quantity—and Drey launches into a tale of a mountain climber whose memories he once sifted through. Jacob and Riva chew thoughtfully as they take in his account, Jake tossing in a few sardonic questions. A subdued laugh ripples through the group that I don't totally understand.

They went through an awful lot before I pushed my way back into their lives. And for a lot of the time afterward, I was working against them, even if I didn't see it that way.

Even sitting right here with them, I can't shake the sense that I haven't really returned. I'm not even as much a part of their group as Dominic is.

And with what *I've* been through and who it's turned me into, this might be the best I'll ever get. Hanging on the fringes, playing a supporting role to the five people who used to be my entire world.

Unless I can prove beyond a shadow of a doubt how fully I'm standing with them.

EIGHT

Riva

I rest my fingers lightly on the doorknob and give it the gentlest turn. My supernatural strength, which could wrench an ordinary knob right out of its socket, also allows me minute control.

My testing gets me nowhere, though. After less than half an inch of give, the knob jars against its lock.

Thanks to my care, no sound comes with the resistance. If Balthazar has guards posted in the western wing as a second line of defense against intrusion, they should have no idea what I attempted.

I sit back on my heels in the dark hallway. I can barely see the door in front of me, even with my eyes adjusted to the night.

Other doors around me are shut, and the hall has no windows of its own. Only the faintest hint of diluted light seeps from under one or another room to keep this part of the villa from being cloaked in pitch blackness.

In what's become my usual late-night rounds of the villa, I've already checked the other two doors that have stayed locked to us. After the last lights inside the building have been off for an hour, I slink through the lofty halls, hoping we might gain a little more ground off some staff person's mistake.

What would I actually find if one night I do get through? Maybe just more grand rooms full of elegant furniture.

But possibly some evidence of Balthazar's plans that he doesn't want us to see because we could use it against him. Maybe I'd even stumble on the man himself.

My fingers flex at the thought with a prick of my claws in my fingertips.

I've never seen our captor in person except in my brief moment of consciousness when he loomed over me on the roadside by the bashed truck, but I can imagine gouging open his throat like I did to Clancy with perfect clarity.

Everything here revolves around his whims. Anytime Toni or Matteo speaks to us, it's because "Mr. Balthazar says" or "Mr. Balthazar wants."

Get rid of him, and I think we'd be free even faster than it would have worked with Clancy. Balthazar doesn't have the rest of the Guardianship waiting in the wings to take over. He's gone rogue.

Do the guardians—however they're organized now, whoever's leading them—have the slightest idea where we are or who has us? I know they have some kind of a "board" with its own authority, one that already was vying to take over from Clancy, but their representative assumed Balthazar was totally out of the picture.

Imagining them sweeping in to battle him for us gives me a whiff of relief that makes me queasy in turn.

The guardians aren't our saviors, not by a long shot.

But it might be easier to escape them again than to challenge Balthazar. They never asked us to kill random people without explanation.

They never killed *us* at random, just to perform a demonstration.

Balthazar knows his former colleagues a lot better than I do, though. It's hard to imagine he hasn't taken every precaution to ensure that they never realize what he's up to.

I slink back to the stretch of hall that holds our bedrooms, my feet moving silently over the tiled floor, my skin itching with frustration.

Just yesterday, Balthazar sent Jacob and Zian out on another mission, to steal a safe that could contain anything. A couple of days before that, he had Andreas join Booker and Ajax in mingling with a bunch of lobbyists at some political luncheon, recording their moods and stray thoughts and memories associated with a few figures he showed Drey photos of.

Obviously he has some kind of political interest, but nothing that adds up to an escape route so far.

We don't know even one of his political goals. I couldn't say whether he had me kill the man at the gala because he's against the guy's support of fossil fuels or because he saw him as competition for a role Balthazar wanted to fill.

As I head to my room, my uncertainties gnaw at me. But despite the tension twisting inside me, I catch a sharp intake of breath even though it's muted by the closed door between me and its source.

I freeze, my ears pricking. Covers rustle with the abrupt jerk of limbs; a thin whimper trickles out.

That's Griffin's bedroom.

My heart lurches. I leap for the door, my mind blanking under a wave of panic.

When I push inside, my feet stall for a moment. A faint spill of moonlight illuminates a scene I'm not sure I should barge into.

Griffin is sprawled in the middle of his bed, tangled in the sheets, his eyes closed. Furrows mark his forehead beneath the slant of his blond hair, but he's lying still now.

I don't want to disturb his sleep if what I heard was just a brief blip of distress.

As I waver in my uncertainty, Griffin stirs again. His hand clenches around a fold of blanket while another pained sound slips from his lips.

I hurry to the bed and clamber onto it to touch his shoulder. "Griffin. Griffin, wake up."

I speak softly, but my touch and my voice are enough to snap him out of the nightmare. His body twitches, and then his eyes pop open.

He blinks a few times as if catching up with reality. His head tilts back so he can peer up at me. "Riva?"

I offer a crooked smile. "I think you were dreaming. About something not so great. You sounded upset—I didn't want to leave you like that."

He swallows audibly and reaches to take my hand in his. "Thank you. I'm sorry I worried you, Moonbeam."

I always love hearing his old nickname for me in that

fond tone, but I wrinkle my nose at the rest of his words. "You don't have to apologize for that. If something's bothering you, I'd always want to help."

I pause, letting my mind linger on the stroke of his thumb over the back of my hand and the tingles lighting up in its wake before I venture farther. "Do you want to talk about it?"

Griffin grimaces. "There's nothing to talk about. Sometimes my old 'training' comes back to me when I'm sleeping. I'm sure it'll happen less as I get more used to feeling things again."

Oh, God. He told us briefly what the guardians put him through to suppress his emotions, and even that pared-down account made me want to tear the assholes apart on his behalf.

And now he's reliving their torture in his dreams?

I ease down on the bed next to him, tucking myself under the sheets as I do. I can't chase away the horrors of his past, but I know that I can give him a little comfort.

An escape into feelings with no connection to the torment the guardians put him through.

Griffin welcomes me, nestling my head under his chin so my breath washes down his neck, sliding his arm around my back beneath my long-sleeved tee. Everywhere our bare skin touches, heat and longing sparks.

Griffin only just found his way back to us—to me. We haven't solidified the bond between us, partly because of the uncertainties lingering between us until recently and partly because Clancy would have used the intimate act to gather data for his own purposes.

I haven't let myself get all that physically close to any

of my guys since we arrived in the villa. My frustration at our loss of freedom, my fear of our unhinged captor, and the constant feeling of being watched haven't exactly put me in the mood.

But right now, with Griffin's warmth wrapping around me, I'm not sure if it's made sense to draw that boundary instead of taking every bit of comfort and pleasure I could from the men I love.

Balthazar hasn't shown the slightest interest in the bonds we've formed. I'm not sure if he even knows we *have* formed them.

Clancy only figured it out because he heard Jacob and me talking about it after the first time we had sex. He might not have made any official report about it, waiting until he had more data to share.

And even if he did make an official report, would Balthazar have had access to it? The guardians seemed to believe he'd vanished years ago.

If the psychopath wants to perv on our hook-ups for some other reason, suddenly I'm finding it very hard to care. How would that be worse than anything he's already subjecting us to?

At least we'd get something good out of it at the same time.

Those thoughts are condensing in my mind, my muscles loosening with acceptance where my body has aligned with Griffin's, when the bedroom door clicks open again.

Jacob's voice, drowsy but urgent, follows the squeak of the hinges. "Griff? I woke up with a bad feeling and—"

As I twist to look at him, he's already jerking to a halt

on the threshold. He stares at us with a flex of his jaw that makes my stomach knot.

Jacob would do anything for his twin. He's killed to protect him.

But I also know that he's struggled since as long as he's wanted me with the assumption that I'd want his brother more.

"Sorry," he says, stepping backward. "I didn't realize—"

"Jake." I hold out my hand from beneath the covers, beckoning him over. The soft squeeze of Griffin's arm still slung around my waist tells me he approves of my invitation.

Jacob stops retreating, but he doesn't move toward us either. I don't know how to read his shadowed expression.

Griffin props himself up on an elbow to look past me to his brother. "I had a nightmare—Riva came in to snap me out of it. You're not interrupting anything."

He pauses, and I have the sense that he's gauging both our emotions. Then he adds, "She wants you to stay. And so do I."

Jacob's mouth opens and closes again without any sound coming out. Then he strides in, kicking the door shut behind him, and stalks straight to the bed.

He stops at the edge, his eyes smoldering in the dimness. But the next thing he says is directed at Griffin. "Are you okay now?"

Griffin nods. "Sorry if you picked up on my bad dream. But… we're all awake… and I think Riva has ideas other than going right back to sleep."

I nudge him with a teasing jab of my elbow and motion to Jacob again. "Come here."

He lets out a sigh, his muscular frame relaxing just a little in the tee and pajama bottoms he wore to bed. Then he eases onto the edge of the mattress.

Griffin and I scoot over to make more room. I guess I have one reason to thank Balthazar for the nice beds.

I peel back the covers so Jake can slide under them, and he tips his head close to mine. His voice comes out rough. "Already all warmed up, Wildcat?"

A gentler smile tugs at my lips. "Just a little. I was hoping for more."

"I can help with that."

He lowers his mouth to meet mine, searing hot from the moment we meld together. My pulse thrums faster as I twine my fingers into his smooth hair.

From behind, Griffin nuzzles the back of my neck. His thumb strokes a giddy arc over my belly.

Now I really am on fire.

I kiss Jacob hard, with all the longing in me that's driven both by my love for these men and the essence in my blood always hungry to join with theirs. He deepens the kiss, offering my first taste of the passion I know he can bring like a thunderstorm.

But his touch stays careful. He traces my jaw and the slope of my shoulder, my side down to where Griffin's arm is wrapped around me and then back up to the curve of my breasts, tender rather than demanding in his affection.

I curl my fingers into his hair hard enough to tug at his scalp, but all he does is groan, muffled against my lips.

Is he ever going to forgive himself for how he hurt me

in the past—which he only did because of how much he was hurting? I have.

I don't know how else to convince him of that.

And right now the tension bottled up inside me wants the whole fucking storm. I want to feel just how fierce he can be, enough to rival the enemies we've found ourselves imprisoned by.

As he rolls my nipple between his fingers, I press into his hand, and his grasp tightens into a pinch. I gasp at the bolt of pleasure—and Jacob releases my breast in an instant.

"I'm fine," I murmur quickly, stealing a hasty peck between reassurances. "It was *good*."

Jacob palms my breast again, tension radiating off him. He's pulled taut as a bowstring but refusing to give in to the pressure.

Griffin grazes his fingers down over the waistband of my sweatpants and speaks in a soft but steady murmur. "Jake, do you really think she'd lie to you about what she wants? She isn't afraid. She's burning up with how much she wants you."

His brother makes a strangled noise low in his throat. He caresses my breast again, more forcefully this time.

I press into his touch and into Griffin's hand where it's curled between my legs. A needy growl reverberates from my lungs.

Hell, yes. I've been restraining myself too, for way too long.

I need these men. They're my blood, and I'm theirs, and nothing any captor can do will change that.

Jacob dips his head to nip at the most sensitive strip of

my neck. The scrape of his teeth sends a quiver of delight through me.

I yank on his hair a little harder, and he outright bites me, not quite but on the verge of breaking the skin. My whole body shudders with eagerness.

Jacob exhales raggedly, his breath rushing over my skin. As I undulate between him and his twin, my hip brushes the bulge that's protruding against his pajama pants. But he still holds himself back, resting his forehead firmly against mine.

When he speaks again, it's not to me. "Tell her, like you told me. Tell her how much I love her. I don't know— I don't have the words for all of it—but you—maybe you can say everything."

Griffin's hand slows in its blissful massage between my thighs. He brands my shoulder with a lingering kiss before answering.

"It's always there, Riva. Even when you're not in the same room. Like an ember smoldering through everything else he's feeling. Wanting to protect and help you. Wanting *you*. And when you're there—when you smile at him or touch him—it flares into a forest fire, blazing through everything else, capturing every part of him. He'd do anything for you, and then he'd do it all over again, and the only thing that would matter is that it made you happy."

Jacob takes another shaky breath. The press of his forehead and his hand still cupping my breast, the relentless thump of his pulse reverberating into me from his body—all of it gives life to Griffin's words and tells the truth of his story.

A lump rises in my throat. I pull Jake's lips back to mine and kiss him with everything I have in me before I answer.

"I know. I know, and I love you too, so much. You don't need to prove anything to me."

Jake grabs me in another kiss, so scorching it sends tingles all the way to my toes. Then he glances over my shoulder at Griffin. "Thank you."

His gaze drops to meet mine again, and I'd swear I can see that forest fire flickering in the back of his sky-blue eyes. "What do you want, Wildcat? Ask, and you've got it."

I wet my lips, the depth of my longing momentarily drowning my words. "Take me as hard as you can—so hard it could almost break us free."

A startled chuckle tumbles from his lips, and then they're crashing into mine.

Jacob wrenches at my shirt, releasing me from his kiss only long enough to yank it over my head. The force of his eagerness is so thrilling I'm not even distracted by the sleeve's momentary snag on one of my manacles.

Jake reaches for my pants next. Griffin hooks his fingers around the waistband to help his twin tug them down my legs.

As Griffin dapples kisses across my shoulder blades, the strange sensation rises up inside me that this coming together isn't just about me being with each of them but a conversation between the brothers as well. A negotiation or a peace-making or I don't know what else.

And I'm okay with that. I want both of them, and I

want them to recover all of the understanding they once had that the guardians ripped to pieces.

I manage to peel Jacob's tee off his sculpted chest, and then he's pulling back on the bed, dragging me with him to the edge. Somehow he manages to fling aside my panties and drop his pants in the same string of motion.

Standing next to the bed, he hefts me up by my ass. My legs brace against his chest, my heels just below his shoulders.

He rubs the head of his cock over my slick folds with one hand while the other digs into my ass. "I'd fuck you to the ends of the earth," he rasps, "and keep going right over the edge."

Through the rush of giddy anticipation, all I can manage is a mewling of encouragement. My fingers clamp around his wrist just below his manacle, and he tightens his grip on my ass.

Jacob plunges into me so swift and hard he's fully sheathed in the space of a heartbeat. I clamp my teeth against a cry that would have rung right through the villa. Pleasure sears through my body as if he's passed the flames burning inside him into me.

He stops just for a second, and my pulse stutters with the thought that he might shy away from my request after all. But then Griffin kneels by my shoulder, stroking my hair back from my face and flicking his thumb over the peak of my breast.

"She wants more," he tells his brother. "Just like that. She's loving it."

When I first cuddled up to him tonight, I thought I might mark him and be marked in turn like I already have with Jacob. A twinge of guilt filters through the roar of bliss.

But as Jacob growls and drives into me, harder and faster with every stroke, my head tips back with the rising waves of furious ecstasy. I glimpse Griffin's face over me as he offers his own brand of worship.

He's smiling, bright with joy and maybe a little relief. And I can feel, almost as if I've borrowed his talent for an instant, that this is how he'd want our interlude to be.

Seeing his brother and me forge our own understanding with each other makes him happier than any collision between his body and mine could have.

Having me to himself isn't enough for Jacob, though. He slams into me again and again, massaging my ass, gripping my knee, and watches my free hand drift to caress his brother's arm.

"Can you take him too?" he says between grunts of exertion. "Can you bring Griffin with us?"

It's a challenge I can't resist as soon as it's out in the air. My fingers curl into the fabric of the boxers Griffin was sleeping in, and I urge him closer.

Griffin might not have been looking for more attention, but it's not as if he's unaffected. His chest hitches as my hand curls around his straining erection.

I rock with Jacob's thrusts and delve my fingers right inside Griffin's boxers to pump him at the same time. Griffin lets out a choked groan and bows over to kiss me nearly as hard as his brother did before.

As if in reward, a new pressure flows over my body. Jacob's invisible touch, propelled by the powers I can't see like extra hands exploring every inch of me.

His talent coils around my breasts to clamp on my nipples and tangles in my hair to tug it from my scalp with pinpricks of painful delight. He lowers one actual hand to pulse his thumb against my clit as fiercely as he's pounding into me.

I whimper and nudge Griffin a little farther back. Then I lean over to muffle a sharper cry around his cock.

My tongue laps around the head, and Griffin jerks into my hold, his breath fragmenting.

"Fucking hell, Moonbeam," he mutters, need fragmenting his voice. "That feels so fucking good."

I work my hand up and down his length as I suck his softly musky flavor into my mouth. My head is spinning with bliss, and every nerve is on fire.

When Griffin's body quivers and he moves to pull away, I lock my fingers tighter around him and propel his release into my waiting mouth. He sags toward me, mumbling curses and praise in a jumbled chorus.

Jacob lets out a groan of his own. I clutch his wrist, my claws slipping out to nick his skin, and he rakes his fingernails across my ass with a hiss.

His power tweaks my breasts and scalp with even more force, his thumb swivels over my clit, and the dam inside me bursts with his next slam home. I bite my lip hard enough to draw blood, muffling my moan of release.

"Love you, love you, love you," Jake says in a breathless chant, bucking into me through the deluge of pleasure. He leans over me as he spills himself inside me, claiming my mouth, bleeding lip and all.

My muscles sag, my body wrung out. Jacob gazes

down at me, a flicker of worry passing through his expression as the haze of desire clears from his eyes.

"I didn't mean to—it wasn't too much for—"

I drag him down onto the bed with me before he can finish the question. "It was perfect. Fucking *perfect*."

As his expression relaxes, I think he might finally totally believe me.

But in the wake of the flood of bliss, it turns out the frustrations that gnawed at me before weren't washed away. While I lie there between two of the men I love, my worries sprout up like weeds after a rainfall.

I don't want this kind of escape to be the closest thing we have to freedom. I don't want every moment of intimacy to exist under Balthazar's watch.

There has to be a way to fight him.

NINE

Riva

Sully slumps into the chair across from me at the dining table, having just returned for lunch after a session with Matteo. He lets out a rough sigh. "I don't know why he keeps making us go through that crap when it isn't doing anything."

Zian lifts his head from the roast beef sandwich he was polishing off a couple of seats down, his eyebrows lifting. "The procedures haven't affected your powers at all?"

The younger boy shakes his head, his broad face gloomy. "Matt's always asking me to make the illusions clearer and hold them longer. Or sometimes to draw them bigger. But it never works."

He pauses, and the lines of his frown pull deeper. "Sometimes I think he's hoping I'll make something that's not even an illusion—that I'll conjure something that turns out to be real. That's crazy, right?"

The six of us Firsts exchange a glance around the table.

None of us can conjure objects out of thin air, but given the unearthly things we *can* do, it doesn't seem impossible.

But from what we know, the younger shadowbloods were created from a weaker formula than our own genetic engineering, however exactly that worked.

Ursula Engel, one of the founding guardians and the scientist who worked out how to mingle human and shadowkind essence to create us, was scared when she saw how we Firsts were developing. She wanted us dead from when we were little kids.

The rest of the Guardianship refused, shut her out, and demanded her work so they could create more shadowbloods. The notes we found on her laptop indicated that she modified the instructions she sent them.

I suspect she was hoping her refined methods wouldn't work at all. That wasn't the case, but all of the younger shadowbloods we've met have powers much weaker than ours.

Balthazar must have been hoping that his staff's "procedures" would wake up new potential in them. Between the injections Matteo has given me and the mental and physical exercises he's insisted I perform, my own abilities have been steadily progressing.

Yesterday, I killed a rat in a second with a shriek that emitted almost no sound at all. Matteo was testing with a piece of tissue paper by my mouth that fluttered only a fraction with the hint of expelled breath.

I don't know what makes me queasier: the thought of how many innocent animals I've slaughtered over the past week or the moment when I almost *missed* Clancy.

The man who presided over the island facility had sick

ideas and was driven by greed, but he was also the only guardian who ever tried to teach me how my brutal power could be used to do things *other* than maim and kill. I'd much rather be practicing how to hold a creature in place without doing any actual harm than how to snuff out its life as quickly as possible.

Of course, if anyone bothered to give us an actual choice like a human being should have, I wouldn't be practicing at all. I'd be shoving down my hunger as far into the depths of my being as I could.

If we didn't have guardians and whoever else hunting us, I'd never need to bring it out again.

Andreas, with typical easygoing diplomacy, side-steps Sully's question of craziness altogether. "Maybe it's working on us faster because our abilities have already had more time to expand before now. I don't know how my talent with memories could develop much farther, but…"

He grips the arm of his wooden chair. With a flex of his fingers, both his hand and the chair disappear, leaving him sitting on what appears to be thin air.

I stare, my breath catching in my throat. I've seen Andreas turn completely invisible himself, but never only partly. And never making an object larger than he could fit in his pocket vanish as well.

He releases the chair, which blinks back into view instantaneously, and shrugs at us. "I have no idea if that's the direction Balthazar would have wanted my powers to go, but that's what I've gotten."

Booker frowns. "I'm not seeing auras brighter than I did before—or seeing anything new in them. Nadia's said it hasn't made any difference for her glowing either."

His stance tenses, and I suspect he's thinking of his girlfriend being led away by Matteo just minutes ago, after he returned Sully to us.

Booker glances at Ajax, who makes a face. "I still can't control when I pick up thoughts or go any deeper than I used to. As much as I wish I could."

The younger teen hesitates after that sentence, not voicing what I think he'd have added. If he could read minds more purposefully and clearly, he might be able to find us information that would get us out of Balthazar's grasp.

We don't mind talking about the things our captor definitely knows or could easily guess. Trying to keep totally closed-lipped about our real thoughts would drive us all insane.

But we all know it wouldn't be wise to openly discuss total rebellion.

Ajax turns to Zian, his dark eyes full of thoughtful curiosity. "You've seen a difference?"

Zian tips his head with an obvious reluctance that makes me want to give his arm a comforting squeeze. I wish he could welcome that contact instead of being afraid it'd set off his past trauma.

"I've been getting... bigger, when I transform," he says. "And some of the wolfish features more prominent. Matteo has been trying to see if anything will change with my X-ray vision too but not much there yet."

His shoulders hunch as he takes a careful bite of his sandwich, and my stomach tightens.

Zian already hated the way he transforms and the

monstrous rage that can provoke a shift. Now Balthazar's people are amplifying that part of him even more.

How many ways will we be tormented before we can find real freedom?

I force myself to tear into my own sandwich, but the layers of fresh bread and sliced meat taste like sawdust. Tension winds through my muscles, begging for action.

But what action could I take? The deadly manacles that hold all of us captive clink against the table with the movements of our arms.

There's been no sign that anyone's reacted to the note I tucked into that man's pocket at the gala a week ago. Did he not notice my plea for help?

Or maybe he thought it was a prank. Maybe he had no idea who Mr. Balthazar would even be.

My jaw clenches with the impression that the painted walls are closing in on us.

Farther down the table, Griffin's head jerks up. His expression goes distant as if he's focusing on something beyond this room.

We're all on edge enough to pick up on his shift in mood. Jacob is already pushing back his chair. "What? What's happening?"

Griffin's lips purse in concentration before his attention comes back to us. He pauses as if he's not sure how to answer.

Then he simply stands up. "Come with me. There's something I want to check."

Something he doesn't want to overtly tip off to anyone listening in. I scramble to my feet, my pulse kicking up a notch.

We all hustle after Griffin, abandoning our lunch. He doesn't give any indication about what he's noticed as he strides down the hall and pushes open the door at the back of the villa.

Nothing about the grounds outside or the sprawling mountain landscape beyond them looks different from usual. Griffin doesn't linger on them anyway, heading a little farther across the back patio toward a garden area with grassy paths winding between low hedges.

He pauses there, his head cocked. The rest of us gather behind him in silence.

After a minute, Griffin glances over his shoulder. "Jake, I think I can start this, but I might need you to... hold things in place."

He's still speaking vaguely for discretion. Jacob looks puzzled but nods without hesitation. "I'm ready."

Griffin closes his eyes.

For the space of several more breaths, we waver in bewildered anticipation. Then a form materializes between two of the nearby hedges: the portly, chestnut-haired shadowkind man we saw by the outer wall several days ago.

He's staring at us, his expression twitching between a smile and flickers of echoed bewilderment. Understanding hits me.

Griffin must have sensed the man was here at the villa —I told him what we'd seen. I bet shadowkind emotions have a distinctive flavor compared to any other visitors.

I also told him how the man ran away when we tried to talk to him. He's used his emotional compulsion to make the guy feel like he *wanted* to appear to us.

But the supernatural being is clearly fighting Griffin's sway. Jacob's eyes narrow, and the man's limbs lock in place.

Keeping his attention trained on the man, Jake motions to me. "I don't think me physically holding him will be enough if he decides to leave. You froze the shadowkind with your scream once."

I did. A chill washes over me, remembering that moment—the moment I slaughtered one of Rollick's associates who'd turned on us and then almost killed Billy, the sweet faun who'd only been trying to help.

But Jacob is right. We've never been able to stop shadowkind from vanishing into the shadows by physical force in the past.

My scream is the only thing that's ever totally constricted them. I can use it if I have to.

Griffin's persuasion seems to be keeping enough of the man's good will for now. I blurt out the first questions that pop into my head before I can't use my voice to speak anymore. "What are you doing here? Do you work for Balthazar?"

"Work?" The man's lip curls with a hint of a sneer. "Oh, he makes me work."

Griffin blinks, and something in the man's demeanor changes, his chin lifting at a more defiant angle. I tense to let out a scream, but the shadowkind doesn't make any other move.

It isn't us Griffin's encouraged his defiance against.

"What do you do for him?" Andreas asks.

A twitch ripples through the man's rounded frame. "Not anything it'd be good for me to talk to you about."

Zian steps forward. "Do you know a demon named Rollick? Or a succubus who works with him—Pearl?"

The blankness of the man's expression answers the question before he opens his mouth. I break in before he needs to. "If you know anyone who'd help us—we're trapped here—Balthazar has worked with people who want to *destroy* beings like you. We'd help—"

The shadowkind man cuts me off with a derisive snort. "*You're* trapped?"

Those two words say enough. I'm abruptly certain that the being in front of us, whatever his supernatural powers are, feels just as imprisoned by his association with Balthazar as we do.

How the hell did our captor manage that?

"Please," Ajax says quietly, but I've already caught the shift in the man's posture. He's shaking Griffin's emotional hold.

And I'm not sure it'd really be in our best interests to force him to stay any longer.

My lips part anyway, but before I can decide whether to make one more plea or to shriek his compliance, a horrible crackling, tearing sound bursts through the air from behind me.

Sully cries out with a choked sound, and Booker yelps. I spin around to see Sully flailing, his hands dangling from severed wrists, blood and dark essence pouring from his gouged forearms where his bracelets have ripped them open.

Like they did to Lindsay. Oh, fuck, no.

I leap to him like I did with her, even though I couldn't do anything before. Horrified adrenaline rushes through me, giving my awareness the heightened, disorienting feel of a nightmare.

Blood streams over the grass, painting the blades crimson. The meaty metallic smell saturating the air turns my stomach.

At the same time, the shadowy smoke billows upward, draining him in a very different way.

I clamp both hands around one of Sully's arms, willing myself to find a way to hold his flesh together, to stem the tide. But like with Lindsay, the gouge is too wide, too deep.

Zian is struggling to help Sully at his other side, but I already know even his thick hands can't seal these wounds. Sully sways on his feet, his face blanched, his eyes wide.

"I—I—" he mumbles, and his voice breaks with a desperate sob.

The other shadowbloods have closed in around him, the shadowkind man forgotten. "Put him down!" Jacob yells. "Maybe—maybe that'll slow the bleeding."

"Tear his shirt," Andreas says in a quieter but equally fraught voice. "If there's any way to bandage them…"

Zian tears at the fabric. Jacob kneels by us, his face hardening with concentration.

The flesh beneath my hands clamps together, but blood and smoke still seep from along Sully's wrist beneath the manacle. Jacob narrows his eyes, but his strained exhalation shows how much effort it's taking to work his talent that precisely.

His voice comes out with a rasp. "I can't hold both at the same time—can't concentrate like that…"

I glance around frantically through the haze of essence,

and my gaze snags on a familiar figure watching us from the house. I hadn't noticed Toni coming out.

"Please!" I shout at her. "Don't let Balthazar do this. Sully didn't do anything wrong. He was just—he was just *here*."

"You were told not to approach that man," Toni says in a rigid voice. "I hope you won't need another warning."

I stare at her. "He's just a *kid*. You can't really think this is okay."

Apparently she does. She simply turns away without another word.

And something snaps inside me.

Fury sears through me, sharp and prickling, rattling my lungs. Stoking a fresh scream into the base of my throat.

The shadowkind man wouldn't help us. None of the human beings here will either.

They've all turned their backs on us. They don't give a shit what Balthazar does to us.

There isn't a single person out there we can turn to except ourselves.

My throat resonates with the rising anger. I think I'd have shrieked it all out at Toni, shattered her from feet to head in the most painful way possible, if Sully hadn't lurched toward me right then.

We've lowered him partly to the ground, but he's managed to roll. My gaze jerks back to him as he squirms next to me.

"Help," he mumbles. "Help. Help."

I can see it's already too late. Blood drenches his

clothes and the grass beneath him. His voice is faltering with every iteration of his plea.

And it's all Balthazar's fault. Him and every person who's let him continue his reign.

The rage blares on inside me, burning away all my hopelessness and fear.

I won't be one of those people. I've destroyed everyone who tried to cage and torture us before.

I will not rest until I've shredded every organ in that psychopath's body and ended this madness once and for all.

TEN

Jacob

Matteo adjusts the target with a press of a button behind the transparent wall of his booth. The ringed circle mounted on its wooden board shifts to the left and rotates several degrees.

"All right," he says in his obnoxiously pedantic voice. "Let's see what kind of impact you can achieve with that."

I grit my teeth and flex my forearm against the arm of the chair, focusing on my awareness of the spines I can form beneath my skin. A prickle runs through my nerves all the way up to my shoulder.

When those toxic spikes first emerged from the side of my arm during the guardians' tests a couple of years ago, I thought they were permanent. Attached to my bones somehow, extending and contracting like Riva and Zian can with their claws.

It turns out they're more mobile than that. A couple of weeks ago on our last mission for Clancy, I shot them straight out of my arm into a man who was about to open fire on Riva.

I haven't mentioned that to Matteo. He believes that his special "procedures" have opened up this new dimension to my supernatural skills.

So he's been prodding me over and over since he first discovered the change, checking how far and how forcefully I can expel them, how quickly my body can produce new ones, and how accurately I can aim them.

And I can't pretend weakness or ineptitude, because the shitty chemical he always injects at the start of these sessions makes me nauseatingly compliant.

After trying to resist and failing every time during my first couple of sessions, I've achieved some kind of inner peace. I'll accept that I can't resist... and focus on gathering all the information *I* can about my own abilities.

Because Lord knows I'm looking forward to the day I can spear the man on the other side of that thick window with my poison quills.

I fix my gaze on the target and apply the mental pressure that I've learned primes my spines. The first time I launched them, it was all protective instinct.

Now I know how to control the firing. I adjust the angle of my arm and give a push that's a combination of will and muscle.

The row of spines pierces my skin and hurtles into the target. One only skims the edge and taps against the wall, but the others thud deep into its wooden surface.

I grimace at the minor error, but behind the pane, Matteo is smiling. "Now use your telekinesis to pry them out and fling them in opposite directions. Half to the left and half to the right."

As I automatically obey with no real say in the matter, a clammy sensation wraps around my gut.

Part of me is proud of the strides I've made under my unwanted teacher's watchful gaze. I've honed not just my skill with the spines but the invisible force I can inflict on the world too.

But I'm not totally sure it's a *good* thing that those powers are growing even more.

Before, it'd have been a strain to fling multiple objects in opposing directions simultaneously. Now, my talent clamps around the spines and flicks them away from each other without wavering.

Less than two weeks ago, I hesitated to heft Riva through a second-floor window. Now, I suspect I could propel her or any of the guys across a distance like that without any fear of missing my mark.

Not long before that, I shook an entire mountainside with Dominic's help, feeding me strength. Now… I might be able to rattle the entire plateau Balthazar's villa is perched on all by myself.

Which would be fantastic if I could count on only applying that strength when I want to. But my temper still has at least as much control over my talent as my rational mind does.

I've broken things I didn't mean to before. I don't like the idea that I could screw up even worse.

Because there are definitely no shortage of things pissing me off in our current situation.

And I still couldn't save Sully when he was bleeding

out. Couldn't figure out how to apply constant pressure to every place he needed it without loosening my grip somewhere else.

Funny how Matteo never wants to teach me about fixing things rather than attacking them.

After a few more exercises, the mellowing effect of Matteo's drug starts to fade. He taps some notes into his computer and then pushes a button that releases the clamps around my ankles. "Good session. You can go now."

He doesn't even look my way as he dismisses me. My hands clench—and the target cracks down the middle before I can catch the flare of anger.

Shit.

With shame quivering through my fury, I stride out of the room before I have to hear what Matteo will say about that slip when he notices.

The worst part about my unsteady self-control is that I could screw us over even if I only damage our enemies. If my power strikes out at anything or anyone Balthazar values, will he tear open another shadowblood's arteries and leave them to die drenched in their own blood?

The image of Sully's shaking, crimson splattered body flashes through my mind. I walk even faster back to the hall where we have our rooms as if I can outrun it.

Riva is there. The one supernatural ability I'm one hundred percent on board with is the fact that I can pinpoint her location through the tingling of the mark on my sternum.

She's nearby. She's okay.

The knowledge flows through me on repeat with every

thump of my pulse, taking the slightest edge off my frustration.

As I get closer, a less welcome sensation quivers through our bond. A jitter of agitation, like a scalding needle stinging me.

I push myself to a jog and reach the row of bedrooms just as Riva steps out of one. Her bright brown eyes shine with a cold glint I'm not used to.

"Here." She tosses a towel at me that I snatch out of the air automatically. "We're going swimming."

Tension winds through her limbs and the sharpened planes of her face. As I grip the towel, something tightens in my chest in response. "What? Why?"

Our friends are emerging from their own rooms to join us, looking like Riva has already informed them of this plan. She flicks her errant braid back over her shoulder and skims her fingers down her arm nearly to the silver manacle circling her wrist. "I think taking a dip could help us relax."

It's not hard to catch on. I should have thought of this myself.

We're still not sure how much information Balthazar's manacles are picking up. If he and his staff are recording audio through them, immersing them in water will cut that function off.

We'll be able to talk more freely, just this once.

It's a good plan, but as I turn to walk with Riva to one of the outer doors, the uneasy ache remains inside me.

Since Sully died yesterday, she's been so keyed up. She hasn't exactly *done* anything, but I can taste how furious she is as easily as breathing.

For the first time since we cleared up the misunderstandings between us, I'm really not sure what lengths she might go to. And I know she's capable of an awful lot.

I don't have even a flicker of fear that she might hurt *me* or any of the other shadowbloods. I'm not so sure about hurting herself by pushing too far.

My gaze veers to my brother, just ahead of me in the hall. Griffin hasn't commented on anything he's noticed about Riva's emotional state.

But then, he probably wouldn't want to point it out when Balthazar could be taking notes.

He could calm her down if he used that part of his talent on her—but for how long? She'd be twice as pissed off once she realized.

And she could end up too complacent to defend herself when she needs to. No, that would definitely not be the right tactic.

Maybe my twin will come up with some other brainstorm, with all his emotional expertise. He's... he's been good for her, now that he's more like himself.

I always knew he would be.

We step past the doorway and head across the patio to the pool with its warmed water. Riva marches right to the edge and starts stripping down to her bra and panties with brisk, jerky movements.

I glance over at Andreas and catch a matching worry in the slant of his mouth as our gazes meet. This isn't what we're used to from the woman we love.

Has that fucker Balthazar pushed her over some edge

already? How the hell are we going to drag her back from it?

My own anger ripples through me again. My power whips out—and I just snatch it back, an instant from battering one of the nearby planters.

My next breath shudders through me, thick with frustration... and guilt.

I can recognize the unnerving potential of Riva's rage because it's such a familiar emotion for me. Fuck, is this how my friends have felt the whole past four years, while I stewed and seethed over the murder and betrayal that never actually happened?

I've been there. *I* should know how to talk her down, not be sitting around hoping Griffin can handle it.

I don't want to be a volatile presence in her life, like a volcano constantly on the verge of erupting. I want to be a steady force she can count on.

But I've never fully gotten my own vicious impulses under control. How can I rein her fury in when I barely know how to do it with my own?

Those questions tangle in my gut as I peel off most of my own clothes. Balthazar didn't give us swimsuits, but boxers work just as well.

The chilly fall air washes over my bare skin, and then I'm sliding into the water. Its warmth closes around me with more relief than I'd like to feel while enjoying this bastard's property.

I stick close to Riva, wanting her within reach even if I'm not really sure how to hold on to her right now. The other shadowbloods slip into the water around us.

A fresh pang of horror jolts through me as I take in the

younger ones. There were five kids with us when we first woke up here. Now we're down to three.

Booker stays next to Nadia, his arm hooked around hers, his usually easy-going expression hardened. I haven't seen him leave her side since she got back from her session with Matteo yesterday.

He's got to know that if she'd been with us when we confronted the shadowkind man out here, chances are Balthazar would have had *her* killed instead of Sully. She was the one he marked as expendable from the start.

Apparently our captor decided Sully was expendable enough. It wouldn't have been as much of a punishment if the slaughter hadn't happened right in front of us.

I sink into the water up to my shoulders, holding my wrists well under the surface. The others are doing the same.

Riva motions us closer with a twitch of her chin. The pool is shallow enough at this end that even she can stand on the bottom, if on tiptoe, rather than treading water.

We gather in a huddle as if seeking more warmth from each other, away from the edges of the pool where other surveillance devices could be hidden.

Riva drops her voice to a whisper. Even that quiet, a thread of agitation thrums through it.

"I need to know everything you've all learned about Balthazar and this villa. Even if it didn't seem important at the time. There *has* to be a way to get to him."

Zian's forehead furrows. "What are you planning to do, Shrimp?" he asks, just as softly. He can't manage to give the playful nickname any amusement.

Riva shrugs. "It doesn't matter yet. I just want to know

what we're working with. Let's go, one by one, every little detail you can think of."

As she turns to Booker at her left, his arm still locked around Nadia, my stomach sinks. She says it doesn't matter, but I can tell she's already got a goal in mind.

If her rage is even slightly like mine, she wants to destroy this place and everyone in it. Especially the man who brought us here.

But how much of the woman I adore will she sacrifice to reach her goal?

ELEVEN

Riva

I can't sit still, even though I have no sense of direction right now. My hatred for our beautiful prison and the man who's keeping us here burns through my veins, gnawing at me to do *something*.

I stalk through the villa's hallways in the fading evening light, my claws arcing from my fingertips. The urge grips me to scratch at the delicate frescos decorating the walls, but I hold myself back.

The building itself hasn't hurt me. Destroying it won't do anything but ruin the only things that *are* appealing in this place.

For all I know, Balthazar won't even care. I have no idea why he picked this place to hold us or how much it means to him—or doesn't.

Maybe it was simply the first building he could find with plenty of rooms and isolation from the rest of society.

He definitely doesn't seem bothered about spilling blood all over the tiled artwork of the floors.

The memories of Lindsay's and Sully's deaths make my clawed fingers flex. Tufts of fur shoot from the shifting tips of my ears as my full morph takes over.

I wish I could transform into an actual cat and slip through all the spaces I can't as a human being. Shake off these stupid manacles.

I prowl all the way to the front door and glare across the courtyard at the drawbridge I've only seen raised. Not that we could reach it even lowered, as Sully demonstrated on our first day.

As I spin on my heel to stalk back the way I came, Nadia ventures into the hall, coming toward me. Dark circles mark her smooth brown skin beneath her eyes, and her once spunky pixie cut droops in limp waves.

She catches my eyes, tucking her hands a little deeper in the baggy sweater she's got on. It's a deep navy blue, striking on her but with completely the wrong vibe.

She's meant to be in neons. Balthazar hasn't bothered to think about our clothing preferences.

It's a silly thing to criticize him for, but hell, even Clancy made that basic gesture toward earning our loyalty.

Our new captor hasn't considered loyalty. He wants our spirits crushed into total obedience.

"Hey," Nadia says. "I was thinking it might be nice to hang out a bit, listen to one of those records in your room?"

I don't know if I can do anything that would help her, but it's better than striding aimlessly around the villa. "Of course."

She stays silent as we walk up to my bedroom. I pick out a record at random from the small stash Andreas brought me and fiddle with the controls until I get it playing, a process I'm still teaching myself.

The bouncy beats of an old pop song crackle out into the air, a sharp contrast with the atmosphere in the room. At another time, in another place, it'd have made me want to dance.

Now it only reminds me of how far I am from being able to enjoy music the way I used to.

Nadia sinks down on the edge of my bed, close to the vanity where I have the player set up. She pats the spot next to her, so I sit there.

As I settle myself, she lifts her arms and emphasizes the tug of her sleeves over her hands. Over her bracelets—hoping to muffle them?

Catching on, I adjust my own sleeves and tuck my hands into the kangaroo pocket of my hoodie to add an extra layer of fabric. This must be why she wanted the music too—to cover our conversation.

Nadia offers a tight smile. She tilts her head close to mine, speaking quietly as an extra precaution. "I think I saw something you might want to check out."

I nod to show I'm listening.

She tips her head farther, indicating the back end of the villa. "I was taking a walk outside with Booker a little while ago, and around the back, close to the western wing, I noticed a window. Second floor, small and square. Definitely haven't seen it in any rooms we've had access to from the inside."

I sort back through my memories. "I haven't seen one

like that either." Most of the villa's windows are tall and arched.

"So it must be a room we couldn't normally get into," Nadia goes on. "Stuff they're keeping hidden. And someone moved past the window while I was looking at it, so they're up to something in there too."

She pauses, adjusting her sleeves again. "The other thing is, at least when I saw the window, they'd left it a little bit open, so it can't be locked. I'm not sure how to get up there, but it's small enough that I don't think anyone could fit through the frame except you or maybe Ajax."

I look down at my hands, bulges in my pocket. I can climb—I've scaled the outside of buildings before.

A tremor of anticipation races through my nerves. "Thank you. I'll see what I can make of it tonight."

Nadia sighs as if relieved to have gotten the information out unscathed and straightens up again. But her shoulders stay a bit slumped, her expression still weary.

My throat tightens as I take those details in. "How are you holding up?"

She rubs her mouth and shakes herself, but the strain doesn't leave her face. "Hanging in there. Honestly, I'm more worried about Booker than me right now. Matteo interrupted our walk to bring him to a session, and he didn't want to leave me. I think he might have tried to fight the guy if I hadn't gotten through to him how much I *didn't* want that."

After seeing how determinedly Booker has been sticking by Nadia's side since Sully's death, I'm not surprised. But she's right—it wouldn't have ended well for him.

"He cares about you a lot," I say.

Nadia's mouth twists. "Yeah. Maybe too much. Everyone knows I'm useless. The procedures aren't doing anything—I still just *glow*."

The anguish in her voice sets off a fresh flare of my anger. "You're not *useless*." And fuck Balthazar for making her think that way.

Nadia raises her head to meet my gaze again, unflinching. "That's the whole reason I'm here. Like a fucking hostage. A damsel in distress." She lets out a rough laugh.

I shake my head vehemently. "No. That's how the psychopath who stuck us here sees it, but he doesn't know anything. All it means is he doesn't see a way to use you for whatever exactly he wants to do. If he was trying to explore dark places, you'd be the only one who matters."

Nadia sounds as if she's choked on a more genuine giggle. "Okay, I guess that's true."

I turn toward her, drawing my legs up on the bed. "And—if there's one thing I figured out on the island, it's that we shouldn't have to use our powers. We didn't ask the guardians to make us this way, and we don't owe them or anyone else anything. We're still people. We shouldn't have to be *useful* to deserve our lives. If you weren't a shadowblood, no one would expect that."

The song peters out, and there's a faint hiss before the next one starts.

Nadia lowers her gaze again. "But we are shadowbloods. That's just how it is."

My hands clench. I want to tear apart the people who made her feel this way.

Of course, it's possible I already have.

Just not enough of them, clearly.

"We're people too," I insist. "We're people *first*. No matter what the guardians or anyone else see. I see a whole lot more than your power to glow."

Nadia is silent for a moment. "What does it matter if we never get the chance to be more?"

The impatient fury churns in my gut with a searing ache. "We will."

I swallow thickly and grope for something to say that might make her feel better in the moment. "What would you want to do in a normal life, as a normal seventeen-year-old?"

I asked that question to a few of the other younger shadowbloods back on the island. Like them, Nadia hesitates, looking almost confused by the idea.

But as she thinks about it, a light comes into her face that wasn't there before. Enough to soothe the sharpest edges of my rage.

She tips her head back, her eyes hazy with her daydream. "It probably sounds silly, but I kind of want to go to a real school. Experience all the drama and stuff… I mean, it's probably hardly anything like the TV shows and movies. But still. Getting to know all those people. Learning normal stuff. Different outfits every day, hanging out after class without anyone shoving you in a cell or hauling you off to training."

The corner of my mouth curls upward. "Yeah, that could be fun."

Nadia fidgets with the hem of her sweater before going on. "I also always liked the cop shows. You know, when there'd be a woman in uniform tracking down the crooks and bringing them to justice. I feel like I could be good at that. 'Stop right there. Put your hands up!'"

She laughs, but it's a softer sound this time. My heart squeezes with pained affection.

I want her to have those dreams. I want all the kids who've grown up like me and my guys to have a chance at a normal future.

"It could happen," I say, even though I don't know how. "We're not done yet."

When I sneak out of the villa to examine the window Nadia mentioned, the night closes in around me in a cloak of shadows. I waited until it was fully dark like I normally have for my secret prowls, although impatience itched at me like a bad case of poison ivy.

A few security lights beam at long intervals along the wall at the edge of the grounds. I stick close to the villa where the darkness is thickest.

As I come around the back of the massive house, I scan the second floor for the small, square window. Close to the western wing, Nadia said.

The panes of glass reflect shimmers of the distant light. I'm a little more than halfway along the back of the villa when I spot the right one.

I must have seen it before; I've circled the building

plenty of times since we arrived. I just never paid much attention to it.

But Nadia's right. I haven't been inside any rooms that hold a window like that.

If someone on Balthazar's staff—or the man himself—spends time in there, it could be important. And just as when Nadia saw it, there's a gap of about an inch between the frame and the sliding pane.

I've tested a few of the windows on the first floor of the western wing as surreptitiously as I could, and none of them budged. Short of smashing through the glass, which would have me discovered in an instant, I'm not getting through those.

Now I can take advantage of someone's lapse of caution.

I flick out my claws and raise my hands to the old bricks. In the past several days, Matteo has pushed me to stretch my speed and strength as well as my scream.

This climb is going to be a piece of cake thanks to the training I've gotten from the pricks I'm working against.

With a little leap, I'm scaling the wall, moving my hands swiftly and precisely so my claws make only a faint click of sound each time they dig in.

It takes only a few beats of my heart before I reach the window ledge. I squeeze my hand into the gap beneath the sliding pane and shove it upward.

It rises with a rasp that has me holding my breath. But only stillness follows.

Even with my tiny frame, it's a tight squeeze wriggling through the open space. With shoulders hunched inward and then a twist of my hips, I finally squirm into a landing I catch with my spread hands on another tiled floor.

Maybe that's why they were careless with the window. They assumed none of us would be able to enter through it anyway.

I roll into a crouch and peer around me, rubbing the sore spots on my shoulders where I expect I'll be bruised tomorrow.

Like the window, the room is small. Maybe ten feet long and wide, a far cry from the grand chambers the rest of the villa boasts.

With my first impression, my spirits deflate. It doesn't look like an office or workroom or anything I'd expect to find sensitive information about Balthazar's dealings in.

There's a twin bed in one corner, the headboard carved with a mountain range like the vista outside. The wood is painted a pale yellow like the dresser on the opposite wall and the bookshelf next to the window.

After that first glance, I move to the door. If this room will give me access to more of the secured part of the villa…

My thoughts are already leaping ahead with a surge of vengeful determination. I could dart through the halls, crash into Balthazar's room, rake my claws through his vital organs before he's fully woken up—

No such luck. My tentative twist of the knob tells me it's locked—and well. I don't think I could break the deadbolt without enough noise to alert anyone nearby.

Shit. Well, I might as well see what I can make of what I do have access to.

I slink around the room, confusion tickling up through my steady burn of enraged resolve.

The bed is a little shorter than the one I've been sleeping in as well as narrower—a kid's bed. Underneath it, my exploring hand encounters a box full of trading cards for some game I've never played.

The bookcase holds picture books and novels with bright covers and large print. A model boat sits on a shelf next to some of them.

When I move to the dresser, I freeze. In the darkness, I barely made out the rectangular objects poised on top of it until I was right in front of them.

They're framed photographs.

I pick up the first of the three and angle it so the faint light seeping from the window can illuminate it. Three little boys grin at me, their arms looped over each other's shoulders, their faces painted like cartoon animals.

The next has the boy from the middle of the first group, recognizable by his light auburn hair and prominent ears, perched on the lap of a man in a Santa suit.

And the third…

The third I stop and stare at as time slips away from me.

The boy is there again, maybe a little older than in the first two pictures but no more than seven or eight as well as I can estimate. He's standing between a man and a woman I assume are his parents, their arms crossing each other's as they both rest a hand affectionately on his shoulders, all three of them beaming at the camera.

The man is Balthazar.

It must be from a while ago, because his hair is all tawny in the picture, no gray showing yet. He's just as broad and imposing as the man I've talked to, but the glint in his eyes doesn't look quite so feral.

He might actually be… happy.

This guy has a family? He murders kids on a whim and then goes back to his wife and son like it was just another day at the office?

I study the woman next. Her ruddy hair obviously contributed to their son's auburn.

She's slim, almost fragile-looking, especially next to Balthazar's hulking frame. There's a sweetness to her smile that sends an odd pang through my chest.

I feel like I would want to get to know her. How can she be with such a monster of a man?

Maybe she isn't anymore. Maybe she figured out what he's like and left him.

I don't think the family could be living *here*, after all, and Balthazar wouldn't spend weeks on end away from them, right?

But then, I don't actually know that he *has* been here himself this whole time. He could be zipping away on trips back to his real home without us catching on.

My mind skims back through all the minor observations my fellow shadowbloods have scrounged together over the past several days. Has anything they've seen or overheard related to Balthazar's home life?

Nothing clicks into place. I scowl and peer at the photo even more intently.

And that's when I notice there are four figures in the image.

The family is standing in front of a stretch of lush forest, probably a park somewhere. And in the background off to the side, slightly blurred but still recognizable, stands a tall, wiry woman with sleek black hair and a square jaw.

Toni's hair is a little longer in the picture, down to her shoulders rather than her current chin-length bob, and there's more youthful softness to her features. But that's definitely her.

So, she's been working with him for a while now—at least since whenever this photo was taken. She's met his family.

I set the picture back on the dresser, the wheels turning in my head. That's something we didn't know before.

Now how can I use it to bring Balthazar down?

TWELVE

Riva

I come out of my bedroom the next morning on my way to breakfast and find Toni standing in the hall just outside my door as if she's waiting for me.

As I jerk to a stop, my pulse hitches. Did she somehow realize what I got up to last night?

Has she come to deliver some horrible new punishment?

She simply tilts her head toward the end of the hall with a swing of her bobbed hair. "Mr. Balthazar wants to speak with you."

I guess it'd be a little much to expect even a "Good morning" from one of his close associates.

My hands rise to fidget with the deadly manacles around my wrists. I push myself to follow her, my nerves prickling.

What does the psychopath want with me now? Can I get anything out of him that will help *my* goals?

How much longer will it be until I can splatter his blood all over the villa's walls?

As the familiar anger sears through my limbs, I glance at the woman beside me. The sight of her square jaw and the firm line of her lips above it reminds me of the photo I stumbled on last night.

What can I get from *her*? She must know all kinds of things about her boss.

She's been working with him for a long time—she's stuck with him through all the horrors he's carrying out. She can't be totally unaffected, right?

Even if whatever she does feel about the situation is in favor of his methods.

"Is it really worth risking your life for this jerk?" I ask abruptly. Surprise seems more likely to get me an unusual reaction than being coy about the subject.

Toni stops and turns toward me with a slight arch of one eyebrow. "Risking my life?"

I fold my arms over my chest, gazing steadily back at her. "I could kill you right now if I wanted to. Before these bracelets could stop me. He's *training* me to kill as fast as possible. And I'm not the only one here who could." Or who'd want to, although spelling out our desire for vengeance feels unwise.

Toni's expression doesn't even twitch. Her tone stays mild. "I don't think you will, though. You know the others would suffer for it. Balthazar would be awfully angry. Who's to say whether they'd all even survive?"

My jaw clenches despite my intention of staying cool and calm. I temper my voice. "You're so sure he'd care that much? He might be pissed off that we destroyed one of his tools, but I haven't seen any reason to believe you're any more of a person to him than we are."

One corner of Toni's mouth curves upward—just a tad, but enough to notice. She thinks the point I just made is fucking *funny*.

"You don't know very much, kid," she says dryly. "I would focus more on keeping yourself safe than on threatening me."

Before she can start walking again, I snatch at another tactic. "And how much does his wife know? Or his son? Are they oh-so-happy that their—"

I haven't even finished hurling the questions at her when an emotion I can't identify blazes in her eyes. "You know nothing about that either," she snaps, cutting me off. "You've got no idea what family even means, lab rat."

I hit a sore spot—but she's managed to prod one of my own too.

My shoulders stiffen with a flare of anger I can't contain. "I guess you don't know much either, then. The guys I grew up with are closer than family—closer than I bet you or your boss could understand. We've *only* had each other. And here you are trying to tear us apart. What does that say about you?"

Toni glares at me for a moment before she visibly reins in her irritation with me. "Enough. Let's get going. He won't be happy if you make him wait."

She heads down the hall again, and I stride after her, following her down the grand staircase. "Why should I care about making him happy? He doesn't give a shit about what I want. Is he going to start killing off my 'family' over a five-minute delay now? That's the kind of lunatic you're supporting?"

This time, Toni doesn't even answer. Her silence gnaws at me.

Something I said got to her. I provoked her out of her professional front.

How can I do it again?

"They don't know, do they?" I venture, speaking quickly to get as much out as I can before she interrupts again. "*His* family. You're helping him go behind their backs while they figure—"

Toni lets out a laugh so dark it sends a chill through my bones. "You really don't have any clue."

I lift my chin. "Then how about you tell me? Explain to me how this job you're doing is anything other than horrific."

"I don't have to justify myself to you."

She ushers me into the drawing room. In another few seconds, she'll let Balthazar know I've arrived, and I won't get to push any farther.

I fling my arm toward the case that contains Dominic, as still as ever with the medical equipment keeping him stabilized in his coma.

"That's what Balthazar's done to my family. To one of the people I love more than anything in the world. You helped him do it. Maybe you can't be bothered to justify it to me, but if you're more than a total idiot, someday you'll have to justify it to yourself."

Toni looks at Dominic with a faint twist of her mouth

that might actually be discomfort. The moment only lasts a couple of beats of my heart before she returns her dark gaze to me, but the edge in her voice has softened.

"I know who I owe and what they deserve," she says. "We have our own loyalties. You're best off accepting that."

She must give some signal, because the screen begins to hum up from the tabletop across the room. Toni marches out through the doorway.

I find myself staring after her, turning over her words in my mind. Who she owes... Her own loyalties...

Something about her phrasing leaves me with the strange sense that it wasn't Balthazar she was talking about. But who else could she mean?

Could she really see what he's doing to us as a necessary evil? I've certainly slaughtered a lot of people in the interests of protecting the men I'm loyal to.

Of course, those people were outright *attacking* us in most of those cases. If Balthazar hadn't taken us prisoner, we wouldn't have done a thing to him.

We still haven't, as much as I've burned to.

The screen clicks fully upright. I file my thoughts about Toni away in case they'll be useful later and focus on the man whose image is blinking into view before me.

Balthazar rests his thick hands on the desk in front of him. My gaze flicks from it to the walls behind him, searching for some clue about where in the villa he is.

Can I decipher the shape of the room's window from the fall of the light? Guess which floor it's on from the angle of the beams?

Are there any sounds seeping through the speakers

alongside his voice that might help form a clearer picture in my head?

If I knew exactly where he is, I could wait until he summons one of the other shadowbloods to speak and then dash over there. It doesn't matter that I'd need to smash the window if I'd be gutting him an instant later.

Or I might even be able to shriek his death without so much as leaving the grounds.

"Hello, Riva," Balthazar says in his throaty baritone. "I've been glad to hear about your progress in Matteo's sessions."

My fingers flex at my sides, the imagined fatal blow tingling through me. I don't give a fuck about how glad he is. "I do what I have to do."

"But it's impressive seeing your powers grow. Don't you find that too? Isn't it satisfying to know how much you can accomplish?"

A renewed wave of fury washes over me. My voice comes out taut. "I'd rather if I could accomplish things that *I* want to do instead of having to follow someone else's orders."

My captor lets out a low chuckle, but the feral glint that unnerves me keeps dancing in his penetrating eyes. "Sometimes your best interests are served by following someone who has a better idea of the world than you do. When we're finished, when you've seen the full picture, there may be time for you to pursue other things."

"Finished *what*?" I ask, pulling my attention away from him to try to study the room around him again. "Why don't you show me the full picture now, if it'll change my mind?"

"Oh, I'm sure it'll come together as we continue our work. After we're through, the decisions will be in our hands—all of them. What more do you need to know?"

The confidence in his tone rankles me. I can't concentrate on the details of his surroundings. Nothing jumps out at me as identifiable anyway.

I glower my frustration at him. "I have no idea what you're talking about."

He gazes back at me intently. "You aren't happy with this world you've been forced into, are you, Riva? The guardians have had their various complaints, but they've never been willing to go far enough to really fix the grand scheme. Can you really tell me that you wouldn't want to set an awful lot of things right?"

The grand scheme? Setting things right?

He sounds almost like Clancy right now, only puffed up with a hundred times more ambition.

"Are you going to tell me that our missions have been to destroy 'bad' people?" I demand. "Clancy already tried to convince us we were going to be heroes. We figured out the truth."

"James Clancy was a petty man swayed by money and the opinions of his peers. I can see straight through to a wider vision. A world with everything in its proper place. But that takes time." Balthazar cocks his head. "And help. I'm only doing what's necessary to bring about the future we all need."

Are all these vague claims supposed to make me feel better about the murders he's carried out?

I grimace at him, the scream that wouldn't affect him through the transmission anyway vibrating beneath my throat. "Why are you telling me this? I don't care what the fuck you think you're working toward when you're forcing me and the others to go along with it."

He hums to himself. "You're still upset with me. That's understandable. I can't tell you more when you might try to use it to undermine me. But I want you to know that I appreciate the strides you've taken and the assistance you've given so far."

Did he call me in here just to *thank* me? To rub it in my face that I've been forced to carry out his dirty work for him?

I bare my teeth, a dozen caustic responses jangling together at the back of my mouth, but Balthazar goes on first.

A slight smile crosses his face. I have the feeling it's meant to be apologetic, but it doesn't quite hit the mark.

"I will also be limiting your distractions. From now on, you'll have fewer responsibilities to worry about."

My pulse gives a painful lurch. "What are you talking about?"

He straightens up, a move that I know from experience means he's about to end this conversation. "The younger shadowbloods haven't been making any progress with the procedures. Continuing on an unproductive path is pointless. I've arranged to have them sent away."

With that, the screen goes black, leaving his last words ringing in my ears.

Panic jolts through my veins. I haven't seen any of the other shadowbloods since yesterday.

I spin toward the door and sprint to the hallway, heading for the stairs.

The names burst from my lips in a frantic yell. "Nadia? Booker? Ajax?"

No one answers.

THIRTEEN

Zian

Riva stalks back and forth over the patio, her sneakers scraping the stone tiles. A tremor runs through her tiny body.

With a sudden snarl, she lashes out at the nearest planter. With the supernatural strength we both possess, her foot connects and bashes a crack through the polished stone.

The sight of her anguished fury brings a helpless ache into my chest. I want to protect her from her frustration, but I have no idea how.

The other guys look just as worried.

"It could be a good thing," Andreas says tentatively, his dark gray eyes as clouded as the sky overhead. "If the kids aren't here, Balthazar can't use them to punish us. Not the same way he did before."

Riva grimaces. "For all we know, he already killed

them. He didn't think they'd be useful to him after all. Why keep them around?"

For a second, none of us speaks. We can't prove what happened either way, and she has a point.

Then Jacob lets out a huff. "He wouldn't do that. They could still be leverage down the line. That prick doesn't seem like the type to *waste* anything he might be able to use later."

I nod, glad to have an argument against the idea that all three of the remaining kids were murdered. "That's true. He said he kept the rest of the kids too, just somewhere else, so why not them?"

"Maybe he was lying about all of it." Riva resumes her pacing, her hands clenched at her sides. "He didn't even give us a chance to talk to them before he did whatever he did with them. Dragging them off in the middle of the night…"

Griffin speaks up in a gentle tone. "I didn't know the three of them well enough that I can pinpoint their presence at a distance. But I had gotten a little friendly with them. I think if Balthazar's people did anything really horrible to them here at the villa, their emotions would have hit me hard enough to wake me up."

Riva swipes her hands through the air, her manacles flashing beneath the cuffs of her sweatshirt. "So, they weren't in total agony when they left. Who knows what happened after—what could still be happening?"

The ache expands down to my gut. She isn't even trying to hide her anger with Balthazar, even though she knows he could be listening to this entire conversation.

The aggression in her tone and movements resonates

all too closely with my own mood. The thought of that asshole on the screen shoving the kids around after he already slaughtered two of them for no reason at all...

My fangs itch in my jaws. A wolfish growl lodges in my throat with a surge of feral rage.

But I don't like who I am when I let out my beastly side. As much as I long to tear apart every person I can reach in the villa, I know going on a rampage against our captors isn't going to solve anything.

I've done things I hate when I let the wolf-man take over. The last four years of my life have been shadowed by horror and guilt because of it.

If Riva is heading down the same path... That's the last thing I want for the woman I love.

"We'll find them again," Andreas assures her. "I once looked in the head of a guy who finally reunited with his high school best friends after thirty years of losing touch and moving halfway across the world. If he could manage it, we will too."

Riva snorts. "Somehow I don't think his friends were also being imprisoned by a maniac."

Jacob bares his teeth. "We've gotten free from maniacs before. There are always answers. We just have to find them."

"You're very upset," Griffin adds in the same soothing tone as before. "It makes sense. But you'll think more clearly if you give yourself a chance to cool down."

Riva whirls toward him with a flash of her bright brown eyes. "Fuck cooling down. There's nothing about this situation any of us should be cool about!"

Her anger reverberates through her words, sharp enough that I flinch inwardly.

This isn't who Riva should be either. I know her—I know who she is when she's not trapped like a wounded creature in a snare.

She had all the compassion in the world for me and the horrible things I've done. For Jake and his awful mistakes.

She considers every angle and tries to find the fixes that hurt the fewest people.

But not like this. Not when she's practically vibrating with rage.

She's been on edge since Sully died. How much longer can she go on like this before she *really* snaps?

The other guys shift uneasily on their feet, glances passing between us. And I realize that no one wants to say the thing that's at the core of all our suggestions and assurances.

A sense of resolve stiffens my posture. What the hell. It might as well be me.

If she doesn't like hearing it, I'm the one best equipped to receive her wrath, however she deals it out.

I clear the lump from my throat, but my voice still comes out rough. "We're just—we're scared for you, Riva. I'm scared that you're going to do something you'll regret when you're this pissed off. Hell, I'm a little bit scared *of* you."

Riva stares at me for a few beats. Tension lingers in her face, but her shoulders come down from their rigid position. "I—I wouldn't do anything that would hurt any of you."

"I know you wouldn't on purpose," I say quickly. "It's just—I know from personal experience that when you've got anger driving you, sometimes you're not even making the decisions yourself."

She's as aware as the guys how true that was for me. But her wince doesn't make me feel any better than her rage did.

Maybe… maybe she needs me more than the other guys right now, *because* I can speak from my experience.

I hesitate for only a fraction of a second before holding out my hand to her, bracing myself against the jitter of my nerves at the idea of touching her. "Walk with me?"

Riva's throat works, her expression softening. She's also aware of how much the simple gesture means to me.

As she curls her fingers tentatively around mine, my gaze flicks to the other guys again. Jacob's eyes are smoldering, but he tips his head as if encouraging me. Andreas offers a crooked smile, Griffin a milder one.

They're okay with me taking the lead here. I hope I don't screw *this* up, because I don't really have any idea what I'm going to do once Riva and I start walking.

Riva manages to still give me some space, falling into step with me about a foot away from my much larger frame while holding my hand. Her compassion hasn't gone anywhere.

The swell of affection around my heart blunts the edges of the gnawing ache. I grip her hand a little tighter and catch a hint of a smile as my reward.

We stroll across the patio and through one of the grassier stretches of garden, not speaking at first. I look down at our clasped hands with a slow breath to steady myself.

"You never got this upset before. Not when we were on the run or with Clancy."

"I know." Riva swipes her free hand over her face. "It's just been so much, over and over. I'm tired of fighting, but I don't know how else to get out of this. I want it to be *done*."

"What if it can't be yet?"

Her head droops. "Then I guess I have to live with that, huh?"

A different kind of ache spreads through my limbs— the urge to wrap my arm around her and tug her close, to offer every kind of reassurance. But I don't want to fuck up whatever progress I've made with her by setting myself off into a panic.

My gaze snags on a row of smaller clay pots lined up along the outer wall of the grounds. The flowers that once sprouted from the soil have shriveled in the cooling weather.

A spark of inspiration lights in my head. I draw Riva over to them.

Picking up one of the pots, I aim a careful grin at her. "Maybe if we smash some things right now, it'll be easier not to smash anything we really shouldn't later?"

A startled laugh tumbles from Riva's mouth. She considers the pots for a moment and grabs one of her own. "I definitely feel like breaking something."

I hurl mine first, flinging it off into the vista beyond the wall. It careens out into the air and plummets beyond the cliff.

My supernaturally keen ears pick up the faint smash of the clay shattering on the ground far below.

Riva could throw just as far as I can, but I doubt she'd get the satisfaction of hearing the result that far away. With a hint of a smirk, she slams her pot toward the rocky outcropping just beyond the wall.

The smash reverberates through my bones with a weird sense of contentment. Hell, I might have needed this release too.

We both snatch up another of the pots and whip them at the edge of the cliff. Riva lets out another laugh, freer this time, a gleam coming back into her eyes.

A stern voice carries across the grounds. "What are you doing?"

We turn to see Toni marching over. She stops several feet away, taking in our stances and the missing pots.

"I don't see what you think you're going to accomplish like this," she says flatly.

Riva cocks her head, a flicker of anger returning but not as wild as before. "We're letting out some frustration. You should probably appreciate the fact that we found a method that doesn't involve any bloodshed."

I pick up another pot and toss it in my broad hand, watching the woman. "You could give it a try too if you'd like to try. Plenty of flowerpots to go around."

I have to think anyone working under a boss like Balthazar has a little steam to blow off. But I'm not really surprised when Toni's mouth tightens and she spins on her heel without taking me up on the offer.

She stalks away, not ordering us to stop either. I guess

she figures it is better that we smash a few flowerpots than anything more important.

"More for us!" Riva declares, and snatches up one of the remaining pots.

We work our way through the entire row, cracking some right below the wall, launching others far out across the landscape. When there are none left, Riva gazes down at the browned strip of lawn where they were resting.

Her attention shifts to her empty hands. Her stance falters.

I'm not at all prepared for the tears that streak down her cheeks.

"Shit," she mumbles immediately, dabbing at her eyes with her sleeves. "Sorry." Her breath comes out in a hitch.

I don't know what to do. *I* caused this. I started us smashing flowerpots and somehow that cracked open something in her.

My body moves on instinct. I step toward her and freeze, my nerves clanging with alarm.

But there's nothing in the impulse that feels at all like the horrible moment years ago when I ripped the woman the guardians hired to pieces. All I want is to comfort *this* woman however I can.

My arms slip around her. Riva startles and then tips her head against my shoulder.

"I want him dead," she murmurs in a watery voice, so quietly I don't think anyone other than me would be able to hear her even this close. "I want that psychopath dead and gone so this can be finished."

I hold her against my chest, so much love and worry

flowing through me that it sweeps away every other consideration. "I know. I get it."

There's nothing else I can say, but it seems to be enough. Riva's breaths start to even out.

She risks hugging me back, not too tight, and my pulse only stutters a little. But the softly sweet scent of her fills my nose, and the moment starts to feel dangerous.

Riva eases back before I have to and gives me a shaky smile. "Thank you. For everything."

She's obviously not *okay*, but I have the sense that I managed to settle down the storm in her a little bit.

I smile back. "Any time, Shrimp."

As Riva guffaws, another chuckle tugs at my attention. I lift my head and realize the other guys have followed us over, watching from the edge of the garden.

Andreas's smile is wider now, and Jacob looks almost pleased—as close as he ever gets, these days. We amble over to join them, my spirits lifting with a strange rush of relief.

I guess I'm more than just a raging brute, aren't I? I've got compassion too—enough that I got through to Riva even in her own rage.

Is it possible I haven't needed to be so scared of myself after all?

Griffin tilts his head toward the villa with a thoughtful expression. "She wanted to, you know. Just for a moment."

It takes me a second to figure out what he's talking about. He indicated the direction Toni stalked off in.

From what he picked up of her feelings, some part of her liked the idea of joining our smash-fest?

I look down at my wrists, wondering how much it's

safe to say in answer. And a fresh chill prickles through my veins, sharper than the breeze.

Riva wants to kill Balthazar. But the manacles he's locked us up with will work even if he's gone.

We won't be able to leave the villa. Unless we can figure out how to access and alter his security system, we'll still be just as trapped.

Which means we're going to need someone else here on our side. Someone who can get them off.

It's going to take a lot more than a brief interest in hurling pottery to manage that.

But I guess we have to start somewhere.

I'm not sure how to express those thoughts to the others either, not here. We'll have to take another swim to talk properly as a group.

Before I can suggest that, Balthazar's other top employee comes striding into view. Matteo rubs his hands together and fixes his piercing gaze on me.

"Zian. You're due for a session."

My body wants to balk, but I force it to relax. "All right."

As I stroll over, I size him up, trying to think of anything I've noticed that might help me win him over. Because he's not just an enemy but another opportunity, isn't he?

Reaching him, I roll my shoulders as if eager to get started. "What are we working on today?"

FOURTEEN

Riva

The silver manacles might not weigh much, but they're starting to chafe my wrists.

I can't stop myself from adjusting them, as little as they budge against my skin. Even with the dampening of sweat that's forming on my arms, they barely move a fraction of an inch.

My gaze stays fixed on the mirrored high rise visible through the van's windshield, looming farther up the street.

We parked a few minutes ago within view of the shallow courtyard outside the shiny office building. Unfortunately, to avoid looking suspicious, we had to turn off the engine.

Can't leave the air conditioning running without wearing out the battery. We don't know quite how long we'll have to wait here for the moment Balthazar is counting on.

The air is already stuffy from the sunlight streaking past the downtown buildings. I wet my lips and take a sip from the bottle of water that's also quickly warming.

Then I glance around at the guys: Jacob in the driver's seat across from me, Andreas and Zian in the open area behind us. "Any idea what city this is?"

Andreas leans against the back of my seat. "I haven't recognized any of the buildings. I'm not sure what kind of writing that is on the signs either."

Zian grimaces. "If Drey hasn't seen it before, I definitely haven't."

Jacob kicks restlessly at the underside of the dash and touches one of his own manacles. "It's not like we can go out and ask anyone."

His statement encompasses various other things he leaves unspoken. He'd like to find out. He knows that if we deviate that far from the task Balthazar has assigned us, it won't be worth the consequences.

We're unlikely to find anyone who'd understand us and answer us clearly before our keeper makes us regret it anyway.

Does Balthazar have another team stationed nearby, monitoring us? Employees who don't have our abilities but could sweep in to collect us if we go off script and he needs to knock us out?

I'm not sure anymore just how valuable or not we are to him. I trusted that our former captors wouldn't risk our lives, but Balthazar…

Balthazar might not be sane enough to worry how many tools he goes through on his way to achieving his goals. Whatever those goals are.

My teeth set against each other with an edge of tension, but the raging frustration that's gripped me more and more in the past several days has dulled to a low simmer of anger. The longer it burns in my gut, the more I have the sense that it's searing away everything else I might be feeling.

Like curiosity. Like defiance.

Like hope.

Does it really matter why we're here or what Balthazar plans to accomplish if we can't do anything about it anyway? If he's going to keep using us and using us some more until he's done or we die?

The dull simmer of anger burns away the queasiness of those questions too. It's hollowing me out.

But a certain sort of clarity comes with the emptiness. I peer up and down the street, considering the instructions our captor gave us, and uncover a lingering flicker of defiance after all.

"Balthazar was right," I say carefully. "It's going to be hard. There's such a limited window of time when we'll have our chance. And we don't know how quickly people inside will notice something's wrong and come to help."

Jacob studies me, his bright blue eyes sharpening like only they can. "He can't expect us to do more than our best. We aren't miracle-workers."

A hint of a smile curves my lips, tight with relief that he understands. My gaze slides to the others as well. "We'll just have to do that—give it our all."

As I speak, I shake my head, slowly and firmly.

A matching rigid smile crosses Andreas's lips.

Zian stares at all of us and clenches his jaw. "He'd

better not be upset if he's given us a job that's too hard," he mutters.

I can tell without anyone speaking another word that we all understand each other. It *is* a difficult job—that's why Balthazar sent all four of us.

The first gambit only requires me and Jake. But he wanted Drey and Zee with us too in case we fail.

And if even he can admit failure is an option, then why shouldn't we make sure of it? Why the hell should we help him if we can get away with doing the opposite?

We just have to give every appearance that we tried our hardest so he doesn't suspect purposeful sabotage.

I lift one leg and then the other, peeling them off the increasingly sticky leather seat, and rein in my impatience as well as I can. I'm so tired of living under Balthazar's thumb, feeling like he has it pressed against the back of my neck, shoving my face into the dirt.

Nothing I've done had gotten us closer to escape. This scrap of rebellion is the best I can give my guys.

Andreas rests his hand on the back of my head with a soft stroke of my hair. "We'll get through this, Tink."

His gentle tone sends a wavering ache through me, a pang of pain that's consumed by the angry simmer within seconds.

He means our current captivity, not just the job ahead. He's worried about me.

I grope for a response that might soothe his worry at least a little. The ping of the screen on the van's dash breaks in, making my nerves jolt.

A message appears along with the sound. *Target is five minutes out. Get in position.*

Yes, someone on Balthazar's team is definitely stationed nearby if they can track the man we're waiting for that closely.

I reach up instinctively to give Drey's hand a quick squeeze. He returns the gesture and bends to kiss the top of my head. "We'll see you soon."

I catch Zian's eyes, and he bobs his head to me before pulling on a thin cloth mask to disguise his face. Then he and Andreas slip out through the van's back doors.

They're the ones in the most direct danger—the ones who'll actually get close to our target if Jacob and I fail.

Not if now. *When.*

I swallow thickly and tuck my legs into a crossed position. Jacob lets out a huff and jabs at the controls. "We can get away with a few minutes of air conditioning. Who can think when it's this stuffy?"

I don't protest as a hiss of cool air gusts over my skin. I do need to concentrate—maybe even harder on messing up the mission than on seeing it through successfully.

Today, Balthazar doesn't want me to kill anyone. I'm supposed to hold them with my scream but not give in to the hunger for pain.

I've never actually tried that effect with people before, only the animals Matteo had me practice on. But I suspect Balthazar won't be too upset if I slip and mangle a security officer or two.

As long as we get him whatever's in that fucking briefcase he wants so much.

Too bad. Not happening. We don't have to dance to his tune in every possible way.

The vibration of a scream tickles at the base of my

throat. The fury that feeds it is aimed at our captor, not the strangers he's set us against, but it'll fuel the power in whatever direction I decide to aim it.

I rest my hands on my lap, flex them, and clench them. Jacob watches me, his gaze penetrating enough that I can feel it even when I have my head turned toward the street.

"Our powers keep expanding," he says. "Whatever we can do now, we have no idea what we might be capable of in another week or two."

He's trying to reassure me too. To stoke my hopes.

Jacob of all people is attempting to play the optimist. The knowledge gnaws at me more than Andreas's expected tenderness did.

I give a brusque nod without looking at him. "I know. We'll just have to wait and see."

Like we already have been. While Dominic lies in his transparent coffin and Balthazar orchestrates who knows what other terrors, and we just sit there helplessly, ready to jump when he calls—

The thrum of an engine cuts through my bitter reverie. When a black limousine cruises into view, I sit up straighter in my seat.

This will be him. The man with the briefcase—I haven't got a name.

Jacob braces himself in his seat too. We follow the limo's course as it slows in front of the mirrored building and pulls up next to the courtyard.

My heart thumps fast but steady. Here we go.

The limo stops completely. The driver will be putting it into park.

One door opens and then another. Three broad-shouldered men in subdued suits clamber out first and form a protective ring around the fourth man who emerges from within.

A briefcase swings in the fourth's hand, secured to his wrist by a handcuff. One he chose to wear to ensure the case never left his possession, not like our manacles.

A fresh prickle of anger jabs through the constant simmer. My lips part as the shriek reverberates up my throat.

I don't have any trouble doing it near-silently now, like a breath expelled. The trick is moderating the impact.

I aim it at all four of the men and the driver in the car for good measure, to show I've been thorough. With a tremor over my tongue, my power smacks into them and locks them in place.

The itch to snap bones and tear flesh, to provoke the pain some part of me craves, digs in deep. My body tenses against it.

The men lurch and stiffen. In the next instant, a few armed guards charge out of the building toward them.

My pulse hiccups, and I almost lose my self-control. No one inside should have realized anything was wrong that quickly.

Unless they were alerted ahead of time. The faint tingle on my collarbone tells me that Andreas has ventured farther than expected, right into the building.

He'll have turned himself invisible, as was always part of the plan, but there are plenty of ways he could sound the alarm even in that state.

As Jacob pushes forward in his seat to fulfill his role,

my lips twitch into a more genuine smile. One thing has already gone wrong in an unexpected way.

Balthazar definitely can't expect us to come out of this job victorious now.

Jacob makes a show of trying anyway. His arm shoots out, his power wrenching at the briefcase and the cuff.

A shiver of pain courses into me with his cracking of the man's hand. I drink it in, watching the cuff yank free of the crumpled mass.

The briefcase heaves up into the air—

And is tackled by one of the guards who hurtled over. The burly man slams the case and its contents to the ground.

Jacob bares his teeth and lets out a grunt, but we don't want to drag the man straight to us.

Good. It's all good.

I keep up my stream of muted sound, clutching tighter around my targets. The other guys have to try too. I can't let go too soon… or too late.

Zian barrels into the courtyard, his bulky body moving impossibly fast for his size—at least, it'd be impossible if he were an ordinary human being. He crashes into the guard who pinned the briefcase, rolling both the man and the object over.

That's Andreas's cue. He's supposed to run in there invisibly and snatch up the case.

But the other guards are drawing their guns. Zian jerks to the side just as shots boom.

My lungs constrict. Now?

Yes—now, before they hurt him. Before they—

I snap my mouth shut, cutting off the scream. The

previously cuffed man crumples with a wail as he cradles his smashed hand.

His security detail whirls around, drawing their own guns. Zian bolts for the parked limo to duck around it as shelter.

Bullets thunder after him. There's no way Andreas could spring into the fray now, not without catching one of those projectiles in his invisible body.

The guard who grabbed the briefcase scoops it up and dashes for the building's door, other men racing with him, a couple pursuing Zian. Zee stays low, running around the limo and then on toward the van.

My hand flies to the door. What if we've gone too far —what if they catch him or the rest of us before we can drive off?

Dominic can't heal us now.

Is this how the job is going to end? Roaring off with bullets pelting after us, knowing nothing more than we did before?

My frustration surges, and I throw open the door. Only two men—I can take them without even a scream, guns or not.

I can say I leapt out to defend Zian, but if I can grab a badge or a name tag, anything with a logo or some information that would at least tell me who they might be working for or why they're important... If I can buy Andreas enough time to paw through their memories...

Maybe all this effort will actually be worth it.

The men see me. One raises his gun to point it my way instead of at Zian's retreating form.

As I lunge at him, I can't tell if I even care whether he

shoots me or not. At least I won't have to worry about failing in all sorts of other ways if my journey ends here.

I collide with him, knocking his gun hand to the side. My clawed fingers scrape over his suit in search of a lump in a pocket that might be revealing.

Shouts blare from somewhere farther away. Footsteps smack the tiles in the courtyard.

I ram the man's arm against the sidewalk and snarl at him. "Who *are* you?"

Somewhere not-that-distant, the safety clicks off a gun. Fuck them. Fuck all of them.

I need answers, or what's the point of fighting to stay alive anyway?

The man stares up at me, uncomprehending. Then solid arms wrap around me from behind.

I stagger backward in a determined embrace I recognize as Drey's. My limbs start to thrash out—he's pulling me away from my goal, my only chance to make this moment worth something—

His voice murmurs in my ear, low and ragged. "Please. Riva, please."

The desperation of the plea unravels me. I sag in his grasp for long enough that his invisible form can haul me into the van, just as the next round of shots ring out.

"Go—*go!*" Zian shouts, and Jacob hits the gas.

As the van tears off down the road, Andreas wavers back into sight, his expression taut as he cups my face. A whiff of frightened pheromones tickles my nose, and a matching emotion shivers through our bond.

As if he's more scared now, after we've raced away from the threat, than he was in the middle of it.

"Don't do that again," he says hoarsely. "That wasn't—you didn't need to—"

My body curls in on itself, my claws still out as I hug my arms across my chest. My voice has barely any more sound than my scream. "I didn't want it to all be for nothing."

"It wasn't. It never would be. Not while we're here with you."

I don't know how much he understands what I was trying to do or why. But as the van sways around a bend, the anger in me simmers on, eating up any ability I have to believe that he's right.

We won, but we also lost. Again.

How many more times can I do this before there's nothing left inside me to care at all?

FIFTEEN

Riva

I thought we gave a pretty good performance of working our asses off and coming up short. But when we step out of the car onto the villa's grounds, Toni is waiting for us in the thickening dusk with the expression of a disapproving headmaster from some boarding school story.

"The four of you couldn't manage to retrieve one briefcase?" she asks tartly.

I study her warily. "They reacted too quickly. I've never had to use my powers like that before."

Jacob comes up to rest his hand on my shoulder as if he thinks I'll need his protection. But Toni only lets out a brisk huff. "You can give your excuses to Mr. Balthazar. Let's go."

She motions for us to follow her into the house. As we tramp through the wide hall toward the drawing room,

Zian spares a longing glance at the kitchen. "Can't we get something to eat? We haven't—"

"You'll talk to Mr. Balthazar first. He'll decide what to do with you next."

My own stomach grumbles despite my best attempt at appearing unaffected. We had a hasty lunch of sandwiches on the trip over to the job site, but nothing except bottles of water for our return.

Would we have found a feast waiting for us if we'd pleased our captor rather than disappointing him? I can all too easily picture Balthazar's people keeping a delicious spread shut away to spoil rather than offering it to us after our failure.

Waste is nothing to him. He's wasted kids' lives for the sake of making a point.

My throat tightens, but as we march into the drawing room, my roiling anger overwhelms any fear or grief. I'm tired of letting him hurt me.

The drawing room is empty other than Dominic's slack form. The screen hasn't risen from the table.

Andreas sinks into one of the armchairs and sprawls out in an attempt at looking casual. He's hiding his own uneasy nerves, but he's apprehensive enough that a flash of the emotion quivers through the mark that binds us.

"We're here," he says nonchalantly. "Where's the boss?"

Toni swivels on her heel. "He'll speak to you on his own schedule."

Jacob's head jerks around as she heads for the doorway. "Where's my brother?"

"Griffin wasn't part of the job. He doesn't need to account for it."

She leaves without another word. The rapping of her shoes against the tiled floor fades away down the hall.

The guys and I glance around at each other. Zian rests his hand on his stomach, his mouth slanting.

Technically we could stroll back over to the kitchen and make ourselves a meal. There's no one here to stop us.

Other than whoever's monitoring us through our bracelets and whatever other surveillance equipment Balthazar has in place.

None of us even moves toward the door. He has us that cowed.

I flex my jaw to keep from clenching it and pitch my voice a little louder than normal to be clear that I'm not talking to anyone in the room. "We're here. If you want us to tell you what happened out there, let's get on with it."

All of us wait in tense stillness. No one arrives, by screen or in person.

Jacob stirs and starts to pace through the room. "He can't send us on impossible jobs and then get mad that we couldn't pull them off perfectly."

"Maybe he's not mad?" Zian says, his tone doubtful despite the hope in his words. "Maybe he's just really busy."

Andreas pushes himself up straighter in the chair. "Toni was upset. I don't think that's a good sign."

I swallow hard. We all agreed, and I don't think any of the guys even hesitated, but defying Balthazar was *my* idea.

We probably could have retrieved the briefcase if we'd given it our all. If Drey hadn't sent more guards running out the moment we launched our assault.

Balthazar can't know that. But if he even suspects it, does it make a difference whether he can prove his theory?

Do I wish I could go back and carry out his job properly?

No. I don't know if that fact makes it better or worse, but the thought of having fulfilled his mission and presenting his prize to him makes the rage in my gut sear twice as hot.

We have to fight somehow. We have to be more than his slaves.

I drift over to Dominic's bed and rest my hands against the transparent shell. The machines buzz and beep. His chest rises and falls with a halting breath.

How long can Balthazar keep him like this? In the soap opera I used to watch with avid attention, people would fall into comas for years—decades, even—and then wake up like they'd never been sick. Other than sometimes they'd lost all their memories.

But those were silly stories with only a loose connection to reality. I have no clue whether a human being really can survive unconscious for that long.

Is Dom at all aware in the cage Balthazar has made of his body? Can he hear us, think about us?

My lips part. I'm going to say something; I just haven't decided what yet—

A sharper beep blares from one of the machines. I flinch, and before my eyes, Dominic's body seems to sag even more than it had before.

My heart leaps to my throat. "Dom!"

I'm smacking the shell that covers him before I've even

thought about what I'm doing, as if the bang of the impact might wake him up.

It doesn't, of course. He just lies there with more color leaching from beneath his light brown skin as the machine spews its frantic alarm into the air.

The other guys rush to join me. Jacob stares down at Dominic, his hands braced against the shell. "What happened?"

Zian's eyes have gone wide. "Is he okay?"

The only answer I can give both of them tumbles from my lips like a moan of horror. "I don't know."

I spin around, searching the room I already know is empty. "Help! There's a doctor around here somewhere, isn't there? Someone needs to look after Dominic!"

My strained plea splits through the air... and is met only by the whir of the screen finally rising from the table in the middle of the room.

I dash over to it, my fingers curling into my palms, claws I can't will back into my fingertips pricking my skin. Balthazar controls everything here—if Dominic has taken a turn for the worse, our captor can order someone to save him.

But when the screen flickers to reveal Balthazar's bulky form, his expression is utterly detached.

Doesn't he already know that something's gone wrong? He's got to have alerts connected to the medical equipment—hell, he'll hear the shrill beeping through the transmission right now.

"Something's happened to Dominic," I burst out before he can say anything. "You need to send your doctor —now."

Balthazar blinks at me languidly, showing no more concern than before. "I don't *need* to do anything simply because you say so. Haven't you learned that by now?"

"He could be dying," Jacob snaps where he's hustled over beside me. "How does that help your master plan?"

Balthazar simply sets his broad hands on the desk in front of him, interlacing his thick fingers. "As far as I can tell, none of you are proving to be all that useful to my plans at the moment. Or you wouldn't have returned empty-handed."

A chill stabs through the center of me. "We tried. We almost got shot out there—there were too many people. You didn't want us slaughtering them all."

"Oh, I think you held yourself back a little more than just from murder. I suppose I should have expected as much, but I can fix my mistakes. It isn't that hard to ensure you're sufficiently motivated."

Sufficiently motivated. My gaze flicks toward Dominic, and I think I might vomit if I had anything in my stomach.

Andreas steps forward, his handsome face harder than I've ever seen it. "What did you do to him?"

Balthazar lifts his shoulders in a measured shrug. "I withdrew a little of my support. His body will keep fighting to live, but it's a losing battle now. I'd give him a week or so."

No. My claws dig deeper into my palms, but I barely feel the jabs of pain. "Why? What do you want from us?"

An eerie smile crosses Balthazar's lips. "Ah. Now you're interested in giving me what I want. Perfect."

A vase whips off a side table and smashes against the

wall. The tick of a muscle in Jacob's cheek is the only sign that it was his talent on the fritz.

He glares at the screen. "Tell us what the fuck we have to do so you'll save him."

"And so impatient now." Our captor lets out a light chuckle that brings the thrum of a scream into the base of my throat.

I don't want to shriek him dead, though. That wouldn't be concrete enough. The urge grips me to rip out his own throat and dance in his spraying blood.

If I could reach him. But I can't—I can't.

I'm so sorry, Dom. This is my fault.

Andreas's voice only wavers a little. "You have our attention. Are you going to ask for anything from us or not?"

Balthazar lifts his chin, triumph glinting in his eyes. "There's something I want very much. Something it'll be very difficult for you to get. You may die in the attempt. I expect you to risk your lives as necessary. If you come back empty-handed, there is no deal."

A spurt of hope rushes through me only to sputter out a second later. "And then what?" I demand. "Then you'll heal Dom just enough so that he's back in his coma like before?"

Is that really better? We don't even know if he's still with us.

He could be nothing more than a husk of a body, another tool for Balthazar to manipulate us.

The sense of fatalism that filled me during our last job rises up again. Whatever Balthazar is trying to do, we haven't been able to make any dent in stopping him. I know his intentions can't be good.

It might be better for both us and the rest of the world if we were all dead instead of doing his bidding.

At least that's one way we can screw him over.

The glitter in our captor's eyes sparks a little brighter. "I can do better than that. If you bring me what I'm after, I'll revive him completely."

My heart stops for a few seconds before it lurches back into motion. "He'll—he'll be conscious again? Talking, walking—everything?"

I hate the smug smirk that curls Balthazar's lips now. "Everything. Is that a good enough reward for you?"

The swell of emotion that crashes over me knocks the breath from my lungs. I don't like the man in front of me seeing the tears that spring into my eyes. I hurt and hope and grieve like a hurricane passing through me.

It floods the vacant space my anger burned away inside me. I'm drowning in so many feelings that'd gone dead in the past few days.

In a distant part of my mind, I find myself remembering what Jacob said to me that night on the boat in Havana when he brought me the severed hands of the men who'd tried to kill me. When he meant to cut off his own arm in penance.

He told me how empty he felt after Griffin supposedly died, empty of everything but rage. That he'd wanted to kill himself and had only held back to get vengeance for his brother.

And then he saw me racing toward a train that could

have been my doom, and so many other feelings broke in. *I cared, so fucking much.*

My own fury is still burning inside me, raised from a simmer to a raging boil. How *dare* this asshole dangle our friend, this man I love so much, in front of us like a fucking carrot on a stick?

But it's not the only sensation swaying me now. It's not even the loudest.

Balthazar has slammed me back into full awareness like the impact of a speeding locomotive.

I do love Dom, with everything in me. I don't know what I wouldn't give to see life light up in his face, to hear his voice, to receive his smile.

There's more love in me than there is anger, even if the rage drowned it out for a little while.

Is this how Jacob felt, the way he cracked, when he saw the train hurtling along the tracks toward me?

The hollow emptiness with its caustic simmer before... is that how he spent four whole years? After just days of it, I already ache all over.

I lift my head and swipe at the tears that have trickled over my cheeks. Balthazar gazes at me with an expectant air that sets off another flare of anger.

Not enough to change the answer I have to give, though.

I glare back at him. "Fine. I'm in. What do you want us to steal for you?"

Sixteen

Riva

The rattle of the tracks shakes my nerves, jostling free memories I'd rather not dwell on. In the back of my mind, a different train roars toward me in the night.

I'm not sure the echo of that old hopelessness is the worst of the memories. Other fragments rise up of the early days on the run with my guys before they started to trust me again, when every word I spoke and action I made was met with wary glances or hostile remarks.

We're stowed away in a cargo car just like some of those times, crouched in the darkness between stacks of crates. Across from me, barely visible in the dim light that flickers through the partly open doorway, Jacob's mouth is set in a tight line.

Is he remembering those past journeys too?

Andreas has hunkered down next to me. He takes my hand in his and runs his fingers lightly over my knuckles.

The affectionate gesture adds a jab of pain to the turmoil that's been stewing inside me since Balthazar offered his deal. There's so much I need to say, but I'm afraid if I start, it'll all spill out too fast, too awkwardly.

Griffin watches us from where he's leaning against a crate near the door. He's got to sense the roaring whirl of emotion I'm holding in, but he hasn't said anything about it.

He wouldn't. He's always given me the space to decide how much I want to say and when.

Zian paces from one end of the car to the other, the floor creaking under his massive frame. "Should we get closer and scope things out? We don't even know exactly what we're dealing with yet."

Jacob raises his head. "Balthazar seemed pretty sure about how well the secure car will be guarded. I don't think we should risk getting close until it's almost time to act."

Andreas leans forward to peer through the gap at the landscape whipping by outside. We're passing a stretch of warehouses now, security lamps washing over the tracks with a faint yellow glow.

"A little ways past this city, we should go by that smaller town," he says. "It's about a half hour after that when we'll be in the ideal position to reach our pick-up vehicle."

I drag all my attention to the task in front of us. "A half an hour sounds like a good amount of time to check things out and then take action. Once we're on the attack, we'll need to move quickly."

Jake nods. "After the town, we move. We only need to go a few cars ahead. We can get there pretty quickly."

As long as we're not spotted beforehand. As long as we don't stumble on any protective measures we aren't prepared for.

Balthazar wasn't sure all of us would make it back alive.

The last of the buildings on the fringes of the city give way to open fields. It's a matter of minutes before we reach the town now.

If I'm going to say something, it has to be soon.

I close my eyes and reach through the chaos inside me to the one feeling that's kept me steady over the past couple of days. The thrum of love, swelling to overwhelm the fear and anger when I picture Dominic's eyes opening, his quiet smile curving his lips.

We're going to make it back to him—all of us. We're going to bring Balthazar what he wants and see our friend restored to life.

And the guys around me need to know how true that is too.

I look around the train car again, gathering myself. I don't think I really move, but Zian pauses in his pacing as if he's sensed that something's coming.

I had some idea of making a carefully crafted speech, but when my lips part, the first thing that tumbles out is simply, "I'm sorry."

Drey grips my hand and tugs it closer to him. Griffin lifts his head with thoughtful intensity.

Jacob's frown cuts through the shadows. "Sorry? What the hell do you have to be sorry about?"

My head droops, but I keep my shoulders squared. "I —I know I've gone a bit off the rails since Balthazar grabbed us. It was so hard to see how we could ever be happy again, and I started shutting down, but I hated that too, and I just…"

I don't know how to go on. But it turns out I don't need to.

Andreas wraps his arms right around me. Jacob pushes himself away from the crates and kneels by my side, touching my cheek.

When I meet Jake's gaze, his eyes are shimmering with anguished passion. "It's okay, Wildcat. I told you before that you don't need to be strong all the time, didn't I? None of us expects you to take all the crap without ever wobbling."

My throat chokes up. "But I—I haven't been careful enough. I took risks I shouldn't have because it was hard to care. What if Balthazar had decided to go ahead and *kill* Dominic?"

"He didn't," Griffin says softly. "And you don't know if he'd have made us this deal if he hadn't realized you weren't going to follow his orders perfectly every time, just because he said so."

Zian lets out a strained grunt and takes a few steps toward me. He stops just behind Jacob, his expression taut. "I don't know how to make any of this better either, Riva. But we are still in it together. We're right here with you, no matter what."

Andreas hugs me and presses a brief kiss to my cheek. "Always. Even when it's hard. Even if you stumble."

Their devotion encircles me just as Drey's embrace has,

melting the edges off all the prickly emotions still churning in my chest. My next breath comes a little easier.

I tuck my hand around Andreas's forearm and reach to grasp Jacob's arm as well. My gaze lifts from them to the other two guys standing over me. "We have to finish this job, get what he wants, and make it back. For us. For Dominic."

"We can," Andreas says firmly. "Because we're in it together. No one's ever managed to stop us for long."

He means not just the guards who'll stand in our way on this mission but Balthazar as well, though we all know better than to speak our hopes of rebellion that blatantly. I inhale deeply and absorb the warmth of my men's love down to my bones.

Zian manages a small smile. "We've even stolen a laptop before. This is just a hard drive. We've got practice."

I sputter a laugh. "The laptop wasn't behind a gazillion locks with very living guards standing between us and it— ones we're not supposed to kill."

Jacob shrugs. "There are plenty of ways to disable people without murdering them. Balthazar never said we had to leave them *happy*."

The corner of my mouth ticks upward. It's true—our keeper even gave us direct permission to get "creative."

I'm not sure why Balthazar is against outright killing the guards, but I can't say I mind. We have no idea whether they've done anything worse than get in the way of a man who's clearly a sadistic psychopath.

It's pretty obvious that we aren't on the side of justice at the moment.

"We shouldn't hurt them too badly," I point out.

Griffin nods. "Nothing worse than necessary to get the job done. I'll be placating them as well as I can the whole time."

"I know." I lean into Andreas's chest for one more fleeting moment and then push to my feet to approach the door.

Tall grass sways in the fields beyond the tracks. When I crane my neck, I can make out the lights of civilization up ahead.

I turn back to the guys. "The town's in sight. It's almost time."

I slide the door mostly closed to hide our presence. The guys gather around me, all of us peeking through the narrow gap as the train sways through a stretch of industrial buildings, apartment complexes, houses, and then more factories.

By the time the last of the structures falls away behind us, leaving only forest outside the window, my pulse is thumping at a brisk rhythm. I focus on that beat and the love that's keeping me anchored.

"Let's move."

This time, we all pull on thin masks—even Andreas, in case he needs to blink back into visibility in front of our adversaries.

We already identified the secure car in the line of more typical freight cars before we got on the train. When we ease out into the night, one after the other, and haul ourselves onto the top of ours, I can see the darker, flatter armored surface three cars up.

We don't know exactly how much manpower is stationed around and inside it, though. Or how many other precautions the owners of the apparently very valuable hard drive may have taken against theft.

A twinge of curiosity tugs at me—why does Balthazar want the contents of this drive so much anyway?—but I can't jeopardize the job and Dominic's recovery with a search for answers.

We slink along the top of the car and spring from ours to the next roof. It's an easy jump for me and Zian. Zee holds out his arms to help catch the others and make sure they don't lose their balance.

We repeat the process at the next car, but stay at the far end. Griffin cocks his head, his eyes going distant as he feels out the additional human presence nearby.

"They're all in pretty similar moods," he says after a moment. "A little bored, but still alert and determined to see through their jobs. It's hard to distinguish all of them, but I think there are six. I can't tell you exactly where."

Jacob claps his brother on the shoulder. "That's plenty. Zian, you can figure out more."

Zee crouches down and creeps toward the secure car on all fours, staying low so his form blends into the shadowed roof. He narrows his eyes at the back wall.

There's no door or window there, but Zian's vision can pierce right through when he exerts his power. He stares at it for several seconds and then crawls back to us.

"There are some inner walls too," he says. "It was hard to see through all of them. It looks like there's an outer area and then a smaller room inside the car that's secure too. Four men in the outer area: two right by the door on the side of the car and the other two spread out a little more by the edges. Two more inside the smaller room."

I make a face. "Armed?"

He nods. "Semi-automatic rifles. We don't want to be caught in that fire."

Not without Dominic to set us right again.

Andreas glances at me. "You can freeze them with a scream without seeing them, right? If we want to paralyze everyone in the car."

"I think so." I swipe at my mouth nervously. "I haven't tried quite like that before. And I don't know what'll happen once any of you go inside too."

Jacob cracks his knuckles. "We'll just have to find out. You lock them down, Zee and I will wrench the outer door open, and we take it from there."

I restrain a shiver. "I'm coming with you. If I need to adjust my power, I want to be able to do it with the targets in sight."

"I'll be there too," Andreas puts in with a crooked grin. "It never hurts to have an invisible ally on your side. I wish I could pass on the ability to you too."

We talked about that potential strategy when we were first discussing the job, but while Drey's ability to make objects he's touching disappear might extend to human bodies as well, so far he has to be touching them to hold them like that. We can't compromise our maneuverability that much.

And it's not like the guards will somehow fail to notice us busting our way in through the door, no matter what they can see of our bodies.

It's on me to go first, to clear the way. I slink to the front of the roof like Zian did and brace my hands against the ridge at its edge.

Six men. Six human figures within the boxy shape right in front of me. I need to pin them all with my scream.

I fix my gaze on the dark shape of the train car and let a vibration of my anger ripple through the softer emotions that've grounded me. My lips part automatically.

The nearly silent shriek warbles up my throat and rushes out into the air. It whips through the steel walls of the secure car.

My heightened senses spark with the awareness of the three—now five—now all six of the bodies my power latches on to. A tremor of pain careens back into me before I clamp down my self-control.

I hurt one of them—snapped his shin bone. Through the knot of guilt in my gut, I remind myself that it could have been worse.

I can't talk to the guys while I'm emitting my banshee scream, so I simply dip my head to let them know it's done. They all file past me except for Griffin, who crouches down at my side.

We talked about this next part as if it'd be simple. Well, I guess it is *simple*, in terms of how straightforward the act is, but it's definitely not *easy*.

Jacob, then Zian, and then Andreas—wavering out of sight as he goes—clamber carefully down the side of our car. They take the wide step across to the secure car one at a time.

But there's no ledge along the side wall leading to the door they need to open. With the train rushing along the tracks, it's not as if they can stand on the ground for leverage.

How are they even going to reach it while the car is in motion?

As Jacob and Zian bend their heads together in muttered conversation, my throat starts to prickle. The hunger inside me is gnawing at me for more shards of pain.

No. Not yet. Not today.

I'd like to say *Not ever*, but no part of me really believes I can do away with the vicious need inside me forever anymore.

Zian boosts Jacob onto the roof of the secure car—slowly, so no thump gives away our presence—and then repeats the gesture for Andreas's invisible form. He hefts himself up after them using his supernatural strength.

They creep to the edge overlooking the door. Zee sprawls on his stomach and manages to lean down far enough to grasp the handle.

I think—I fucking hope—that Andreas is holding on to his legs to make sure he doesn't slide right off. We could die here without taking a single bullet, skulls smashed on the ground whipping by below us.

Jacob makes a furtive gesture, peering down at the door. Then the metal starts to groan.

He's wrenching at it with his telekinetic powers while Zian hauls with his wolf-man power. I push a little more emphasis into my scream, wincing at the thought of automatic gunfire.

But my shriek holds. And Jake has gotten even stronger since he shook up an entire mountain.

I don't know whether he undoes the lock or simply breaks it, but the steel slab of the door crumples as he and

Zee pull. Like it was made of nothing more than cardboard he's dented to the side.

Zian jerks back a few inches for better balance and grasps Jacob's hands. Without missing a beat, he swings Jake in through the opening.

Griffin sets a tentative hand on my back. I almost forgot he was there.

"I'm keeping them as calm as I can manage," he says, just loud enough to be heard over the clatter of the train. "Are you going over there too?"

That was the plan. An abrupt jolt of panic shoots through me at the thought of maintaining my shriek while making the jump.

But I told the guys I'd be there with them. And I might need to be if they're going to make it through alive.

I risk a shallow gulp of air with only a waver of my shriek. Then I spring across to the opposite car.

Zian has already tossed himself inside after Jacob. I assume Andreas has followed them, one way or another.

Hooking my hand under the doorway, I stabilize my fingers and then fling myself around the frame with a hasty tumble.

I land on my feet with a lurch of my chest—and a hitch of my shriek. One of the guards braced around us twitches his gun closer to aiming it at Jacob.

Shit. I steady my voice and motion hastily at the guys I can see. Zian snatches the handle of the inner door while Jacob tenses in preparation to exert his powers—

And the car thumps over a broken bit of track.

The floor heaves under my feet, tossing me onto my ass. My shriek breaks completely.

As I suck in a gasp of air, one of the guards tackles me to the ground.

He slams my head into the floor face-first. My mouth is crushed against the metal surface.

I couldn't scream again right now if I wanted to.

At least not the usual way.

Panic flares through my thoughts in the split-second when I'm captured, and a bolt of heady defiance races up in its wake. In the back of my mind, I see Dominic slumped on the hospital bed, waiting for us.

Dominic, who healed me even when he thought he should hate me. Dominic, who was the first boy to ever kiss me without a disaster. Who showed me I could be loved without everything I cared about falling apart.

I will not lose him. I refuse to lose *any* of them.

A flare bursts within my skull, and this time it's as if my brain itself shrieks, hunger and fury and desperation melding together in a silent, mouthless wail of vengeance.

The man holding me down buckles with a pained grunt. I taste the crack of two ribs and the puncture of a spleen before the understanding catches up with me that I'm really doing this somehow.

I'm screaming without even opening my mouth.

I jerk around, lips clamped tight, my mental shriek expanding to collide with the other four guards on this side of the doorway.

One of them has his gun under Zian's chin. I break his hand.

The other two have converged on Jacob. As I fracture one's pelvis so he drops to the floor, Jake twists his hand, and the other man's knees give beneath him.

Not a killing strike. We haven't disobeyed our orders.

Two of the rifles soar out the doorway into the night. Andreas is tossing them away so there's no chance of the guards turning them on us again.

I start to reach for another but hesitate, unsure how easily I can keep my hold on our opponents with this newfound dimension to my power.

Jacob and Zian kick the other weapons out of the train. Zee pauses to stare down at me. "Riva?"

I have to control the men inside the smaller room too. I close my eyes and push my awareness and my mental shriek beyond the wall.

There. There. They seize up in the grip of my power, pain flooding me just from their bewilderment and fear.

I wave a hand vaguely toward the door. The guys leap forward.

Jacob and Zian haul that door open inch by screeching inch. They each tackle one of the guards inside, smacking them hard enough in the right spot to knock them temporarily unconscious.

Which is a good thing, because a headache is starting to expand through my brain with the effort of the telepathic scream.

"Fuck!" Jacob snaps from inside. "There are too many goddamn security boxes in here. Which one is the hard drive in?"

Zee must scan them with his X-ray vision. "Here," he says. "But I don't think—the door on this thing is too small and thick."

He hesitates, and I can't help looking up even as I pin the remaining injured men with my power.

Zian blinks. Then his eyes spark, and a glowing line sears through one of the panels embedded in the inner wall.

Our wolf-man's powers have grown in new ways too. The line crackles through the metal in a rough rectangle, which Jacob yanks out with his telekinesis the second it's complete.

Andreas reappears. "Come on. We just passed the marker by the side of the tracks. Let's get out of here!"

Zian tucks the sleek metal case of the hard drive he's retrieved against his chest, sheltered by his arms.

Jacob turns in the doorway to look toward the car behind us. "Griffin! We're leaving."

Zian stiffens for a second and then slings one arm around me too. Squeezing me against him with as much care as he gave our cargo, he leaps into the brush along the side of the road.

He hits the cushioning of the shrubs shoulder-first, his brawn sheltering me from the worst of the impact. As I scramble up, three more thuds sound in quick succession.

The silent scream fades from my mind as the train whisks the guards away from us.

I let out a rasping sound and clear my throat so I can speak. "Everyone okay?"

Jacob mutters a curse. "I think Griffin sprained his ankle."

"I'll be fine," his brother replies. "The hard part is over, right?"

Yes. We just have to get to the planned meetup spot, deliver the hard drive to Balthazar, and…

And what guarantee do we actually have that he'll fulfill his side of the deal? A deal made with a madman?

As the guys gather around us, Griffin limping, my stomach sinks like a stone. My gaze catches on the vague shine of the device in Zian's arms.

Balthazar wants it. He wants it enough that he played his trump card to force us to get it.

Why can't it be *our* trump card now?

I wet my lips, a weird mix of hope and trepidation tickling through my veins. "Before we go back... I have an idea."

Seventeen

Riva

I'm expecting a brutal welcoming party when we arrive at the villa. Balthazar must already know that he isn't getting his prize as easily as he hoped.

But no one is waiting to intimidate us into submission. When the drawbridge rumbles to a halt at the top of its raised position, the courtyard stands eerily silent.

Somehow that's worse than if a brigade of goons had marched out to meet us. Like our keeper is still perfectly content to wait for us to come to him.

Like nothing we've done actually matters.

As we head into the villa, Jacob catches my hand. Griffin takes the other, while Andreas shoots me a reassuring glance and Zian lets out a protective growl.

We'll meet whatever's waiting for us together. We all made it back in one piece, and that's what matters the most.

I only dozed on the flight and drive back, nothing that

I could call real sleep. My weary legs would like to walk me right into my bedroom and toss me onto the bed.

But I can't rest until Dominic is returned to us. And that means confronting the man holding him captive in his own body.

We stride through the dawn-lit halls together, the twist of tension in my gut contrasting with the delicate frescos painted on the walls we're passing. This place should be beautiful, but to us it's only become more horrifying with each passing day.

Balthazar clearly knows we've arrived. When we file into the drawing room, the screen is already raised from the tabletop, though it's currently dark.

The machine by Dominic's bed continues its shrill, faster beeping. Does his skin look even more washed out than before?

I mean to watch him for a breath—to count how long he's taking between them—but then the screen blinks to a view of our captor.

Balthazar peers out at us, looking even more the predatory lion than usual. A few locks of his graying tawny hair shade his penetrating eyes. "It appears you've failed in your mission."

My spine stiffens. I glower back at him. "We didn't fail. We got the hard drive you wanted."

"Then where is it?"

The twins tighten their grip on my hands. Jacob speaks before I can, even though this gambit was my idea. "You're not getting it until Dominic is awake. Otherwise how are we supposed to believe that you're actually going to pay us back for the job?"

Balthazar lets out a low huff. "If you've left the device somewhere it'll be damaged, it isn't worth the sweat on your skin."

I resist the urge to clench my jaw. "We made sure it was safe. And that it's somewhere you're never going to find on your own. It was a long walk between the train tracks and the pickup car."

A hint of a smirk touches Andreas's lips. "And something that small is very easy to hide when you've got an entire forest to work with."

A growl ripples through Balthazar's otherwise even tone. "It doesn't do me any good if *you* can't even find it again either."

"You don't have to worry about that," Zian insists. "We're not stupid."

"I don't see how I have any guarantees of *your* good faith."

I slip my hands from the guys' grasp to take a determined step toward the screen. "Why are you trying so hard not to give us what you promised? If we can't give your people directions to find your prize, then it's not as if you can't knock Dom out—or worse—all over again. Do you think *we* could possibly not realize that, after everything you've already done? That we'd risk losing him right after we've gotten him back?"

Balthazar studies me through the screen with an unreadable expression that sends alarm clanging through my nerves. "I could simply start cutting down your remaining companions until you cough up the information."

I hold myself steady against the hitch of my pulse, my

glower sharpening into a glare. "Try me. If you do that, then we know you're never going to be good to your word. There's no point in us giving you anything if we're all going to end up as worm food before long anyway."

A few days ago, I'd have meant those words whole-heartedly. Now, with the promise of Dominic's restoration dangling over me and the warmth of affection soothing the worse of my hopeless anger, the idea of giving up sends an ache through every part of my body.

But what I said is true regardless. I want to live and love however I can.

If I *can't*, if this man is going to make it impossible, then it would be better to die on our own terms.

My skin continues to creep under our captor's intense attention, but I don't break from his gaze. After another moment, the corners of his lips lift—is that the start of a *smile*?

It remains so subtle and vanishes so quickly I'm not sure if I only imagined it. He reaches toward something out of view on his desk. "You are a force to be reckoned with, aren't you, Riva? Let's see if we can't come out of this deal with both of us satisfied rather than disappointed."

My spirits lift. Does he really mean…?

I don't quite believe it until two figures hustle into the room: a plump woman and her scrawny male assistant who walk straight past us to Dominic's bed. They don't even bother to look at us.

As the woman unlocks the case over Dominic's limp body, Zian moves as if to barge over. I catch his arm, just for long enough to stop him before yanking my fingers away.

When he glances at me, I shake my head. We can't risk interfering with anything they're doing.

I *want* them to give Dom their full concentration.

After lifting the case, the woman adjusts several controls on the machines while her assistant prepares a couple of syringes. My stomach knots at the sight of the vicious needles, but I hold my own defensive urges in check too.

We made our bargain. Now we have to give it a chance to be fulfilled.

The woman takes one syringe, injects it into Dominic's neck, and monitors the display on the machines for an endless minute before holding her hand out for the second needle. This one, she applies to his wrist.

The machine's beeping has slowly eased back to its normal pace. Gingerly, the woman removes the tubes and wires that encircled Dominic's form, and then shuts off the machines completely.

She gives us one brief look. "Give him a few more minutes."

Then the two of them sweep out of the room so quickly that in a matter of seconds it's as if they were never here.

All five of us venture closer to Dominic's bed. His breath is coming in what looks like a more regular rhythm now.

But his eyes remain closed, his expression slack.

What if it doesn't work? What if Balthazar miscalculated, and Dom was too far gone already?

Even as a pang of fear reverberates through my chest,

Dominic's eyelashes twitch. I'm just sucking in a gasp when his eyelids lift.

He blinks a few times, staring up at the ceiling. A flinch runs through his frame that isn't provoked by anything I can see—maybe a memory flashing through his mind.

I can't bear to hang back any longer. I dart forward to rest a tentative hand on his arm, leaning over him.

Dom stares up at me. His lips part, and for a stutter of my heart, I think he's going to knit his brow in confusion.

"Riva?" he croaks.

My face splits with the widest smile I've ever made. I tip farther to hug him, just as carefully as my initial touch. "How do you feel? You've been… out for a long time."

He coughs and flexes his muscles. The next second, Zian is there at his other side, sliding a strong hand under Dom's shoulders to help him sit up.

All of the other guys cluster tighter around the hospital bed as Dominic finds his balance. He slings a wobbly arm around me and gives me an equally wobbly smile.

"You don't have to look so worried, Sugar," he says softly though hoarsely. "There isn't much that'll knock me and my tentacles down for good."

As I choke back a startled laugh, he loops one of those tentacles around my waist. Then his gaze drifts from me to the other guys and to the room beyond us.

At the scene he takes in, his brow does knit. He studies our surroundings for several breaths before returning his attention to us. "Where the hell have we ended up now?"

The laugh I sputter at his question holds no humor at

all. "It's a long story. And most of it isn't good. I'm just glad you're back with us."

Glad is the understatement of the year. The glow of joy lighting me up at his embrace and his words could power an entire city.

"Let's get you up," Jacob says, a little gruffly, and holds out his arm. "I don't know how well those assholes actually healed you. If you need to draw energy from someone—"

Andreas knocks Jacob's ribs with his elbow. "You don't have to go all self-sacrificing, Jake. There are plenty of shrubs and hedges outside that'll do the trick."

Jacob makes a face as if he was actually looking forward to offering himself up—which knowing him he might have been—but he doesn't argue.

I help Dominic off the bed. Zian quickly comes around to join us, but Dom manages to walk with only a little extra support keeping him steady.

His head swings one way and another on our tramp down the hall to one of the outer doors. He manages a weak whistle. "This is definitely our fanciest prison yet."

I guess it's not hard for him to figure out that we're not exactly free here. Not just from the way we're acting, but from the metal bands that bind his wrists just like all of ours.

I brush a kiss to his shoulder. "You could say that. This one holds us with a different kind of chains."

To my surprise, none of Balthazar's underlings rush over to demand the location of his prize. We meander out into the chilly early morning air unimpeded.

Dominic's feet stall under him while he takes in the

mountain vista surrounding us. "Well, that's… that's something," he manages to mumble.

We help him over to a stone bench near a couple of particularly vibrant shrubs… which might not remain that way for long.

Jacob jerks his head toward one of the bushes. "Heal up anything that's still not quite right inside you. Who knows how much damage the prick who's keeping us here actually did to you?"

Dom stretches his back and snakes one of his tentacles over to the shrub. "I don't feel *bad*, exactly, just worn out and a little sore."

"You should do what you can, just to be sure," I say, my throat constricting.

What if Balthazar's doctors only healed him enough to make him *look* okay, and he'll collapse again tomorrow?

Dominic's monstrous appendage twines around the shrub's bristly branches. He closes his eyes and relaxes against the back of the bench.

Before my eyes, the shrub's thin evergreen leaves turn brown around the spot where Dominic's tentacle rests. The closest branches shrivel and sag.

But when he releases the plant, he's only left a dull patch on the larger form. As far as I can tell, not being a gardener, it should survive with a bit of pruning.

A more vibrant color has come back into Dom's face, a brighter light in his eyes. When he smiles at us now, my heart lifts.

"I think that'll do it," he says. "How about you show me around and fill me in now?"

I lift one arm to indicate my manacle. "As much as we can."

Dominic's mouth slants. He's been through enough troubles with us to understand my implication.

"Let's get you to the kitchen," Zian suggests. "You haven't eaten in more than a week—you've got to be starving!"

Dom chuckles in agreement and ambles back to the villa with us without any support needed. I can't tear my eyes off him, as if, if I glance away for a second, his recovery might reverse itself.

We really did it. We bargained with Balthazar... and got what we wanted.

Of course, he still needs to get what *he* wanted. We've just stepped inside when Toni appears in the shadowed hallway.

"The boss will have your directions now," she says brusquely.

Andreas steps forward. "I can project my memory of the landmarks you need to look for to whoever you want to send for it. I can come along too, if you want that extra confirmation."

She lets out a grunt that doesn't sound entirely pleased but motions for him to follow her. As I watch him walk away, my heart wrenches even though this was always part of the plan.

I have to believe that Drey will come back to us like Dominic did. I have to believe that we can find our way out of this mess with our wits rather than by tearing everything apart.

All the anger that fueled me before didn't get me

anywhere except close to getting torn apart myself... and if I'd given in to that impulse, Dominic wouldn't be standing here next to me.

We don't need Balthazar dead. We don't need revenge for the murders he's committed or the torments he's inflicted, as much as I'd still like to have those things.

All that matters is getting away. Rescuing the younger shadowbloods who are counting on us.

And then finding the freedom I've always dreamed of with the men I love.

We've just learned that we can negotiate at least part of our progress along that journey. There has to be a smart way of navigating this prison that'll work better than the brutal method I imagined but couldn't carry out.

Shoring up my resolve inside me and swathing it in the glow of joy and love sparked by Dom's presence, I grab his hand and stride on.

Eighteen

Dominic

Riva glances from my plate to my face, worry and happiness flickering together in her expression. "Are you sure you've had enough?"

I consider the sandwich I've eaten about a quarter of, but my stomach rebels. I might not have eaten anything in weeks, but whatever the man who runs this house used to keep me alive, it didn't starve me.

Some part of my body has forgotten that it needs food.

I shake my head and offer a smile I hope is reassuring to offset the refusal. "I think I'm going to have to work up to regular meals. My stomach probably shrunk while I was out. I feel full enough."

Zian is watching me with obvious concern too, his own lunch long since polished off. "Are you feeling at all sick anymore?"

I redirect my smile to him. "Not at all. I seem to have

healed myself up no problem. It's just… a bit of an adjustment."

I don't exactly feel sore or unsteady now, not like when I first woke up. My power can't sense any bacterial invaders to destroy or injuries to heal within my body.

But I can't say I'm totally back to normal in the few hours I've been awake either. A vague sense of fatigue hovers at the edges of my senses.

It's not like I've been the strongest of our group even at my best.

As I stand up, *all* of my friends look me over, the same worries echoing across their faces. My gut twists with guilt.

I was the weakest of the six of us. I was the one this Balthazar guy felt was expendable enough to be used as leverage against the others.

They haven't talked in much detail about what's gone on while I was in my coma, but I've gotten the gist. Even the brief accounts left me queasy.

I don't know how to make up for the things they've done out of fear of what would happen to me if they didn't. For the things they did in exchange for our new captor waking me up.

I don't know how to make sure he doesn't turn me into an unconscious hostage all over again.

Riva has gotten up too, grabbing my plate to carry it to the kitchen as if she's afraid to leave me with even that minor burden. "There isn't a ton to do here when we're left to our own devices," she says, "but one of the sitting rooms has some pretty packed bookshelves. There could be something in there you'll find interesting."

I tip my head in thanks and am about to ask her if she'll join me when a middle-aged man appears in the dining room doorway. His bony frame and sharply pointed beard would give him a menacing vibe even if I were meeting him at a beach club rather than an isolated mountain villa.

"Dominic," he says briskly. "You've been exempt from our procedures so far by necessity. It's time to see about bringing you up to speed."

My body tenses automatically, my tentacles recoiling against the fabric of the T-shirt I shed my hospital gown for. Zian ripped the tee's neckline for me so my monstrous appendages could move freely.

The others have told me about the procedures and some of how their powers have expanded. I got the sense from subtle hints of body language that there's more they've discovered that our captors aren't aware of yet, things they'd like to keep secret if they can.

We were able to hide just how far we were progressing from our old keepers in the facility, what feels like years ago. But the situation under the insane dictator they've described feels much more precarious.

And I'm not sure I *want* to stretch my abilities any farther. I can already heal every illness and wound I've been faced with. I managed to patch Riva back together from the verge of death after the train hit her.

The other side of my abilities—the giddy strength I can absorb by siphoning off life energy from other creatures beyond what I need to keep my good health— already horrifies me enough as it is.

When I hesitate, my friends push to their feet around

me. As they step closer as if forming a guard around me, Matteo's cold eyes narrow.

I stride forward before he needs to make a threat. It's not as if we have much choice—and I don't want the others suffering on my behalf any more than they wanted me to for them.

I think I know what to expect. I'm not surprised by the plain modern room Matteo leads me into or the steel chair or the syringe he brings out to begin his procedure.

He lets me stand, leaving my limbs unencumbered, and motions to a table set up next to the chair that holds a variety of not particularly unnerving objects—bricks and slabs of stone and woven cords. "We're going to see how far you can take that borrowed strength of yours."

That's when my stomach starts sinking. It drops even farther when he slips behind the partition at one end of the room and presses a control that pushes a cage full of half a dozen white rabbits toward my feet.

Matteo's gaze pins me in place through the tempered glass. "We'll take it one at a time. Follow my instructions carefully. You can kill the first now."

I want to resist. A pang of defiance stabs through me.

But my nerves have gone pliant from the chemical he injected into me, just like the others described. Even as my gut wrenches, I kneel down in front of one of the cages and snake a tentacle through the bars.

While afternoon fades into evening, I lie on my bed in the room Balthazar has assigned to me and try to judge whether Matteo's drug has worn off. Is the heaviness in my muscles an aftereffect of his procedure or simply my horror weighing me down?

None of the rush brought on by my power remains— that's for sure. Thinking about the life I drained from the helpless animals only makes my stomach lurch queasily.

Voices murmur in the hallway. The others are probably even more worried about me now that I've holed up in here, but I can't bring myself to face them, not yet.

For the first few hours since Matteo released me from his tests, they've respected my closed door. As I run my hand over my face, it finally eases open.

Riva slips inside and shuts the door behind her. She stays by it as if she isn't sure whether I'll yell at her to leave.

"I had to check on you," she says.

There's so much anguish tangled in her tone and shining in her eyes that I can't turn her away. She's spent too long already scared for my wellbeing.

Mutely, I extend my hand to her. She darts across the tiled floor and scrambles onto the bed.

We fit together as if our bodies are meant to interlock, my chin tucking over her head, our arms looping over each other's sides, her legs nestling against mine. I hold her close, absorbing her warmth for the more welcome strength it brings me without any supernatural powers necessary.

Riva brushes a delicate kiss to my sternum, just below the mark that connects us. "Do you want to talk about it?"

"Not really." There isn't much to say. Matteo had me kill one rabbit, then two, then three at once. And in between each slaughter, he ordered me through tests of my physical might.

After the final rabbits, I snapped the thickest stone slab with my bare hands. Matteo looked pleased.

He told me he was happy we'd been able to establish a "baseline." Just remembering that word sends a fresh wave of nausea through me.

"How often do they bring you in for the procedures?" I can't help asking.

"I think on average it's been once every couple of days." Riva pauses. "But from the way Matteo was talking, he might bring you in more. Since he figures you're behind."

Fuck. I try to suppress my flinch, but a trace of my discomfort must show. Riva's arms tighten around me.

Her voice comes out strained. "I'm sorry—we wanted you back with us. I didn't even think about the downsides of you being awake."

My own throat chokes up. I hug her back just as tightly. "It's okay. I'd rather be going through this and here with you and the guys the rest of the time than half-dead and used as a threat."

"I just wish there was more… I wish there was a better option."

"I think you made the best choice you could have, considering the situation we're all in," I say honestly. "I promise you, there isn't a single particle of me that's upset about being revived."

"Okay." Riva manages to snuggle even closer to me. "I missed you so much. You guys have always said it wasn't the same when I was gone… It wasn't the same without you either, Dom."

I doubt my absence had quite the same impact on our group as hers did, but a burn of tears forms in the back of my eyes anyway. Because I can hear how much it mattered to her.

We stay like that for a long stretch, our bodies gradually relaxing together, Riva's presence melting the worst of my lingering distress. Gradually, other impulses wake up beneath my skin.

With her breaths, her breasts shift against my chest. One of my tentacles has fallen across her thigh.

The sharply sweet smell of her floods my lungs when I inhale. I can almost taste her on my lips, but I'm weirdly afraid to move to make it real, as if this could be a dream —as if I could be lost in a coma still, only imagining her.

Riva's enhanced senses must pick up the signs of my desire. She lifts her head and lets her lips graze my neck, my jaw.

My pulse jumps. When she raises her head higher, it would have taken an iron will I sure as hell don't have not to claim her mouth with mine.

Riva nudges me onto my back and straddles me. The feel of my dick settling between her legs has me stiffening even with the layers of clothing between us.

She leans over me, kissing me again and again, as I slide my hands beneath her shirt. As my tentacles circle her waist and dip right between her thighs to conjure more pleasure for her.

The hem of her shirt catches on the slim bracelets

wrapped around my wrists—the silver bands the others have called "manacles." Just for a second, I hesitate.

Back in the island facility, Riva would never have taken things this far. Not while she suspected the guardians were listening in.

I don't think she enjoys the thought of Balthazar and his people monitoring us any more than she did with our previous captors. But she's decided… that she doesn't care?

It could be rebellion. Or it could be desperation—the fraught uncertainty of whether we'll ever get to do this again if not now.

Riva draws back and gazes down at me with her bright eyes. "Are you okay?"

The longing in her gaze is more than just hunger. And I'd be lying if I didn't want her just as much.

Fuck this house. Fuck the people who are keeping us here.

Whatever her reasons, we can confirm our bond and still kick their asses when we get the chance later.

I nod and tug her back down over me.

As she starts to rock against me, Riva doesn't make any move to strip off my clothes. Maybe that's her concession to privacy, as little as we have.

I follow her lead, stroking all the bliss I can into her body working around her outfit.

My breaths go hoarse as hers turn ragged. She unzips my jeans and frees my cock, then wriggles her leggings and panties down as far as she needs to.

When she sinks over me, taking me into the slick heat of her pussy, every thought flees my mind but the heady joy of joining together with her like this again.

I thrust up to meet her, electric quivers racing through my veins. I'm not going to last long, but I'll be damned if I don't bring her with me.

With one tentacle's suckers, I massage at her clit. The other applies its cups to the curve of her breast while I work over the other with swivels of my thumb.

Riva moans and pumps faster over me. My jaw clenches as I hold myself back against the swell of release. I clamp down on the sizzling need until she shudders over me, and my control snaps in a blaze of ecstasy.

We sway against each other a few more times before settling into a slack embrace. I feel like I can't hug Riva close enough.

There has to be more I can do for the woman I love than offer up a temporary physical escape.

Whatever that is, it isn't coming to me in this moment. We cuddle together in a silence that's as contented as it can be, given the circumstances.

Then there's a tentative knock on the door. Zian's voice carries through. "Dominic? Riva? We made some dinner, if you're hungry."

I sit up slowly with Riva in my arms. A weight still drags down my spirits, but not as badly as before.

And a jab of hunger prods at my stomach.

"That would be great," I say. "Thank you."

Riva gives me one more kiss and squirms back into her leggings. When we open the door, Zian is waiting in the hall.

His gaze travels from her to me, not judging, just with a glimmer of envy that tells me he knows we weren't only having a friendly chat.

My gut twists. I wish I knew how to do more for my friend too.

The wounds getting in his way aren't the kind my powers can seal over.

As we head down the hall, Zian drifts back behind me. Sensing he's got something on his mind, I let Riva pull ahead of us.

He glances sideways at me, and the corner of his mouth lifts despite his previous solemn expression. "Getting your mojo back, huh?"

A faint flush tingles across my cheeks, but it's hard to be really embarrassed around any of my friends when we've shared Riva together. "It's not that hard when I have her as inspiration."

"Yeah." Zian pauses and seems to gather himself. "I— Dom— There's something I've been thinking about. I don't know when I'll be ready to try it. But I think I could use your help."

A flash of hope lights in my chest, small but potent. I tap his arm with my knuckles. "If I can, I will. Why don't you tell me about it after dinner?"

Nineteen

Riva

It's hard to say how exactly I stumble on the hidden passage. Maybe it's luck or random chance, but it feels almost like some higher power took pity on our troubles, finally, and showed me the way.

The night after Dominic was returned to us, I'm even more restless than usual. I prowl through room after room in the blanket of darkness, never making a sound.

I've been in all of those rooms before. I've scanned every inch of them. But Balthazar's people use them too, and it's always possible they'll have left some hint of their work behind that I can use.

At least that's what I've told myself night after night. By the time I slink into the sitting room that holds the bookcases, the idea is striking me as about as plausible as the possibility that Martians will beam down from outer space and rescue us.

And then I see the book on the floor.

It's lying a few feet from the nearest bookcase, just beyond the edge of a table by one of the armchairs. Like maybe someone sat there reading it and set it down so idly it teetered off after they left.

I'd swear it wasn't there when Dominic, Griffin, and I wandered in here after dinner. Dom and Griffin each took a book to pass the time, but they brought those back to their bedrooms.

Did one of the other guys come in even later? It's hard for me to imagine any of them lingering in one of the common rooms alone, relaxing with a book.

I steal over and crouch down to pick up the book. The heft of it and the bland title—*Theories on Geographic Migration*—convince me that there's no way any of us was reading this for fun.

So who was reading it? And does it matter why?

While I'm hunkered down like that, my gaze skims the darkness again—and catches on a crooked tile right where the dim strip of security light streaks through the far window.

In this room, along the two walls that aren't covered by bookcases, the tiles creep right up from the floor to about knee height. The upper ones are maybe a foot squared, a yellowish tan with a typical intricate leaf-and-flower design painted across it.

They've always stood in a straight row, but now one cants just a smidge to the side like a slightly crooked tooth.

Weird.

With apprehension creeping over my skin, I stay close

to the floor as I ease over. My slim fingers probe the edges of the tile.

It shifts—and swings around on a hidden hinge.

A square of thicker blackness gapes open on the other side. I reach my arm in, and my fingers encounter only smooth, cool walls falling away into the darkness.

It's some kind of hidden passage. Leading where?

What am I even doing here if I don't find out?

My hand rises to my chest, reaching for my now long-gone necklace and the reassurance it offered. I'd almost forgotten that one small thing Balthazar took from me in my anger over all his other crimes.

I might not be able to get it back, but I have to take every chance I come across that could point us to our freedom. I ease forward into the hole in the wall.

Like with the window in the western wing I squeezed through what feels like years ago, like the air ducts I wriggled through what must be centuries ago to investigate an old facility, I'm the only one who could investigate. None of the guys could possibly contort their larger bodies to fit into this space.

After the first couple of feet, while I still have my hips outside, my groping hands mark a widening of the passage. Still not enough that anyone but me could fit through, but giving me enough space to be sure I won't get stuck.

Not enough to turn around. If I hit a dead end, I'll just have to count on my supernatural muscles to push me out backwards.

Or hope I can yell loud enough to summon Balthazar's people to break me out.

I think of those options in an attempt at reassuring myself, but my lungs still constrict as I squirm farther into the passage. A thread of nausea winds through my gut.

I don't like being clamped in like this. It reminds me too much of both the heavier shackles I've worn and the past times when even my guys saw me as an enemy.

The passage continues forward for only a short distance before it slants downward. I follow it, breathing shallowly, the thud of my pulse echoing in my head.

The minutes slip by with the rasp of my clothes against the surfaces around me. I can't tell whether the sides of the passage are made of stone or plaster.

Then my reaching hand jars against a dead end just in front of me. My heart lurches in the split-second before I register the edge of another square imprint carved into the passage floor right before it.

I flick out my claws to pry the panel out and lean it on the narrow lip between the opening and the end of the passage. Ever so carefully, I lower myself into the space below—head-first by necessity.

I was on the first floor when I found the secret tunnel, so I must be in some kind of basement now. One we haven't found any direct access to by conventional methods.

No windows let in any light. It's as if I'm dropping into a pool of total blackness.

Hooking my feet so that I won't plummet right to the floor, however far down that is, I stretch my arms in every direction. My fingers brush a wall to my left.

They trail along it and bump over a light switch.

I hesitate for a few seconds, but there's no sound in the

stillness around me. Not a breath or a creak.

I'm going to take this gamble.

With a flick of the switch, a pale light floods the room I'm descending into.

I'm dangling only a few feet above a cement floor. The room holds no furnishings, only stacks of cardboard boxes that must have been here a while from the layer of dust on most of them.

But not all. My attention immediately latches on to the two at the top of their stacks that must have been recently opened. And opened regularly, I'd guess, since they don't have so much of a streak of leftover dust on them.

Next to the light switch stands a door that must be the normal way of getting into this room. It's firmly closed. No one bursts in at the sudden flare of light that might have shown under it.

I curl myself and jerk my feet free so I can flip onto the ground.

The first thing I check is the door. The handle doesn't budge—locked.

Not a basic supply room, then.

Keeping my ears pricked for any sound of approach, I move to the boxes next. My fingers unfold the flaps on the first.

I find myself staring at a heap of folded clothing. Tentatively, I pull the top piece out and let it unfurl from my grasp.

It's a dress—light and casual in blue cotton. Made for someone maybe a few inches taller than me.

A faint, clover-like scent drifts off it. The remnants of

that someone's perfume?

The next couple of articles—a blouse and another dress—look to be part of the same wardrobe. The next item I lift up is a band T-shirt that's a very different fashion statement.

It's bigger, too. I don't think it'd fit the same person who wore the dresses and the blouse. The cargo shorts and scuffed jeans I unearth next give me distinctively masculine vibes too.

My mind darts back to the photograph I saw in the western wing. Balthazar with the woman and the little boy.

That was from a while ago, based on Balthazar's and Toni's more youthful appearances. The boy would have grown up.

But why would our captor be keeping pieces of clothing from his wife and son in a locked storage room... and opening the box up to check on them regularly?

My uneasiness grows as I dig farther. In the bottom of the box, I find a wooden jewelry box that holds a few necklaces, rings, and a bracelet that don't look like something you'd just toss aside.

Unless the owner wasn't able to wear them anymore.

Balthazar's wife doesn't need to approve of what he's doing these days if she isn't around to see it.

I swallow hard and return the clothes to the box in as close to their previous order and state as I can manage. After closing it up, I move on to the other recently opened container.

The second box only adds confidence to my suspicions. The books, the deck of cards, the grubby baseball, and the other objects inside all strike me as keepsakes. Memorabilia of times past.

That room in the western wing might simply be a larger version of the same idea. His son's childhood bedroom, preserved like it's in a museum.

How long has Balthazar lived in this villa? What did he do here while his family was with him?

A corner of what looks like a photograph pokes out from the largest of the books. I tug at the faux leather cover to free it and realize it's a scrapbook.

More of the sweet clover smell drifts up when I ease the book open. Did Balthazar's wife put this together?

The scrapbook appears to document their lives after the birth of their son. It starts with photos of the delicate-looking woman I saw before with an even more youthful Balthazar, her belly bulging with pregnancy.

Then there are a couple of pages of the couple with their newborn baby, and more as their son grows from toddler to child to teenager. Family trips, birthday parties, random candids...

My gaze snags on one birthday cake. I can just make out the lettering on the icing: *Happy Birthday Peter!*

Peter. Didn't Andreas mention something about that name when we shared all our observations in the pool?

Ajax had heard it in Balthazar's thoughts years ago, in a memory Drey peeked into. He thought our captor might have been thinking about a colleague.

But he wasn't. Even in the facility, overseeing his work, he'd had his family on his mind.

Continuing through the scrapbook, I pause over a couple of pictures that might hold clues to Balthazar's interests beyond his family. There's one with a slightly older man who might be a colleague, but I don't recognize his face.

In another, Balthazar and his wife are poised outside a building with a polished marble face. A stylized metal symbol like a wave arcing over a cloud is fixed to the wall next to the door, maybe some kind of company logo?

Balthazar has his hand resting on it with a proprietary air. But I've never seen the symbol before, not in or around any of the facilities.

Every photo is painstakingly fixed to the pages with stickers and decorative tape chosen to match the theme. Running my fingers over the textured surface, I can almost taste how much love and care the curator put into her creation.

There are a couple of photos in which the son looks about the same age as Nadia and Booker—late teens. I turn the page and freeze with a hitch of my pulse.

The next pages are blank... of photos and stickers, anyway. Instead, shaky words scrawl across their beige surface in stark permanent marker.

IN A BETTER WORLD, THEY'D LIVE. TO MAKE A BETTER WORLD, I'LL DESTROY THEM ALL. TO DESTROY THEM ALL, I HAVE TO CONTROL ALL.

That's it. The several pages afterward offer nothing at all.

I flip back to the urgent scrawl and suppress the shiver that crawls down my spine.

Somehow I don't think it was the wife who wrote that. Who is it Balthazar thinks he needs to destroy?

Totally unnerved, I shove the scrapbook into the box. Nothing else inside offers up any message.

I close the box up and prowl through the rest of the room, scanning for other signs of activity. All the remaining boxes look undisturbed under their sheen of dust.

I can't pry into them without giving away my presence here.

As I crane my neck to peer between the stacks, a glint off near the far wall catches my eye. I slip over to it, dislodging as little of the dust as possible.

A thin glass tube lies on the floor near the baseboard. One end of it looks vaguely singed.

I have no idea what to make of that. I guess it's just a stray bit of garbage that got left behind.

The urge to get back to my room, to get away from the questions now crowding my head, rises inside me. I scramble onto the dust-free box that's closest to my access point, swing my feet to kick off the light, and scramble back into the passage in the ceiling.

The image of the brief but emphatic manifesto lingers in the back of my mind long after I've crawled into my bed.

I'm heading to breakfast when the hum of the drawbridge brings me to a window instead. By the time I reach the pane, a sedan has parked beyond the rising bridge with Toni stepping out from the driver's seat.

My feet move of my own accord. Hunger vanishing, I hurry to the nearest doorway.

Toni has already marched most of the way to the villa when I reach the door. She slows and peers at me. "Do you need something?"

I have to swallow a wrenching laugh at the thought of all the things I need that she'd never offer me. But there may be one thing she can give me.

I raise my chin, looking her straight in the eyes. "Was he always this insane, or only after his wife and son died?"

Toni stiffens—briefly, but visibly enough that I know I've hit my mark. She pushes forward again with a motion for me to get out of her way. "I don't have time for conversations like this."

"You should," I insist. "You're working for him. Carrying out his crazy jobs. *You* don't seem insane, so you've got to be able to realize how horribly he's treating us."

"Balthazar has bigger dreams. A higher purpose." Toni cuts her gaze toward me again as she brushes past me. "You should remember that. Justice doesn't come pain-free."

This time I do let out a snort. I stride after her, keeping pace. "Oh, yeah? If it's his justice, shouldn't it be his pain?"

When Toni ignores me, I let my voice rise a little. "He can't bring back the dead. You know that. And he's adding to the death toll instead. He's killing people who don't deserve it, who never did anything wrong."

"Then I suppose you'd better follow his orders well

enough that you don't need to be reminded of your mortality, don't you think?"

My jaw clenches. "You know where that logic leads, don't you? If it's okay for him to torment and kill us for *his* justice, then obviously we'd be justified torturing and murdering people to get back at him for what he's taken from us. Why does his justice matter more than anyone else's?"

Toni spins with a flash of her eyes. "It's not your business to question what he does here," she snaps.

Then she sweeps through a doorway. The click of a lock sliding into place sounds in her wake.

My shoulders slump as the rush of my show of defiance ebbs. Did she listen to me at all?

Maybe it was stupid to even try. But I know Matteo doesn't give a shit what happens to us as long as he can run his experiments and gather his data.

Toni at least has shown glimmers of normal emotional reactions. She doesn't like having her conscience nudged.

I summon as much of yesterday's determination as I can and trudge toward the kitchen. Griffin emerges when I'm only a few feet away.

He aims a gentle smile at me with a tip of his head. "I have some good news—and it looks like you could use it."

His words and the smile wrap warmth around me. "Yeah, I'd say so. What's up?"

"I managed to get Balthazar to have a chat with me this morning—through the screen." Griffin motions toward the drawing room. "I pointed out some things about emotional endurance and all that... The point is, in the end he agreed that you need a break before he lays any more responsibilities on you."

I blink at Griffin. "What kind of a break?" And how much of his emotion-warping talent did he manage to impose on Balthazar to get him to agree?

Griffin's smile stretches into a grin. "You're allowed to go into town on a date. With just one of us, your choice, but that's better than nothing. A few hours where you can recover and enjoy a little freedom to do what *you* want."

TWENTY

Andreas

As the car rumbles along the first streets of denser-packed buildings, carrying us toward downtown Florence, I glance across the backseat to where Riva is sitting.

It's strange seeing her wearing a dress, even this fairly casual knit one with a boat neck and a skirt that falls to just below her knees, the long sleeves hidden under a suede jacket for extra warmth. The only other time I have is the fancy evening gown she picked out for the soap-opera-style party I arranged on Rollick's yacht.

When I couldn't help staring at my first sight of her by the car back at the villa, her lips quirked into an awkward smile. "Since this is supposed to be a date, I figured I should dress up a little."

I can't help thinking of all the possible lives she could be living, all the things she might have enjoyed doing in those lives, if the one she has hadn't been so strictly regimented by our keepers.

Dressed up or not, she's still Riva. Still warily alert, still poised as if braced for danger.

She's gazing out the window, her eyes flicking back and forth as she takes in the first semi-local scenery we've had access to beyond the villa's grounds. But her hand stays clamped around mine as if to make sure I don't disappear.

I'm filled with joy at being with her outside the tighter constraints of the villa and the thrill of wondering what we might accomplish with our leashes loosened. Those happier emotions come with a twinge of guilt.

I clear my throat, unable to hold back the question. "Are you sure you wouldn't rather have brought Dominic?"

Riva's attention jerks to me. "What?"

I shrug awkwardly. "I mean—he just woke up. You've had a lot less time with him than the rest of us since all this started."

She studies me for a moment before scooting a little closer on the seat. Her fingers shift to twine with mine instead of just wrapping around them.

"I thought about it," she admits. "But I figured—you're our history-keeper. Our storyteller. You'd be the best one to make the others feel like they got to have a bit of freedom too."

The intensity in her eyes tells me she intends to communicate more than the words she's saying. There's something about my talent with memory that she thinks will be important during our temporary escape—something Balthazar wouldn't be happy about.

I nod with a crooked smile. "That makes sense."

What makes more sense than anything is that she'd be thinking up ways to spin this gift to our advantage, no matter how monitored we are. I'm not totally sure what we can accomplish out here that would work in our favor while the other guys are still trapped back at the villa, but I'm open to ideas.

I also intend to help Riva enjoy this theoretical date in every way possible while we have the chance.

She's seemed more grounded since Dominic came back to us, her vibe of constant agitation and frustration fading. But the signs of tension haven't vanished. Her worries show in the set of her jaw, the flex of her fingers around mine.

How could she *not* still be upset about our situation?

I can't free us permanently from Balthazar when we're on our own, but I can at least remind her of how much we have to look forward to when we do break free. Of all the good things this world has to offer despite the evil we've encountered in it.

The excursion has already told us a bit more about what we're dealing with. We know that Balthazar's villa is in Italy—not a surprise given the look of it, but good to have confirmation—within a few hours of Florence.

Unfortunately, I don't speak any Italian, but it's got some overlap with Spanish. I could probably make myself understood on the basics if I needed to.

Not that going up to someone and trying to convey that we're being held on a mountaintop by a madman is likely to go over well. Somehow I don't think the Florence police department is equipped to tackle Balthazar, even if they believed us.

Even if we could get through the full story before he knocked us out.

As the car slows with the thickening traffic, I take in the buildings outside the window. I'd probably be more awed by the towering yellow and white-washed facades and intricately carved window frames if I hadn't been surrounded by similar architecture for the past two weeks in our fancy jail.

But there is a weird relief to seeing so many normal people walking along the streets: locals striding briskly or ambling with casual confidence, tourists peering at their phones or folded maps. The storefronts and restaurants we pass remind me of the thin wad of cash Toni handed me for this outing.

Fifty euros isn't going to get us far, but it should allow a decent sort-of date.

Our driver parks at the edge of a broad, stone-tiled plaza surrounded by Medieval-looking buildings built out of warmer shades of stone. With a grunt, he motions for us to get out.

Riva and I exchange a glance and slide out on the same side of the car. I assume Balthazar has at least a couple other vehicles staked out nearby, his employees monitoring our movements to ensure we don't make a run for it and scanning our conversations for shows of rebellion.

Still, being able to walk away from the car with just

Riva by my side lifts a weight I hadn't even realized was pressing down on my chest.

Riva cranes her neck toward the street we drove up. "I think I saw a tourist information office. We should grab a map if we're going to make the most of the time we have here."

I let out a dry chuckle. "And to make sure we can get back here when it's pickup time."

Balthazar said he'd give us "a few hours" and that our bracelets would signal us when it was time to return. I suspect he likes keeping us on our toes, not knowing exactly when the call will come.

We set off down the street at a quick pace. Riva points out a sign declaring *Informazioni Turistiche* with a lower case *i* next to it that I recognize as the universal info symbol.

Inside, Riva grabs one of the free maps on offer… and uses her supernatural speed to pilfer one of the pens off the counter when the staff person isn't watching.

"Do you know where you want to go?" I ask as we step back onto the street. The breeze is a bit nippy, but the bright mid-day sun warms the air in its wake.

Riva inspects the map, and a sudden gloom comes over her expression. "I'm not sure."

I hate seeing her spirits sink before my eyes. If she hasn't figured out the best course of action yet either, we might as well get something good out of our time here rather than just stewing on it.

I tuck my hand around her elbow. "Let's start with something simple, then. I'm ready to get something to eat."

Riva nods hesitantly. "I want to take a look around first… Maybe we can just stroll and get an idea of what's in the neighborhood."

Is she looking for something specific? If so, she obviously isn't comfortable saying it out loud.

It could be she's simply hoping for inspiration to strike.

I give her arm a reassuring squeeze. "Sure. Let's admire the scenery."

Riva's grateful smile in return transforms my false cheer into a little more genuine upbeat mood.

We wander along several streets and through a couple of plazas, pausing a couple of times to gaze up at the particularly spectacular buildings. I can't tell what has changed for Riva when she declares, seemingly at random, "All right, let's get some lunch."

I pick out a café that gives me a friendly vibe and do the ordering, since I can make more sense of the menu. Riva rewards me with a grin when a tall glass of lemonade arrives for her.

I have to beam back at her. "I'm sure it's not as sour as your custom creation, but it's been a while since you've gotten to have any."

The anguish of our captivity might be an unspoken presence in the back of both our minds, but I have to take a simple pleasure out of her wordless murmur of pleasure as she digs into the pasta I picked out for her—a spaghetti carbonara with the bacon sprinkled liberally. It's some kind of miracle that I now know this woman well enough to offer *her* a simple pleasure so easily.

She eats quickly, so I gulp down my penne in marinara

sauce to keep pace. But after checking with me about how much cash I still have, she orders another lemonade to go.

There's an air of anticipation around her as we meander back down the street—the way we came, by Riva's choice. She sips at her lemonade, but her small smile fades into a pensive expression.

Something in her face sets with visible resolve. She grabs my hand and tugs me over to a bench.

The chatter of voices in a language neither of us knows winds around us, but we're both aware that's not enough to cover a conversation between us. Riva pulls out the map and pen and writes something on the back.

"There are a few things I'd like to take a look at," she says, and slides the map so I can read what she wrote. *Your memories of Rollick. Any time he talked about helping us. I don't know whether we should have trusted him.*

I'm not totally sure why she's asking, but I turn toward her without hesitation. "Of course. I don't mind letting you call the shots."

Whoever's listening in can assume we're only talking about landmarks to gawk at.

I raise my hand to Riva's cheek as if this is a romantic moment, but from the back of my head, I draw up my recollections of the shadowkind demon who took us under his protection. Fixing my eyes on hers, I let the images flow from my mind to hers.

Some of the moments Riva was there for too: when we first confronted Rollick in his Miami hotel, when he organized his shadowkind underlings to help us practice our powers, when he agreed to give us the resources we needed to rescue some of the younger shadowbloods from an isolated facility.

Others she'll never have seen from any perspective. There was the time when I asked him for permission and the opportunity to make amends with Riva by way of that party, which the demon agreed to without argument. A conversation while she hid away after she'd accidentally hurt one of our shadowkind friends, when Rollick assured me he wasn't going to retaliate.

I believed in him. I can't say with certainty what happened after we got the kids free from the facility that turned out to be a trap for us, but no part of me can imagine that Rollick purposefully had the younger shadowbloods slaughtered.

If they're dead at shadowkind hands, it was in spite of him, not because of him.

My feelings won't come across in the memories, but maybe that's beside the point. Riva wants an objective perspective to add to her own recollections.

And I can do that. I can show her a broader view of reality.

As I jump from one memory to another, a different sort of satisfaction wells up inside me.

Riva called me the shadowbloods' history-keeper and storyteller, but those things mean more than just entertaining people. I can show the truth with the glimpses of the past I hold in my head—truths that might be lost to us otherwise.

I've done it before: when I showed Riva how the guardians had deceived us about her role in Griffin's supposed death, when I offered her my perspective of my argument with Jacob after she and I first had sex. I just never thought about it quite that way until now.

Reliving the memories while I project them to Riva's mind only solidifies my own sense of what's true. Rollick wasn't human, and his sense of morality might have been somewhat skewed by that... but not much more so than our own morals are as shadowbloods.

When it mattered, he was there for us. I never saw him show unnecessary cruelty.

When I ease back from the psychic connection, Riva blinks a few times and rubs her forehead. She shoots me a twisted smile that looks more uncomfortable than happy.

"I just want to make sure... that we don't get lost," she says quietly. "Heading in the wrong direction. But I guess pretty much everything we could do is right, comparatively speaking."

More right than what we're experiencing back at the villa? I chuckle softly. "Yeah, I'd say so."

I pause, recognizing the tenor of Riva's uncertainty even if I don't totally understand what she's working through. She's deciding between believing our impressions of Rollick... and what the guardians showed us?

There's a little more I can say—or rather show—on that subject.

I stroke my fingers over her temple. "Something else to consider."

In a fleeting stream, I bring up the memories of the various ways the guardians have betrayed us. Misled us. Manipulated us. Just a glimpse of one and another, enough to stir the unpleasant memories Riva already has without forcing her to dwell in them longer than she needs to.

Wetting my lips, I catch her gaze again in the present. "We know going in that direction definitely wasn't right for us lots of times."

We have no direct proof that Rollick ever lied to us. But the guardians did all the time.

Riva's fingers curl around the map. Then she dips her chin in a sharp nod.

"All right. I know where we should start. We never got dessert."

She tugs me farther down the street, around a couple of corners... and toward a pastry shop she must have noticed during our earlier wanderings.

A pastry shop with a small sign announcing an internet café up top.

TWENTY-ONE

Riva

It feels strange, making what might be the most daring move of defiance since Balthazar kidnapped us while chatting idly about the excellent cannoli we're enjoying. I take a bite, the thick, sweet filling coating my tongue, and furtively tap on the keyboard of our rented computer with my free hand.

Andreas looks on with a casual smile but alert eyes. He ushered us over to the computer closest to the boombox that's playing upbeat Italian pop music through the room, to better cover the faint clicking of the keys.

From the moment Griffin told me he'd gotten permission for this "date," the idea of how I could reach out to the demon who once guided us came together in my head. The hardest question wasn't what I could do but whether I should.

I bring up the website for the Beach Bliss Hotel and Nightclub in Miami. The design is flashy but in a refined sort of way, a lot like the building—and the demon himself.

I find the link for the Contact page down at the bottom. When I click on it, it brings me to a sparse page with a simple form.

It'd have been better if there'd been separate email addresses for different levels of the business. Then I'd be more sure of the message reaching Rollick quickly. Or at all.

But this is by far the best strategy I can come up with. Even if I could get access to a phone, I don't have his number memorized. I have no idea what his personal email address is.

The hotel was his primary business and also, as far as I could tell, his home. A significant number of the employees, if not all of them, were shadowkind.

Please, let whoever checks the hotel email be one of those. Or at least a human obedient enough to follow my instructions regardless of how weird the message sounds.

I pop the last of my cannoli into my mouth so I can type with both hands, so focused on the task in front of me I barely notice the crunch of the pastry and the final gulp of sweetness.

This is an urgent message that should be passed on to the owner of the hotel. Don't worry if you don't understand it—he will.

This is Riva. The guys and I are being held by a man who's split off from the guardians and is forcing us to help him. He's already killed at least two of the younger shadowbloods. We haven't found any way to escape without help. We're hoping there's some way you can reach us or send shadowkind who could get us out. His last name is Balthazar, and he has us in a villa on a steep hill in an isolated part of Italy, within a few hours of Florence.

"South," Andreas murmurs as if making commentary on our map to himself.

I revise my last sentence. *Within a few hours south of Florence. There's at least one shadowkind who's being forced to work with him, so you might be able to find out more through your connections. He also has a woman who goes by Toni and a man named Matteo working for him. That's all we really know.*

If you come, please be careful. He has devices on us that can kill us in an instant if he wants to, and I think he might prefer that we're dead rather than let us escape.

I sit back, feeling wrung out, and have Drey read over what I've written. He nods in approval and squeezes my shoulder.

I don't have an email address of my own to put in the form, but then, I doubt I'll get a chance to check it for a response. I write *riva@shadowbloods.com* as if my explanation of who I am in the message itself might not be blatant enough.

Holding my breath, I click send.

My body goes rigid, some part of me anticipating a blare of pain from my manacles or a thunder of pounding footsteps as guards rush into the room. The pop music plays on, the chair stays firm beneath me, and we go unmolested.

I exhale slowly and manage a grin at Andreas despite my queasiness.

I did it. The only thing I could think to do, and a gambit that might not pay off any time soon if at all.

But it's one more flicker of hope to sustain us through whatever our captor throws at us next.

Andreas slips his hand around mine and tugs me to my feet. He tucks the map he was contemplating into his pocket. "I picked out a good route from here. Trust me?"

My next smile comes easier. "Of course."

As we drift down the street outside, Drey strokes his thumb over the back of my hand. "We've gotten through a lot of hard stuff already. This was supposed to be a break for you. Do you think you can set the worries aside and enjoy being here?"

I know that by "hard stuff" he means the email I just sent as well as everything we've endured before. Tension still winds around my gut, but there really isn't anything else I can do to improve our situation right now.

"Yeah," I say. "I can give it a shot, anyway."

Andreas flashes a warm grin at me. "Then I'll do my best to make the rest of the day as enjoyable as possible."

He guides me past some historic buildings I barely paid attention to before and then others beyond them, pointing out details in the architecture. We stop to read plaques offering stories of their significance.

After the first few, Andreas glances over at me. "It's kind of comforting in a strange way, don't you think? That these buildings and the memories attached to them have endured for hundreds of years."

I think I get what he means. "It's nice to know that it's possible."

The horrors we're facing now are just one blip in the

grand history of the world. Balthazar's impact could end up being nothing more than a brief burst of static.

The beautiful things people have created can outlast a whole lot of trouble.

Andreas leads us on from the streets of towering buildings to a sprawling park. No flowers bloom in the gardens in the autumn chill, but impressive statues gaze down over the perfectly shaped hedges that form winding paths through the greenery.

We stop by a breathtaking fountain, taking in the water streaming over the carved stone. The rhythmic warbling settles some of the lingering jitters in my nerves.

Not many tourists are bothering with the park at this time of year. The sound of other voices fades as we venture deeper among the hedges.

Drey's face brightens when he spots a sort of alcove formed between the hedges, like a dead end in a maze. A stone bench stands against the leafy wall.

He draws me down onto it and takes my other hand in his. A glint of mischief gleams in his eyes.

"I've been thinking… Our talents feel like a burden sometimes. Not something we've asked for—something the guardians forced on us so they could use us."

"Something a whole lot of other people seem to want to use—or destroy," I can't help muttering.

"Yeah. But the powers aren't just that. They're *ours* too. There are so many things we couldn't have done for our own benefit if we hadn't been made into what we are."

I can't really feel happy about any of the destruction I've caused with my hunger for pain. On the other hand, I am glad I could cast out my shriek to save us when I've needed to.

And my strength and speed have given me moments of exhilaration I wouldn't have gotten any other way. I like the power that runs through my muscles when I flex them.

In my silent contemplation, Andreas gives my hands a little squeeze. "How would you like to experience one more thing no one else in this city could get to?"

I raise an eyebrow. "What did you have in mind?"

Rather than an answer in words, a tingle glides over my skin, from my hands up my arms and then racing all through my body.

Before my eyes, Andreas fades from view. But not just him. When my gaze jerks to our twined hands where I can still feel the pressure of his grasp, I've vanished too.

I can see right through the spot where our joined hands should be to the bench my no-longer-visible legs are braced against.

Andreas releases one of my hands, and I wave it toward the hedge next to us. I can't see anything but the dense leaves, but they tickle against my arm when I brush it right against them.

An elderly couple strolls by our alcove, glancing into it with bland expressions that show they don't see us at all. My pulse leaps with a giddy hiccup.

"It isn't much," Andreas says in a low voice. "It's only a temporary disappearance. But it means I can do this right here, and no one's going to stop us."

His fingers trace the line of my jaw, and he guides my mouth to his.

When I close my eyes, there's nothing different about

the embrace at all. Andreas is here with me in every way that matters.

The only difference is we don't have to worry about anyone seeing us and judging our PDA.

Because we're shadowbloods. We're *special*.

Even if I hate what the guardians put us through, even if sometimes I hate what they turned us into... there *is* something amazing about our existence too. Only six of us humans in the entire world with powers strong enough to rival actual monsters.

And those powers don't have to be used just for fighting.

The shadows in my veins shiver and flare. My longing for the guy in my arms grows with every second of our kiss, every stroke of his hand from my shoulder to my hip and back again.

It's never been as urgent as it was back when we first collided, when the smoky essence inside us wound together to form our matching marks. But I know that part of me will always call out to part of him, recognizing him as my own.

We're blood.

I kiss him harder, looping my arm around his neck. A pang of hunger radiates from between my thighs.

I have to remember what's really important, no matter what shit we're going through. I *need* this physical connection as much as everything else we share—with all of my guys, or at least all of my guys who are ready for it.

Balthazar might have us cuffed and under threat, but even he doesn't own us. Not entirely.

When I feel for the hem of Andreas's shirt and tease

my hand up under it, his breath catches. His mouth slides along the edge of my jaw to the crook.

He speaks in a low murmur and a hot exhalation. "Riva, we don't have to—"

The desire lacing the air tells me he's just as eager as I am despite his words.

I curl my fingers against the taut lines of muscle that shape his chest. "I know we don't. But I want to. Because we can. Because I always want you."

He makes a strained sound and nips my earlobe. "I always want you too, Tink. We'll have to be quiet, though. I can hide us from eyes but not ears."

I give a soft laugh against the tight curls of his hair. "I've got plenty of practice at that."

My hand slides lower, and Andreas sounds as if he's swallowed a growl. He tips me over so I'm lying on the bench with him braced over me.

His mouth brands my jaw, my neck, the top of my shoulder. "Someday it won't be like this. I look forward to getting to hear you let it all out."

He cups my breast through the fabric of my dress, and I arch up into his touch. When the swipe of his thumb over the peak provokes a whimper, I yank his lips back to mine so he can muffle it for me.

As much as I want to soak up every bit of passion Drey can offer me, I know we can't take our time with this interlude. What if one of the few other visitors to the park decides this bench looks like a nice place to sit?

What if Balthazar summons us back?

With our mouths still melded together, I reach beneath the waist of Andreas's jeans. The brush of my fingertips over his scorching erection earns me a strangled groan.

He yanks up the skirt of my dress and runs his own fingers over my already dampened panties. I rock with his touch, letting my gasp get lost in the meeting of our lips.

It's not just special or exhilarating, being with this man. It feels like some kind of miracle.

We were wrenched apart more than once but found our way back, with a love and trust I never knew I'd be able to have, back in the anxious teenage days with my unspoken crush.

I manage to undo Andreas's fly. As I ease his rigid cock from his boxers, he pulls down my panties.

My knees splay around his hips. He plunges into me with another crash of his mouth against mine.

My shadows sing, and my body bucks to connect with his even more closely. My spine jars against the smooth stone beneath me, but I don't give a shit about the distant pain or the bruises I might be giving myself.

We're in the middle of a sprawling city full of people, but we're also alone together in our own invisible world. No matter what happens next, Balthazar can't steal this moment from us.

He tries. Andreas thrusts deeper with a rasp of breath, and the bands around our wrists give off a faint buzz of an alert.

Before I can even start to tense, Drey grips my thigh and slams deeper. His lips sear against mine.

He doesn't need to speak for me to understand that he's refusing to back down, to give up this stolen intimacy. And the defiance sparks a starker fire inside me.

I sway up to meet him, my fingers digging into his shoulder. He pounds into me even harder, chasing the eager pants of breath I'm now expelling against his cheek.

His cock hits the perfect spot deep inside me, and the manacles thrum again.

"No fucking way," Andreas rasps. "Not until I'm done with you."

The desire in his words and the pulsing pressure inside me tip me over the edge. I come with a moan I can't totally stifle, pleasure flooding every inch of my body.

Drey follows me with a jerk and a groan of his own, his face bowed to my neck. He holds me for several beats of our heart before deigning to lift his head, claim another kiss, and sit up to help me straighten my clothes.

"We're on our way," he says softly for the benefit of the manacles. "Just had a little something to finish up first."

There's no one in sight of our alcove in the hedges to see Andreas's powers at work. He brings us back into visibility, appearing before my eyes with a triumphant grin.

We won this minor battle. Balthazar didn't have us knocked out or harmed for delaying an extra minute.

For all he knew, we really couldn't have returned right away regardless. He couldn't have seen exactly what the circumstances were.

A little loophole in the tangled mess he's wrapped us up in.

I don't know if he'll agree to any more recreational excursions after we've stretched the limits of his patience, but that possibility seems unlikely anyway. All that matters is the lightness that winds through me as Andreas and I find our way back to the waiting car.

The sense of momentary freedom lingers through the drive to the villa as I nestle against Drey in the back seat. It lasts until the car passes over the drawbridge into the grounds, and Toni eyes us as we clamber out.

"You got your fun," she says. "Now Mr. Balthazar has another job for you."

TWENTY-TWO

Riva

Somehow it feels odd to look around and see all the signs up and down the city street printed with English words. Many of them I can't fully make out in the hazy light of streetlamps through the night, but it still gives the neighborhood a sense of home that I hadn't realized I was missing.

This isn't the first time any of our recent keepers have sent us on a mission to an English-speaking place. The gala we attended, where I carried out my political assassination, must have been in the US.

But that one time, our escort dropped us off right at the site of the job. We had no chance to look around, let alone roam.

Every other place Balthazar or even Clancy sent us was someplace beyond the continent where we grew up, often unidentified and made even more indecipherable by that lack of information.

Here, the recognizable language showing in shop windows, over their doors, and on the ads in a bus shelter grounds me. Balthazar and his people didn't tell us what city we were going to, but it's warm for the late autumn. I guess it's possible we're in Australia, but the look of the place, the sounds and smells and the overall atmosphere, strike me with a sense of familiarity.

We're probably somewhere in the southern US. Maybe I'll see a reference to a state or the city itself on one of the buildings we pass.

Not that the information will necessarily tell us much of anything about why we're here or how it matters to Balthazar, but I'll take every scrap we can get.

His driver has chosen our stopping point well for keeping Zian, Andreas, and me in the metaphorical dark as well as the literal, though. Most of the structures we slink by on the short walk to our target are bland office buildings with vague company names that give away nothing about what services or products they offer. If the few street signs we pass include the city name like I've seen some places, it's in a print too small for me to make out in the night.

I spot our destination up ahead: another office building, slabs of concrete around horizontal rectangles of glass. Our instructions said it'd be on the corner, with a large logo like a red daisy cut in half etched on the wall beside the front door.

Pausing on the opposite side of the street, I reach back to touch the small bag slung across my back. Confirming I've got my cargo.

Today we're not stealing anything but dropping

something off. Which somehow seems more ominous, since I can't imagine Balthazar's offering is actually any kind of gift.

For a second, I could imagine I'm alone on the street corner. Only three of us headed out from the villa for this latest job, and Andreas's only role was to use his expanding powers to turn Zian, me, and my cargo invisible. Zee and I left him back in the van.

The faint huff of a breath confirms that Zee is still there beside me. I have the urge to reach toward him, to solidify his presence in my mind with a touch, but that seems particularly risky when he won't even be able to see my hand coming.

"Ready?" I ask under my breath. I don't see anyone around, but the caution comes automatically.

Zian replies with a repetition of the next part of our instructions. "Middle of the south side, twelfth floor." He inhales audibly. "Let's get it done."

Balthazar picked the two of us for the main part of this job mostly for our supernatural strength. None of the other shadowbloods could have fit their fingers and toes into the small ridges in the concrete and hauled themselves up twelve floors without fear of falling.

Okay, not *much* fear. Given the choice, I'd rather have a climbing rope.

But Zian and I clamber upward with no further conversation, only the soft rasp of exertion in our breaths. I sense him just a foot away from me in the shifts of the air with his movements.

When I'm looking straight up, not paying any

attention to the area beside me, my mind fills in his image there as if I could see him after all.

My limbs move even more effortlessly than I'm used to. All of Matteo's "procedures" have continued enhancing my strength and speed as well as my banshee scream.

With my conversation with Andreas in the back of my mind, the things he said about how our powers could work for us as well as other people, exhilaration trickles through me. I don't like that I'm performing this feat for Balthazar's benefit… but there is something thrilling about the fact that I can accomplish the climb at all.

There's one row of the three-by-four windows for every story. Pushing myself a little faster and reveling in my speed, I count them off in my head until I reach twelve.

Then I hook my fingers and the claws I've extended as deep as I can into the small concrete lip I'm clutching, bracing myself to hang there for at least a couple of minutes. "Go ahead."

This part, only Zian could do. Balthazar wants us coming and going without leaving an obvious trace of our presence.

Heat wafts through the air, and a thin ruddy glow spreads along the edges of the window. Zee has honed the cutting edge of his X-ray enough to aim it steadily.

As the heated line runs along the final side, the cut pane starts to wobble. I slip my fingers around the opposite edge to hold it from toppling and shattering on the floor.

When Zian has finished the cutting, he eases his own hand around the other side. Together, we lower the glass to the floor just inside.

It hisses against the vertical blinds that are closed over the window. They warble louder as each of us crawls through the space into the room beyond.

Darkness fills the sprawling office. I don't dare turn on a light, but I do adjust the blinds so they let in some of the city glow and moonlight from outside.

The thin illumination washes over a broad mahogany desk, a row of matching bookshelves behind it, and a cluster of modern armchairs and loveseat around a sleek coffee table at the other end of the room. This dude—or dudette—has an office as big as the vast drawing room back in the villa.

I guess they're someone pretty important. Maybe the head honcho of whatever business we've invaded.

It's not like Balthazar would care about messing with some minor underling, after all.

We need to find somewhere to put his "gift." As I give the room a more thorough scan, fingertips graze my arm.

Zian has reached out to *me*. I hold still, and he lets his hand linger against my elbow, fixing both of us in the space no matter how invisible we are.

He edges a little closer before he speaks. He doesn't touch me anywhere else, but the warmth his unseen body gives off grazes my skin.

His voice is barely more than a breath. "What do you think?"

I cock my head, forcing myself to focus on the scene in front of us rather than the leap of my heart at Zee's closeness. We're supposed to leave the unknown item in its taped paper wrapping somewhere it *can* be found but where it won't catch the eye unless someone knows to look for it.

Carefully, I adjust my arm so I can give his bicep a little nudge toward the bookcases. As we slink over to them, his touch falls away, but he stays close enough for me to feel his presence.

I pause to study the framed certificates on the wall next to the shelves. I was right in my first guess of *dude*—this office appears to belong to someone named Rodney Milner. A Rodney Milner who received an MBA and also a few different awards and commendations he was proud enough of to show them off.

Most of the organizations and honors don't mean anything to me, but one of them is the International Clean Energy Federation. Not that I was aware of that organization either before this moment, but a frown crosses my face as I take it in.

The politician Balthazar had me murder—he had something to do with fossil fuels. Wouldn't this guy be on the opposite side of an energy debate?

Is Balthazar just trying to throw everyone into total chaos, or is there some pattern I'm not grasping?

Zian taps my shoulder, bringing my attention back to the job at hand. I step closer to him, and we inspect the bookcases together.

"Here?" Zian murmurs, guiding my hand tentatively toward a section with some shorter books. "Or would it be too obvious if we just stuck it on top?"

I hum softly. "I think we'd want to tuck it *behind* something so it's a little more hidden. Is there anything on the higher shelves that would obscure it?"

There's a pause before Zee answers. "Mostly books, but there are a couple of liquor bottles and a cigar case."

"How big is the case?"

"About…" He hesitates and then takes both of my hands. With a light grip, he adjusts them so they're about eight inches apart.

A tingle races over my skin at the contact, but I don't push for more. "I think that's too small. And we don't know how often he's taking it out."

I prod Zian farther down the row of shelves. He directs my hand toward a shelf at my chin height. "We could pull these books a little farther out?"

He's found a spot with a row of matching volumes that are all relatively narrow despite their height.

I smile. "Good call. That's perfect."

As I retrieve the package from my bag, Zian pulls out a few of the books to make room for me to slide it into place. I tuck it behind the rest of the row, he replaces the removed books, and I run my fingers over their tops to confirm that the package won't be seen poking up over them.

For now, the package is as literally invisible as we are. But from the recent experimenting Andreas has done with his powers, he said Matteo has determined that if he uses a soft touch, the invisibility will fade within several hours without him needing to intervene.

I step back to take in the wider view and raise one of my wrists to my mouth. "First bookcase on the left, four shelves up," I whisper to the manacle.

Balthazar wanted confirmation of where exactly we left his little present.

The job is done. We could leave now. But as I turn around, my gaze lingers on the desk—the papers and folders piled in the stacked desk trays off to one side, the laptop closed on the thin mat in the middle.

There's no hope in hell of me hacking this guy's computer password, but the documents he's been dealing with might give us more of a clue of his recent activities. Activities that could have prompted Balthazar's hostility.

I've got to take my chances when I can.

Zian says nothing while I guide some of the papers out of the top rack. I shuffle through them carefully, making sure to keep them in their original order.

None of it tells me anything enlightening. They're reports full of numbers and abbreviations I don't know, followed by a few memos that sound like mundane business-speak, not anything controversial.

Gritting my teeth, I set those back and grasp the stack from the next tray down. *Come on, there's got to be some little tidbit…*

I flip open a folder and find that tidbit—but not at all the way I expected it.

The page on top is a color printout of an article about innovations in clean energy. And right below the headline is a graphic I recognize.

It's the stylized wave and cloud symbol I saw in one of the photos in the scrapbook I assumed his wife put together. The metal fixture that Balthazar looked so proud of, attached to the front of a building.

My eyes dart over the page, squinting against the dimness. It's a business logo—*StreamCycle Enterprises, the tech giant that's long been the forerunner in the energy revolution...*

Does Balthazar work for that company—*own* it? He's got to be making the money to maintain that villa and all his vehicles and staff somehow.

I lean closer, wanting to absorb every scrap of information I can out of the article—and Zian grabs my arm.

In the instant as I freeze, the noise his sharp ears must have picked up reaches mine too. A distant but steady hiss of footsteps over carpet.

It's getting louder even in the few seconds I'm listening to it. And it's heading this way.

My heart lurches. I duck down by the desk, feeling Zian move with me.

The footsteps thump closer. Is it a security guard? Or an employee?

What if it's Rodney Milner himself, come to do some urgent late-night work?

He won't be able to see us—but I left the papers out on the top of the desk. If anyone comes in, they could realize we were here.

Another flare of panic races through me, twanging in the base of my throat. I adjust my position to dart upright and shove the papers back into place, but in the same moment, the floor creaks just outside the office door.

My body tenses, a quiver of power shivers up my spine —and a choked yelp breaks through the door.

A shard of agony wafts into me in the same moment.

Oh, shit. I hurt him—I used my power with my mind without even realizing it.

Drowning under a deluge of icy horror, I lock down my hunger for pain with all the will I can bring to bear.

What did I do to him? I was too startled by my panicked reaction to get a clear sense of the injury before I absorbed its impact.

We weren't supposed to leave any mark.

I didn't mean to—my power just flared out of me in my panic—

The figure outside curses under his breath in obvious distress. But he's well enough to hustle away, even if his footsteps sound uneven now.

I run my tongue over the back of my teeth, tasting the flavor of the brief agony I drank in. I think I might have snapped a bone or two in his feet.

Will he assume it was just random chance? That he somehow stepped wrong?

It's not like he's going to imagine that some monstrous girl was lurking around and psychically attacked him... right?

As I muddle through my inner turmoil, Zian's shoulder brushes mine with a shudder. He grips my hand abruptly.

"I closed my eyes as soon as I realized—I didn't mean to do it."

I glance around. On the floor beneath the desk, a small scorch mark has blackened the wood.

Zee's powers slipped away from him too. We were both so nervous.

And we have so much more power than we used to, thanks to Balthazar and Matteo's work. We're filled up to the brim.

Which makes it much too easy for those powers to overflow. Like Jacob's telekinetic ability whipping random objects when he gets upset.

I close my eyes for a second, gathering my scattered emotions.

We both caught ourselves in time. We didn't ruin the job; we didn't get caught.

"It'll be okay," I murmur to Zian. "No one will be looking under there anyway… If they do, they'll have no idea it happened tonight."

I sense his nod. My nerves keep rattling—and the urge to shriek is still lodged in the base of my throat, where I can't necessarily suppress it anymore.

When no footsteps return, I scramble up and reassemble the papers into their previous order. Then we hurry to the window as quickly as we can in our stealth.

We climb out and heft the glass into place. Zian melts the edges he carved out to fuse the pane back together.

If anyone looked particularly closely at the area where the glass meets the frame, it might look strange to them. But not like anything they'd expect a human being could do.

As we descend to the street with none of the exhilaration I enjoyed on the way up, my pulse thuds in a heavy rhythm.

I thought I'd finally come to terms with my powers. I believed I could control how I used them.

Has Balthazar stolen even that peace away from us?

TWENTY-THREE

Jacob

I flop onto one of the stuffy armchairs, but I can't sit there for more than a few seconds before I'm shoving myself off it again. Agitation winds through my limbs.

I glance over at Dominic and Griffin where they're poised at the room's card table, attempting a game of checkers I don't think either of them is all that focused on. "Shouldn't they be finished talking already?"

Dominic's mouth tightens with a hint of a grimace. "We don't know what Balthazar wanted to talk to them about."

Riva, Andreas, and Zian got back from their overnight mission a couple of hours ago. I heard the whir of the drawbridge lowering to admit the car.

But Toni ushered them into the drawing room immediately and shooed us off when we came asking if the job had gone okay. They still haven't emerged.

My gaze fixes on my brother. "How are they feeling? Has anything changed?"

I asked Griffin a similar question when they first returned. He told me then that both Riva and Zian were upset, with some agitation and a little fear, but not hurt. Not in an immediate panic.

Has this long discussion with Balthazar made them feel better or worse?

Griffin leans back in his chair, fully abandoning the game. His eyes take on a distant cast.

He can pick out their separate impressions because he knows them so well. That's how he once helped the guardians track us all across the continent and beyond.

He will always know Riva from the inside out, in ways I never can. He hasn't solidified the connection in our blood with her like I have, with the mark that hums on my breastbone with a faint but clear sense of her presence in the house, but he has a much more direct line to her heart.

It shouldn't bother me anymore. It shouldn't bother me that Balthazar sent her off with Drey and Zee when having my powers in the mix should *always* mean she's better protected.

So I'll just pretend that it doesn't. That's gotten me pretty far already.

"Their agitation has become less intense, but it's still there," Griffin says after a moment. "The general uneasiness has spread to Andreas too. He and Zian are frustrated now—Riva's closer to outright angry."

Dominic is taking all this in as I do. His grimace

lingers. "Whatever Balthazar is telling them, it's not helping."

I can't restrain a snort. "When does it ever?"

But making that snarky comment doesn't help anyone either. I stalk around the room that's part living room with its hearth and upholstered chairs, part games room with the table and the collection of basic board games in a nearby cabinet. "If he's not helping, maybe he should let them go so *they* can tell us what's going on."

Of course, that would serve our purposes rather than the asshole's. He only cares about what he wants.

If I knew exactly which of the rooms on the far side of the villa he's lurking in—if I could barge right in there and wrench his neck around with my powers for that satisfying *snap*.of his spine—

My hands clench, and one of the cabinet doors flings open hard enough to smack into a neighboring side table.

With a waft of shame, I inhale slowly. Then I nudge the door back shut with the same power that yanked it open accidentally.

Griffin and Dominic don't comment on my lapse, but it's not as if they won't have noticed. They're just being polite about it.

I open my mouth, wanting to say something that'll make me sound like I do have *some* self-control, but just then Toni appears in the doorway.

She takes us in with a flick of her cool gaze and jerks her head toward the hall. "Mr. Balthazar wants to see the three of you now."

My pulse speeds up with a searing mix of relief and annoyance. We're going to find out something, finally—

but naturally the bastard made us wait a good long time before he could be bothered.

Toni escorts us down the hall to the drawing room. She steps back while we walk inside and closes the door behind us. I don't know whether she stays outside to guard the doorway or goes off on some other business.

Apparently whatever business is going on in here, it doesn't concern her.

In the past few days, the drawing room has become a lot less ominous. Not having the nearly dead specter of one of our friends lying there attached to unfamiliar hospital equipment will do that.

But today, it feels almost as unsettling as it used to. Even I can pick up on the tension lacing the air.

Riva glances over her shoulder at us from where she's standing between Andreas and Zian in a semi-circle facing Balthazar's screen. Her shoulders are raised, and the tendons show around her tightened jaw.

Zian is sporting an uneasy frown. Andreas holds on to some semblance of his usual easygoing posture, but his dark gray eyes have turned stormy.

It's not just them in the room. To my surprise, Matteo has joined the discussion.

The scrawny, pinched-faced man who loves to poke and goad us stands off to the side between my friends and the screen, studying us new arrivals with an avid air I don't like at all.

From the video transmission, Balthazar acknowledges our entrance with a smooth nod. *He* doesn't look remotely out of sorts. He doesn't look happy either, though.

The worst thing about the prick is that I can rarely tell

how to read him. Even when he does let some emotion slip, it always seems a little off kilter with the situation.

I stride over to join my fellow shadowbloods, my muscles braced. "What's going on?"

Balthazar draws in a breath as if to answer, but Riva beats him to it, her voice taut. "Our expanded powers—it's getting harder for us to contain them. I hurt someone by accident while we were out there, and Zian damaged the office we were in."

Her gaze shoots back to the man on the screen. "Apparently *he* knew that was likely to happen all along and doesn't care."

"Didn't bother to warn us either," Zian adds in a wary mutter.

My own anger flares inside me. I know how badly Riva takes it when her powers get away from her. I'm not sure there's anything she hates *more* than the idea of hurting someone who didn't deserve it.

And this jackass has forced her back into the chains of guilt and self-doubt she worked so hard to throw aside.

I'd like to smash the fucking TV screen and his stupid face with it. But I know that's not going to accomplish anything useful.

Elsewhere in the room, a chair leg cracks.

"Now I'm ensuring that all of you know," Balthazar says in a tone so calm it makes me want to smash a whole lot of other parts of him too. "It's an understandable trade-off for the growth of your powers, but I'm sure you'll adjust in time."

Dominic folds his arms over his chest. "Are you going to help us with that adjustment or just expect us to figure out how to adapt to the changes you've forced on us on our own?"

Balthazar's bland response is barely an answer. "I can see you're all motivated to harness your powers. I doubt it'll be much trouble."

I glower at him. "Fucking bullshit."

Our captor considers me for a moment, his lips curving just slightly. Is he *amused* that we're upset?

Then he turns his attention to Riva. "If you're particularly worried, maybe you should spend more time with Griffin. From what I've seen, he has a steadying effect on all of you."

His gaze flicks back to me. "And it might be best if Jacob keeps his distance from the rest of you while he gets his own issues with control sorted out, since he was dealing with those before Matteo even got started with him."

My jaw starts to clench. "If you don't like my temper acting up on your furniture, maybe you should stop pissing us off."

Matteo tilts his head at a contemplative angle. "You have struggled the most out of all the shadowbloods I've worked with."

Balthazar hums in agreement. "Your companions need to think of what's best for themselves, not just what will pacify you. Why would they want to be around someone unsafe, who doesn't even care enough to keep his destructive emotions reined in?"

My skin burns with a heat that's both fury and shame. I suck in a harsh breath, and Riva shakes her head.

She narrows her eyes at the screen. "Jacob's only ever

struggled because of all the shit the organization *you* helped form put him through. We're not afraid of him."

But has she already eased a little closer to Griffin? How much does she believe her defense of me, deep down under the loyalty that comes instinctively to her?

Is it possible some of the forgiveness she's offered really has been an attempt to placate my temper for her own protection? It's not as if I *didn't* hurt her—and badly—not that long ago.

Balthazar speaks as if he's pulled the conflicted thoughts right out of my skull. "Look at how well you've convinced her that you need coddling. Are you really surprised that she's gravitated toward your brother now that he's back with your group?"

Griffin stiffens, but whatever he says, it's lost in the roar of rage that floods my head. I close my eyes, grappling with the caustic rush of anger turned more venomous by the fear that he might be right.

I can think of times all the others seemed to treat me with kids' gloves. What if they've just been waiting for an excuse to shove me away, to get rid of the problems I make for them?

Have they been fucking *lying* to me all this time, feigning friendship as well as forgiveness?

The darkness behind my eyelids brings me back to the endless nights in my cell while the guilt over Griffin's death—the death that never actually happened—gnawed through my insides. Swallowing a growl of despair, I glare at the screen again.

And catch the glitter of triumph in Balthazar's eyes an instant before the smug prick wills it away.

Understanding hits me in a chilling deluge that douses all my fury.

He wants this. He wants to get me worked up, have me questioning my friends, provoke me into doing something that might encourage them not to trust me in turn.

He almost succeeded.

I don't know why he's trying to carve a fissure through our group, but it can't be for any *good* reason.

I inhale and exhale through my nose so it's not so obvious that I'm expending significant effort to cool myself down. So I can at least keep the appearance that I wasn't on the verge of exploding.

When I'm sure I can speak steadily, I lift my head. "If that's what my friends want, I'll go along with it. I know I've screwed up before, and it's not their job to deal with that—it's mine. But the decision is up to them, not you."

I risk glancing around then, and the expressions that meet me might as well be another punch to the gut. But not in a way I can blame them for.

Griffin doesn't look surprised, but then, Griffin knows me at least as well as I know myself. He'll have followed every shift of my emotions.

The other guys... look relieved. Andreas even shoots me a reassuring smile, as if to say, *Good job.*

They weren't sure whether I'd hold myself together. They were probably afraid I'd explode like our captor hoped I would.

Well, why wouldn't they be? How many times have I gone off half-cocked or pushed myself past my limits and left them to pick up the pieces of whatever I broke?

I've never even really apologized for all of that, have I? I've made my amends with Riva, because I hurt her the worst, but I'm sure I've inflicted a hell of a lot of smaller pains on my friends over the years.

All the times Dominic expended his powers and felt his tentacles growing while he healed me up. All the sharp remarks and barked commands I threw at the three of them.

It wasn't just Riva I was an asshole to.

She's pushed a little closer to the screen, staring Balthazar down. "If that's the only kind of advice you can offer, then you can shove it. I guess we will figure everything out ourselves."

I might still explode, but if I do now, it'll be out of love for this woman who's somehow chosen to be mine.

She spins and strides out of the room, and the rest of us follow without another word. Neither Balthazar nor Matteo tries to stop us.

In the hall, Zian rests his hand on his belly. "Am I the only one who's starving?"

The question is so Zee and so incongruent with the conversation we just ended that it sets off a burst of hilarity. I start chuckling, and Riva breaks into giggles, and then everyone's cracking up, even Zian.

In the middle of our laughter, we manage to make it to the kitchen. Andreas starts poking around in the fridge, and Dominic automatically moves to grab plates out of the cupboard.

And my amusement dies, strangled by the knowledge that *I'm* not actually done with that conversation.

"Guys," I say, feeling unnervingly awkward.

My friends leave off their lunch-making to look at me.

Riva leans against the counter, watching with thoughtful curiosity. I have the sense that she'd leap in to help if she knew where I was going with this.

But the fuck-ups have been mine. I can own them.

I glance from Drey to Zee to Dom. "I just wanted to say—I should have said it sooner—I'm sorry I've been an ass so much of the time. Not just since we went on the run, but before in the facility too. No matter what I was going through, I shouldn't have taken it out on you. I never want to again. Okay?"

Andreas offers another smile, this one slightly crooked. I have apologized to him in part before. "I don't think any of us blames you, Jake. We were all dealing with a lot. I'm sure the rest of us screwed up in all kinds of ways too."

I wince. "Not like I did."

"We're all different people," Zian says carefully. "It affected us in different ways."

"You still shouldn't have had to put up with me acting like a prick."

Dominic smiles too, soft and bittersweet. "No. But did you ever cross the line on purpose? Was there ever a moment when you felt like you could have done something different—better—and just decided not to?"

The memory of the aching emptiness that filled me for so much of those four years nibbles at the edges of my mind with a twinge of lingering horror. A lot of the time it was a wonder I did anything at all.

"No," I say hoarsely. "But that's not an excuse. I *should* have been thinking. I—"

Griffin moves to my side and slips his hand around my

arm. My gaze shoots to him, and my throat constricts even more.

The words spill out of my mouth before he can say whatever he meant to. "I was a prick to you too, back on the island, at first."

My brother lets out a quiet laugh. "*I* deserved it. I definitely screwed up too."

He gives my arm a squeeze. "No one's angry with you. We're in this together, and that means you as much as anyone."

He isn't lying. I'd know it if he was.

My throat constricts even tighter.

These guys—all of them—are my family. It isn't just my love for Riva that's swept away the emptiness that threatened to consume me but the other bonds that go far beyond basic friendship.

I swallow hard, but my voice comes out a little hoarse anyway. "I just—I wanted you all to know that I *am* sorry. And how much getting through this mess with you matters to me. I wouldn't be alive without you, and I'm going to damn well do my best to make sure you all make it out of whatever else we have to face too."

Andreas grins. "I've never doubted that for a second. Now are you going to help us make some sandwiches or what?"

I give him a half-hearted glower, and laughter fills the room again. As I go to grab a loaf of bread, Riva tucks her arm around my waist and gives me a sideways hug.

And I know that no matter what Balthazar says, I have gotten better. I've remembered how to care again—about more people than just her.

I *can* be a proper friend to all of these guys now, like I couldn't really before.

Even if I don't know how yet, that fucker on the screen is going to pay for all his crimes, including trying to tear the only family I've ever known apart.

TWENTY-FOUR

Riva

I t's easy. I *hate* how easy it is.

Several mice, two rabbits, a squirrel, and a ferret have lost their lives to a silent shriek in my head that doesn't even require that I part my lips. When Matteo places a cage holding a tabby in front of the chair I'm locked into, my body balks even more emphatically than it did before.

I can't help thinking of Lua, Griffin's sweet cat that he was forced to leave behind in some unknown jungle near Clancy's island. Is she surviving okay? Has she managed to trek to other people who've taken her in?

I like that imagined version of reality better than the one that seems more likely—that the guardians abandoned her to become a tiger's dinner.

No part of me wants to be responsible for ending this other cat's life. It peers at me through the bars of its cage and lets out a piteous meow.

I lift my gaze to meet Matteo's through the transparent pane that separates us. "No. Haven't you seen enough?"

He smiles, his eyes gleaming with barely suppressed excitement. "But you've been doing so well! You did want to make sure you can control your impulses, didn't you? Practice seems to be the best way of ensuring that."

How can he look so fucking happy—almost *giddy*—about slaughtering innocent animals by the dozen?

Frustration stabs through me, and my power vibrates in my throat. A spike of the vicious energy quivers through my thoughts.

I do have some control—enough to yank my attention away from Balthazar's flunky before I hurt *him*. Because God only knows what agony he'd inflict on my guys if I slipped up that much.

But a soundless blare of my pain-seeking hunger spills out of me anyway, latching on to the only other available target.

The cat flinches and yelps. Its leg twists at an impossible angle.

My stomach lurches. I twist in the chair and gag over the bucket Matteo set there after the first time I puked during this "training" session.

There's nothing left in my stomach to come up. I only sputter a little sour acid.

Matteo tsks his tongue with an air of droll chiding that pisses me off even more on top of my anger with myself for lashing out accidentally. He didn't even inject me with his special serum this time, so I can't blame any chemical compliancy.

What I do here is totally up to me. That's the point. He wants to see how far he can make me go.

I clench my jaw so hard it aches, willing my mind to stay closed. But the cat is trembling and whimpering, and Matteo is watching me expectantly.

He won't do anything to help it. He'd probably have us sit here like this for hours more, the cat wallowing in the pain I inflicted, waiting for me to finish what I started.

Tears prick at the backs of my eyes. I don't know what else to do.

Bracing myself, I send out all the power of my frustration in one sharp mental blast.

The cat's body jerks, its spine snapping the way Jacob often kills his targets. It slumps on the cage floor, now out of its misery.

Matteo's smile widens, and I want to vomit again. "Good, good. Very impressive. I'll need to have more animals brought in—larger, more mentally advanced—to see how you do with them."

I flinch inwardly, barely holding in a protest. What good will arguing do me?

He already knows I don't want to do this. The more I complain, the more he might feel he needs to challenge my resistance.

What if someday he brings *people* for me to practice my powers on?

I restrain a shudder at the chill of that thought and keep my mouth shut as Matteo emerges from his booth. My gaze falls to my lap.

I don't want to look at him. I'll be too tempted to unleash my anger on the man who's directed this session.

It'd be so easy to sever his life without so much as a peep. The hunger inside me shivers with its own giddiness just imagining it.

Not yet. Not when I'd only be condemning all of us to more misery.

Lashing out doesn't do us any good when we still have no way to escape.

I get to my feet, willing my legs not to shake, and walk past Matteo to the door. In the hall outside, I suck in a breath of air that smells just a little fresher.

My gut is still churning. It might be past lunchtime now, and I don't have anything left in my stomach, but I can't imagine trying to eat.

Rubbing my arms, I head back to the section of the villa where we spend most of our free time. Who is Matteo going to bring in for his "procedures" next? What is he going to make *them* do?

Is he going to traumatize my guys even further after everything they've endured in the past?

My fingers curl, the tips of my claws emerging. In the same moment, Toni steps into my path up ahead.

I can tell the moment I see her stern expression that she's here to give orders. It's not like she'd ever inquire about how I'm doing or whether I'm okay, right?

I stop about five feet away from her and trail my fingers over the plaster wall, almost but not quite scratching the faded blue paint. "What do you want?"

Toni tips her head in the direction of the drawing room. "Mr. Balthazar has a new job he needs to talk to you about."

Oh, he *needs* to, does he?

My jaw clenches. I think he needs to shove his expectations up his ass.

I said no to Matteo today, and he ignored me. But I do have a little leverage with our main captor.

He knows that we're capable of disobeying him—and that he won't necessarily be able to tell the difference between an honest failure and a purposeful one. That unless we're sufficiently motivated, failure is definitely an option.

I push my lips into a tight smile. "You can tell Balthazar that I'll deal with his demands when they're actually a deal. I've been doing what he's asked. He needs to do something for me in return if he wants me to continue cooperating."

Toni narrows her eyes at me. "What are you talking about?"

I stare back at her unflinchingly. "He healed Dominic like he promised. Which, by the way, worked in Balthazar's favor too. I think I've done more than enough to cover my side of that bargain. Now I want to know about StreamCycle Enterprises and how his business fits in with all these jobs he's giving us."

A scoffing sound slips from Toni's mouth. "He's not going to talk to you about his personal affairs."

I raise my eyebrows. "They can't be that personal if he's sending six strangers to handle some of them, can they? If he wants our help, I want to know what we're actually doing. More than the nothing he's told us so far, anyway."

Toni's lips purse as if my even making the request is distasteful. "He has security concerns. You don't have a right to that information, so you can forget about getting it."

My frustration blazes to the surface again with a vengeance. The words seem to scorch my tongue. "I don't have the *right*? Where the hell did he get the right to turn me into even more of a monster than I already was?"

My experience with the cat and my apprehension about threatening Balthazar's people in general hold the most cutting part of my temper in check, but only barely. An ache pulses in the middle of my forehead.

"You don't understand the purpose of all this," Toni retorts.

"Which is exactly why I'd like an explanation!"

"You *wouldn't* understand. It's too big—you've barely been outside the cages the guardians kept you in."

"And whose fault is that?" I snap back. "Who's keeping me caged now, while you defend him?"

Toni's gaze sharpens to a glare. "Mr. Balthazar has his reasons, and it'll be better for everyone when he sees them through."

Before she's even finished her response, anger flares white-hot behind my eyes. I have to jerk my gaze away, clenching my hands and digging my claws into my palms so the pinpricks of pain keep me stable.

My voice comes out strained. "It's not better for me. It's not better for any of us shadowbloods. What he's forced on me—I almost killed you right now, you know? I could hurt you so badly without even meaning to, if I wasn't putting everything I have into clamping down on my powers."

"Is that a threat?"

"No," I rasp. "It's just the truth. I wouldn't want to—I don't want to hurt *anyone*. Can you please just stop acting like an asshole and tell him what I said?"

There's silence. The pressure reverberating inside my skull gradually eases.

I risk glancing over at Toni, my fingers relaxing. Her gaze drops to my hands, taking in the streaks of blood from where my claws dug in and the tiny wisps of smoky essence drifting up.

Her jaw works. Her gaze flicks to my face again, and a strange expression comes over it.

A trace of nervous pheromones reaches my nose, mingled with the faintest tang of what I'd have taken for… longing?

I frown. "What?"

Toni shakes her head as if to clear it. "For a second, you almost looked like— Never mind."

She jerks around, away from me. "I'll pass on your message. I can't say he's going to be happy about it, let alone agree to your demand."

"Fine," I mutter. "As long as you tell him."

As she walks off, I stand there in the hall, feeling even more out of sorts than I did before. The effort of holding in my fury has left me wiped out, and I have no idea what to make of Toni's reaction.

My feet drift toward one of the outer doors as if of their own accord. I want to drink in the fresh air, even if it's cold outside with the impending winter.

I want a glimpse of the world beyond our prison even if I can't reach it.

I wander across the lawn and between the hedges. My whirling emotions gradually settle.

Then a sound like a distant voice reaches my ears.

I pause and listen hard. Maybe it was just something from inside the house.

No. A faint but insistent call is carrying from somewhere ahead of me. I can't quite make out the words, but they tingle in my mind on the verge of recognition.

Casually, so no one who happens to be watching would realize something's odd, I stroll toward the sound. As I approach, it becomes clear enough for me to distinguish the faint summons.

"Shadowbloods. Oh, shadowbloods."

The hairs on my arms rise. I crouch down by the wall, following the call.

Here. A small, smooth stone, solid black, little more than a pebble. It's lying amid the grass like it was tossed over the wall carelessly.

But there's nothing careless about this. The moment I pick it up, a faint quiver passes through my skin.

And a voice I now recognize as Rollick's resonates from the stone.

"Hello, little banshee and company. Don't worry—no one without our essence in their blood will be able to hear this message. I just wanted you to know that I got yours. I'm not sure how long it'll take to sort out your latest mess, but I'm on my way."

TWENTY-FIVE

Zian

I rub my hand across my mouth as if I can wipe away my nerves and glance at Dominic where he's standing across from me by the kitchen doorway. "You're sure that you're okay with this?"

His gentle smile takes the edge off my nerves—but only the edge. "I'm honored that you want my help. I think taking this step could be good for all of us. And I want to see you and Riva happier."

We both turn our attention to the far end of the room, where Riva is just finishing washing the dinner dishes. She hands a plate off to Andreas for him to dry, her stance more relaxed than I can remember seeing in ages.

It was just before dinner that Andreas showed all of us his memory of the covert email she sent during their "date" in Florence. He communicated her hopes in a way no one listening in could pick up on.

And then Riva told us, in an even tone but with

excitement shimmering in her eyes, that she thinks she's going to get what she asked for.

I'm not sure what else she's requested that she expects our captors to assume she's talking about, but she clearly meant Rollick's help. She must have seen some sign that the demon is coming to our rescue.

I have no idea how he's going to manage to get us out of here or when—she didn't indicate that we should expect him soon. But she's lit up just a little like she hasn't been since... since the last time we were free, I guess.

Wouldn't it be nice if she could feel that way all the time? If all of us could?

I hope Rollick gets his ass over here and puts Balthazar in his place ASAP.

It seems like as good a time as any to approach her with the proposition I've been mulling over for days. She's in good spirits, and I don't want to leave it long enough that I'll regret my hesitation.

Who knows what Balthazar might do to us next? Whether Rollick's plan will get all of us out of here alive?

Dark thoughts, but necessary if I'm going to kick my own ass into gear.

Riva swipes her hands on a towel and heads toward us. I draw myself up a little straighter, like I'm not already more than a foot taller than her tiny frame.

Fuck. Is this going to work at all? Am I an idiot to even—

I tamp down my worries and manage a smile that's not too tense. "Hey. Could—could you come with me? I was hoping we could... spend some time together."

Riva cocks her head with curiosity darting across her

face. Something about the way her expression softens when I put myself out there like this always gets my heart thumping twice as fast.

"Of course," she says. "What did you have in mind?"

"I, ah, I'll explain in a minute."

Can she already tell from my awkwardness? The back of my neck burns with embarrassment.

But then, it's not as if I've ever been particularly smooth when it comes to Riva.

When she realizes that Dominic is heading down the hall with us, she reaches for his hand automatically. Seeing the simple gesture sends a pang through me that's not pleasant at all.

She'd reach for me too if she thought I'd welcome it. If she wasn't worried that I'd flinch away like I have so many times before.

That's why I have to do this.

If Riva is surprised that we head upstairs rather than outside or into one of the many common rooms, she doesn't show it. I lead her right into my bedroom and then stop just past the threshold, abruptly twice as uncertain.

Dominic keeps his head enough to shut the door behind us. Right. Privacy is a good thing.

Even if nothing about this can be totally private when we've got these fucking manacles clamped around our wrists.

To hell with Balthazar. He and his stooges don't matter.

All that really matters is the woman in front of me.

Riva doesn't look remotely concerned. She lifts a

questioning eyebrow at me, her stance untroubled in her fleece pullover and jeans.

Casual clothes, just the stuff left in the villa for us, but she always looks gorgeous to me no matter what she's wearing. I have the urge to tuck a stray strand of her silvery hair back behind her ear to join her braid.

I swallow thickly and ease a careful step toward her. "I —I've been thinking about what you said before. On the island. About… about how maybe we could try to work through my hang-ups."

Riva blinks. Then she glances from me to the bed and back again, and her eyes widen slightly.

But there's no horror mingled with her surprise. Her cheeks flush. "You were thinking we'd get started on that now?"

"I feel like I've already left the situation the way it is for too long, lost so much time with you…" My throat starts to constrict, and I pause to take a slow breath. "Unless you think it wouldn't be a good idea to try, for reasons like before."

Before, when our former captor shoved us together in the hopes of gathering data about the bond we could form if we have sex—like Riva has with three of my friends already.

Riva brushes her fingers over one of her manacles automatically, but she shakes her head. "I haven't gotten the impression that we need to be worried about those things in our current situation."

I haven't either, but the fact that she's confirmed it relieves me. Balthazar hasn't shown any interest in our personal connections other than how he can use our loyalty to each other to get his way.

From what Clancy said, our current captor hasn't been a part of the Guardianship in years. And even if he was still hearing some news about their progress, I think Clancy would have wanted to keep that particular interest of his pretty quiet.

How many of his colleagues would have approved of him acting like some kind of a supernatural pimp?

"Okay," I say, somehow feeling both exhilarated and even more nervous at the same time. "I figured we could just start and... see how it goes. And, ah, I asked Dominic to be here too, just in case—in case I panic. So he can drain me enough to knock me out before I do anything I'd really regret."

I tense, half expecting Riva to balk at my precaution. Her lips part, and a gleam comes into her eyes that looks more sad than anything.

It's Dom she looks at now. "Are *you* okay with all of this, if you have to step in?"

I should have known she'd ask that. She doesn't want him pushing himself past his limits either—and there are obviously things about his own powers that he's not totally comfortable with.

Before I can feel guilty again about asking him at all, Dominic offers her a smile as gentle as the one he gave me. "I'm glad that I can be a part of making this happen for you two."

His gaze slides back to me. "I'll intervene if it's necessary, but I don't think I'm going to have to. It's mostly about Zee knowing he has a… a fail-safe, I guess you could call it, so that he can relax more."

Riva takes that in. Then she aims a grin that's both shy and sly at me. "Where did you want to start?"

Holy fuck. This is actually happening.

A shudder of apprehension races through my limbs instinctively, but I remind myself that I want this. That I'd never want to hurt Riva.

That what we'll do here is nothing at all like that day with the woman who tried to seduce me against my will.

And if some idiotic part of my brain decides to lash out as if it is like that, Dominic is here to siphon all the vicious energy out of me.

He can heal me again later. But I wouldn't care even if I ended up in a coma like he did.

If I try to hurt Riva, I'll deserve it.

I resist the urge to fidget, feeling totally out of my depth. "I guess the bed would make the most sense?"

Without hesitation, Riva walks over to my bed and clambers onto it. She sits there on the covers, her knees drawn partway to her chest, and waits to see what I'll do.

I haven't even touched her yet, and I'm already fighting to keep my legs from shaking. I follow her and ease onto the covers beside her, leaving about a foot of space between us.

Dominic joins us silently, perching on the edge of the mattress near the headboard, his tentacles looped in front of him. Ready but not intruding, our protective witness.

Maybe it should feel weird to have him here for this moment, but my nerves settle a little as soon as he's in position.

I watched him and the other guys hook up with Riva on my behalf just weeks ago. There was nothing wrong with sharing that moment between us either.

Riva has stayed perfectly still, giving me space to decide how I want to proceed. Making sure I don't feel pressured.

Gazing at her, my heart swells with so much love it chokes me up.

I raise my hand and bring it gingerly to her cheek. Stroke my thumb over her soft skin, up and down, until the frantic thunder of my pulse ebbs.

Her mouth draws my attention, and the thumping rises again. I refocus my self-control. "I—I'd like to kiss you."

Riva beams at me. "I'd like that too."

She turns her shoulders toward me but doesn't lean forward. Still letting me come to her at my own pace.

I've never kissed anyone before, not really. I'm probably going to be horrible at this.

But something about this woman draws me in like a magnet. Even as I tilt toward her, quivers run through my veins as if the smoky essence in my blood is propelling me closer.

My lips brush hers, and heat flares beneath my skin. I can't help pressing my mouth harder against hers, drinking in all the softness and warmth and the pleased little sound that vibrates from her into me.

My head is spinning, but suddenly this doesn't feel so difficult. Everything about the situation *is* different, so different.

It's Riva. My woman—the woman I love. The only woman I've ever wanted.

My fingers trail down to her jaw as I kiss her again. But another tremor ripples through me, my fears still clinging on.

How much farther can I take this? What if there's a moment when my buried panic switches on and the beast comes out?

If I feel it coming, I'll retreat. And if I'm not fast enough, that's why Dom is here.

I can do this. Riva wants me.

And God knows I want her.

Ever so slowly, I let my fingers trail farther. Over her shoulder. Down her side. Across the curve of her hip.

My erection strains against the crotch of my pants. A fresh jolt of fear hits me.

She's so small, and I'm so big… everywhere. Are we really going to be able to—

The shadows singing through my blood call out, *Yes, yes, yes.* And so does everything in the way Riva's responding to me, tipping her head so our mouths can meld together even more temptingly, humming encouragingly at my touch.

I want—I want to really touch her. All of her, skin to skin, nothing between us.

I want to feel how much we belong together in every meaning of that word.

Is this how the other guys all felt when they got this far? Is the act supposed to be so overwhelming?

It doesn't matter. All that matters is how it is for her and me.

I draw back only a few inches. My voice has gone hoarse. "Can I take your shirt off?"

Riva only smiles again and lifts her arms to make it easier for me. My pulse racing, I grip the hem, barely grazing her skin, and peel the shirt off of her.

The sleek curves of her breasts rise and fall with her breath within the plain pink bra she's wearing. I've never seen anything more tantalizing.

Oh, please, if any higher powers exist at all, let me get through this encounter without coming in my pants first.

Keeping a close watch on the whirl of emotions inside me, I tease my fingers along her collarbones. The three thumbprint-like marks she shares with the other guys stand out against her pale skin.

As I let my hand drift downward, her chest gives a little hitch. The flush spreading across it reassures me that the sound was approving rather than frightened.

I chart the path from the base of her throat to her belly button. Splay my fingers across the toned planes of her stomach. Dare to lift my hand higher so I can cradle one breast against my broad palm.

Riva's tongue flicks out to wet her lips. "It feels good, Zee," she says softly. "Really good."

The longing twined through those words wakes up an animal inside me, but not the one I was afraid of. One that wants to throw her beneath me and drive inside her without wasting another instant.

No. That's too dangerous.

But I can't completely hold back. My reservations are fraying.

I roll her nipple under my thumb through the fabric.

Riva quivers and then reaches behind her to the clasp at her back.

She catches my gaze first, waiting for my approval. My mouth goes dry.

"Yes," I rasp. "Please."

She lets the bra slip off her arms. And something in me cracks open.

My mouth crashes into hers, my arms enfolding her. Riva lets out an eager gasp and clutches me in return.

Our tongues collide and dance around each other like licks of flame. I devour her mouth and then brand a path down the side of her neck, over her shoulder, to the slopes I can't resist.

When I lap the peak of her breast into my mouth, she arches to give me better access. A needy whimper spills from her lips, and my cock turns so hard I'm aching.

The shadows inside me leap and jitter, egging me on. Craving everything she can offer.

This isn't enough. I need everything. I need to be *inside* her.

Somewhere in the midst of my passion, my claws have come out. I rid myself of my shirt more by shredding it than tugging it off.

Riva raises her hands to my chest, at first cautiously and then tracing my bulging muscles with more confidence at my encouraging growl. I tip her over on the bed, yanking at her jeans as I do.

She has the presence of mind to undo the fly so she can wriggle out of them. Her fingers hook around the waist of my pants.

And all at once my breath stutters with a spike of panic.

The hired woman. The white-walled room. The nausea on Andreas's face when he returned after she led him away.

The demanding stroke of her hands over my body, trying to tempt my compliance—

I freeze over Riva, panting and trembling, a groan of frustration locked in my throat.

Riva goes still. I can feel Dominic watching, evaluating —deciding he doesn't need to interrupt.

Not yet.

Riva gazes up at me with no judgment at all in her bright eyes. "We don't have to do anything more than this. This was—this was amazing. If you need to stop—"

Fuck, no. The idea of stopping when we're so close, when my need for her is throbbing through every inch of my body, brings a screaming sense of resistance to the front of my mind.

She's mine. I will not let the fucking asshole guardians and their perverted tricks ruin what should be ours.

I inhale her scent, absorb her warmth, and will my sparks of panic to dwindle. When I lower my head to steal another kiss, the heat of it sears away any lingering chill.

I jerk at my pants, and Riva resumes her assistance. She caresses my bare thighs until a groan that's all hunger reverberates out of me.

Then she lifts one hand to my face, holding my gaze. "I love you."

The last fragments of my control shatter. "I love you too. I want you. I *need* you."

Her smile could reignite the sun. "You have me."

I don't know what I'm doing, but my hips sway toward hers as if we were made to fit together. Her legs splay to make room.

My dick slides between her folds, and the rest of the world falls away.

If I'm stretching her more than she was ready for, she shows no sign of it. Her breathy cry sounds only ecstatic.

I can't stop myself from pushing deeper, faster. Reveling in the scorching friction of our joining.

My balls pulse. I'd swear my cock gets even harder.

I slam into her, all restraint lost, and Riva bucks to meet me just as wildly. She clutches my shoulders, her forehead tucking against my chest, her breath breaking with bliss.

The same joy blazes through my veins, igniting the shadows that are craving this moment as much as any other part of me.

My claws jut farther, scoring the bedspread. My fangs spring from my teeth as my jaw lengthens. Fur sprouts along my shoulders.

Before I can feel more than a flash of dismay at my unexpected shift, Riva curls her fingers into the tufts of fur as if she welcomes it.

"It's good," she mumbles. "It's good."

Her body quakes beneath mine, heat floods my groin —and the base of my dick swells in a way I've never felt before, not when I got myself off with my hands in furtive moments of privacy. The sudden bulge locks into place inside her, just as the shadows inside me roar to the surface.

I come harder than I can ever remember, in a rush so

heady it sweeps every other thought out of my mind. Riva moans, gripping me tighter, and I feel the pleasure of the moment wash through her too as if I've totally merged with her, soul as well as body.

I drift to reality to find myself braced over her, my breath rasping, my cock still lodged inside her with that thickened ring that came out of nowhere. I don't know if I can pull out without hurting her.

The bulge starts to shrink with the fading of my wolf-man features. "I'm sorry," I mutter. "I didn't know—"

Riva curls her hand around the back of my neck. "It's all right. It must be something to do with your powers, or the shift—it always seems to happen like that, the first time. We lose control over our abilities a little. But not in a bad way."

She gives me the same brilliant smile, and my heart lights up with the sudden realization.

I did it. I was here for her as a lover as well as a friend, and I didn't fall apart. I didn't go crazy.

My damage hasn't totally ruined me after all.

And now the marks dappling Riva's collarbone balance out. Two on one side and two on the other.

I shift my weight so I can touch the new one, the one that matches the tingle on my breastbone with a connection I can't explain, can barely describe.

"I really did it," I say inanely.

Riva's smile widens. "With undeniable physical proof."

A chuckle tumbles out of me. When I adjust my position, I realize my dick has finally softened, the strange swelling fully contracted.

As I sit back on my heels, Riva pushes herself after me. She slings her arms around my torso and hugs me.

"It was so worth the wait."

There's so much joy in her voice it almost breaks me.

I blink hard and glance over at Dominic. He's grinning too, like nothing could have made him happier than seeing us get to this moment—than seeing me sort out my baggage.

I wrap Riva up in my arms, press a kiss to her forehead, and shoot him a smile in return. "Thank you."

He lifts a shoulder in a mild shrug. "I didn't do anything. You can take all the credit."

I only get another few seconds to linger in the thrill of Riva's embrace before we're interrupted by a sharp rap on the door.

Matteo's even voice filters through. "I'd like all of you to join me in the back garden as soon as you're decent."

My cheeks flare all over again, first with embarrassment and then with an angry suspicion that Balthazar sent him to cut our happiness short. But Riva bobs up to offer me a quick kiss to my lips—a kiss I can accept without even tensing—and I decide I don't give a fuck.

He can be an asshole about it, but I've already won.

We scramble into our clothes and head out to where the other three guys have already gathered. Andreas arches an eyebrow, and Griffin aims a pleased smile our way—of course *he* knows what we just got up to.

Matteo clears his throat impatiently and ushers us all the way to the wall along the edge of the property. He points to the stone surface. "Sit right there. That's as far out as you can get without triggering your bracelets."

Frowning, I do as he said, sticking close to Riva.

The skinny man consults a tablet and eyes us for about a minute. "Do you feel anything you didn't inside the house? Any discomfort or uneasiness?"

"Other than the fear of falling over the edge to our doom?" Andreas says dryly.

Matteo ignores him, his gaze scanning the rest of us. I feel totally normal, so I shake my head.

Riva knits her brow. "I haven't noticed anything. Why?"

He taps his lips. "Interesting. Very interesting. Well, you might as well come off of there now."

We do, Jacob scowling as he pushes away from the wall. "What the hell was that about?"

Matteo turns with a distracted air. "There are protections against the monsters you're partly made from embedded all around this hill. I thought as your powers became more pronounced, you might also experience some similar negative effects... Apparently not. You can go back to your evening activities."

Confusion loosens my voice. "But—there was that shadowkind guy we saw here before—"

I cut myself off, unsure if mentioning the being we were warned not to talk to, the one Balthazar killed Sully over, was a wise move.

Matteo simply shrugs. "We have one possible route, fully under our control. They can only use it if Balthazar lets them in."

He strides off, leaving the rest of us to drift toward the

villa behind him. None of us wants to hang out in the deeper chill now that the sun has sunk below the horizon.

But when I look at Riva, her skin looks even more sallow than I can blame on the security lamps. She catches my gaze, and her mouth tightens.

Then it hits me.

She was counting on Rollick coming to break us out of our prison. But how much can any of the shadowkind help us if the entire hill we're on top of is warded against them?

Twenty-Six

Riva

I wake up too early, with only the faintest trace of sunlight seeping through my window from the impeding dawn.

A strange energy is humming through my body. My bones tingle with it.

Maybe Griffin would be able to tell me what I'm feeling, if he were in the room for me to ask. He's experienced the emotions of hundreds if not thousands of people, and I only have my own for reference.

I can't even tell whether the energy is an impression of something good or bad. It has the flavor of anticipation and a tremor of urgency, shivers of both hope and dread.

And it niggles at me, as faint as the pale dawn light but undeniable, insisting that there's something I need to do.

I try to open my mind up to the idea of what that would be, but nothing occurs to me. I don't know anything more about Rollick's plans than the almost nothing I did before. The same with Balthazar's.

We're still locked into our manacles, still trapped within the boundaries of the villa's grounds until we're sent out on another closely monitored job.

If some part of my brain has figured out a way to deal with any of this situation better, I'd really appreciate if it'd tell me.

I put out that appeal silently into the universe. No such luck.

Sighing, I roll over and bury the side of my face in my pillow. But the nagging hum won't let me relax enough to drift off again.

I push off the covers and go to the closet, deciding I'll take a dawn prowl just in case something turns up that'll clarify my feelings. But I've only just tugged on a hooded sweatshirt and matching leggings when a quiet knock sounds on the door.

My body tenses automatically with the knowledge that it isn't any of my guys. I'm aware of four of them in their own rooms, not stirring, and Griffin would tell me it's him alongside the knock.

Bracing myself, I ease open the door.

Toni is waiting outside, as coolly vigilant as ever. "Since you're up now, this is as good a time as any. Mr. Balthazar has agreed to provide more information."

My pulse stutters. Just like that—now, so early in the day it's barely even morning?

She knew I was awake. My fingers brush over one of the slim metal bracelets.

I hate feeling this monitored. But maybe Balthazar's

agreement is what my mind picked up on—a chance to understand him better and therefore how to escape him.

I nod and step into the hall after Toni. Then a more frightening thought occurs to me.

What if it's the opposite? What if I was wrong, and he has been watching for me to form the inexplicable connection with Zian or Griffin?

What if he wasn't, but some data from the manacles tipped him off that what happened between me and Zee yesterday was more than just getting off?

Neither of us said anything about the supernatural element. I was careful about how I talked afterward. But who the hell knows what he'd already heard from the other guardians...

Shit. Should I have turned Zian down? Not taken the chance?

Getting to be there with Zee while he broke down the barriers inside him and let loose his passion was one of the most amazing things I've ever experienced. I can't wish it hadn't happened for both of our sakes... but indulging in the moment could have been an epic screw-up as well.

By the time we reach the drawing room, my stomach has knotted. As the screen rises from the table at our entrance, a sour taste laces my mouth.

Toni closes the door and stands on guard in front of it. I sink onto one of the armchairs arranged in the semi-circle facing the screen, welcoming the extra bodily support.

Balthazar might not have realized very much. If he asks questions about last night, I'll have to deflect them convincingly. Show no signs of stress.

The screen snaps from black to a now-familiar view of Balthazar sitting behind his desk in what must be his office. I instinctively scan his surroundings for any new clue about his exact whereabouts in the villa, but I still can't even say whether he's on the first floor or the second.

Hell, that light could be artificial and he's down in the basement somewhere.

He seems to wait a beat longer than usual before he speaks, his piercing gaze inspecting me just as closely as I am him. My heart gives another lurch that I conceal as well as I can.

Then he smiles—weirdly soft and somehow more unnerving than the crueler, sharper smiles I've seen from him before. "I understand you've uncovered a few things about my business dealings that you'd like me to explain."

I hesitate, hardly able to trust my relief. Is this meeting really just about the demand I made and nothing else?

I sit up a little straighter, hoping my surprise wasn't obvious. "Yes. I know you have something to do with a company called StreamCycle Enterprises, and that it creates technology for providing clean energy. And I know that at least a couple of the people you've sent us on jobs against are also involved in the energy business one way or another."

"Very canny of you," Balthazar says, sounding approving rather than annoyed that I figured out so much. His whole vibe strikes me as oddly upbeat today.

Has he gotten some kind of good news—has something we did advanced his plans in a major way?

Just because he doesn't seem to care about Zian and

me doesn't mean there's nothing to fear in this conversation.

I fix him with my most determined look. "So, before I take on any more jobs, I want to know how it all fits together. How are you associated with StreamCycle Enterprises? Why are you messing with other people in the same industry?"

Surely he hasn't set this whole operation in motion simply so he can make his business more successful and bring in more money? But then, I never would have thought that Clancy's speeches about making the world a better place were a cover for nothing more than financial greed.

Balthazar looks almost amused. He must suspect what I'm thinking. "I'd appreciate it if you'd give me more credit than assuming my goals are on such a small scale that they'd revolve around one company."

My forehead furrows. "What's the connection, then?"

He gives a careless wave of one broad hand. "Through StreamCycle Enterprises, I get information about the activities of other people who hold sway in various arenas. So it offers a useful starting point. But I'm already reaching far beyond that scope."

"Toward what?" I can't help asking. "What are you even trying to do? You told me before that you're not happy with how things are—what things? What do you think you're going to do about them?"

How have any of the jobs the guys and I have done for him helped him toward those goals?

Balthazar pins me with his penetrating gaze. "You've talked to Ursula Engel. You know what the Guardianship's purpose was. And you've seen the monsters in this world firsthand, haven't you? From what I understand, they nearly killed you more than once."

A chill washes over my skin. He's obviously talking about the shadowkind, even though I'd count the guardians as more monstrous than them.

But yes, some of Rollick's associates did try to kill me. Multiple times.

I cross my arms over my chest, absorbing his words. "But you're not working with the Guardianship anymore. At least, that's how you made it sound."

Oh, fuck, have we still been supporting them and their sick agenda all this time?

Balthazar gives a light snort, though. "Those imbeciles couldn't carve their way out of a paper bag. I tried—I thought it could be something good—"

He shakes his head and gives me another softer look that sets my nerves on edge. "You'll come to realize that the more people become involved in working toward a goal, the more their efforts get muddled. I do much better working on my own, making the hard decisions that need to be settled."

His answer doesn't make me feel any better. "But you —all of the work you're doing is about destroying the sha —the 'monsters' still?"

Balthazar's voice resonates with intensity. "I've tangled with them too, far more than you've had the opportunity to. They've taken more from me than you can imagine. They're a poison in this world, and someone needs to be willing to step in and eliminate them for good."

I restrain a shiver. I can believe he's met some cruel shadowkind—they definitely exist.

But so do beings like the perky succubus Pearl, who befriended me with so much eager curiosity about the human world. Like her friend Billy the faun, who was willing to stand up for me and the other shadowbloods against beings so much stronger than him.

And what Balthazar is saying doesn't even fit with what I've seen in my time here at the villa.

"You have at least one of those 'monsters' working for you," I have to point out.

"I use every resource I have at my disposal. That doesn't mean I *like* the fiends. If I can use them as weapons against each other, so much the better."

I suppress a shudder at his chilly tone. "But none of the jobs you sent us on have anything to do with monsters. It was all human beings."

Balthazar lets out a gruff sound of dismissal. "There are too many of the creatures. They're everywhere, with their claws sunk in, twisting us to their purposes... It's going to take a consolidated effort, more than any tiny secret organization can accomplish, even with tools like you."

I frown at him, both because he's still being annoyingly vague and because of the way he referred to me. "So you left the Guardianship to do something totally on your own? You have even fewer people!"

On the other side of the screen, the leonine man's eyes shine with a predatory gleam. "Fewer people I speak to directly. When I'm done, I'll have the strength of every government and military behind me."

I stare at him for a moment, the pieces clicking into

place but my mind not quite willing to accept it at first. But then, I've known our captor was insane from our very first conversation.

"You think you're going to take over the entire world," I say, a little roughly. "You're—what—building political influence, corporate leverage…?"

I don't even know the right words for all of it. The idea is batshit crazy.

And there's a speck of icy fear starting to expand in my gut that tells me I'm not convinced he's incapable of pulling it off.

While using us to do so.

Would even the might of all the world's major governments and armies be enough to wipe out the shadowkind from the mortal world? It's not as if mortal weapons have much impact on them.

I suppose if Balthazar was able to sway entire military forces into using the materials that do weaken or even kill the "monsters," if he focused every country's resources on that goal—

What would happen to every other part of society then? How many people's lives will he wreck chasing his maniacal goal?

No wonder he doesn't mind telling me. Who the hell would believe anyone would even attempt this kind of global domination if I could manage to warn them?

They'll think it's crazy too. And they won't know Balthazar to realize that his brand of insanity is disturbingly effective.

Balthazar hasn't said anything, just watched me take it all in.

I lift my gaze to meet his again. "Why does it matter to you so much? What have the 'monsters' done that's so much worse than all the crap humans are constantly doing to each other?"

If I hadn't already been aware of some of the totally human atrocities from the books and movies we had access to in the facility, my time carrying out Clancy's assignments would have filled in the blanks amply.

Balthazar's expression hardens so abruptly that my pulse jumps as if he's aimed a gun at me. "They don't care. They can't be bargained or reasoned with. All they know are their sick, monstrous cravings, and they'll destroy the most beautiful things to get their way."

I decide it's better not to mention that his words could describe various human beings I've been subjected to— including the man who just said them.

He leans toward the screen, making my skin creep with the intensity of his gaze. "You can sense it, can't you? That this is what you were meant for."

The hairs on the back of my neck stand on end. "What Engel made me for, you mean? Even she didn't think she'd done a good job of it after all."

"She gave up too easily," Balthazar snarls, and then seems to gather himself. His voice smooths out. "You've discovered some things about my family."

I open my mouth and close it again, confused by the abrupt shift in the conversation. Well, he'll have already heard me confronting Toni about the things I saw or guessed.

"You had a wife and a son," I say. "But they both died." Oh. "They were killed by 'monsters'?"

Would that have been enough to set him on this megalomaniac journey? I guess if he'd already been unhinged and it just nudged him over the final edge…

Balthazar is nodding grimly, but there's something too avid in his face that contrasts with his supposed grief. "They're gone, because of so much brutality and incompetence. But I still have— You've looked at the pictures. You must have suspected at least a little."

I resist the urge to hug myself. "Suspected what? I don't know what you're talking about."

"Engel needed genetic material for her work. The human elements to mingle with the monstrous aspects. She guarded her work closely, but we founders all had access to every part of the facilities."

The prickling cold spreads through my abdomen. The words catch in my throat before I can force them out. "What are you saying?"

That small, soft smile plays across Balthazar's lips again. "When my son was born, they told Willa that she wouldn't be able to have another child. She always wanted a daughter. So I did what I could to give her one, one I thought she'd eventually be able to meet. If they hadn't— But you're still here. You're here where you belong now. You can take your place in the family."

A strained noise reaches my ears from where Toni is standing near the door, but I'm too frozen in shock to look over my shoulder and check her reaction.

My limbs have gone rigid, locked in place. I feel like I'm choking and drowning all at once.

Balthazar goes on as if he hasn't registered my horror at his announcement. "You're my daughter as well as hers, no matter what else went into your creation. You can stand beside me. We'll work together and set things right. Don't you see it?"

My stomach lurches. I would puke my response if I had anything in my stomach to vomit.

I *can't* see it. My brain wants to reject the very possibility that any part of me is tied to this psychotic man.

There's nothing I can see that would disprove it either, though. My complexion is similar to his and his wife's. I'm not built anything like his substantial frame, but she looked pretty petite and delicate in the photos I've seen of her.

I wasn't thinking about it at the time, but the shape of her face was like mine, wasn't it? Rounded cheeks and a pointed chin.

And my eyes... Staring back into Balthazar's, I can't help noticing that his bright brown irises are only a shade or two darker than mine.

"No," I sputter. Somehow I'm on my feet, though I still don't feel like I'm fully in control of my legs. "If the way you treat family is the way you've treated me, then I don't want anything to do with it. I'm not your anything."

His piercing eyes narrow. My hands clench into fists, and a shriek scrabbles in the base of my throat, wishing he was actually in front of me so I could unleash it on him.

"You're not thinking clearly," Balthazar says with a cold edge. "You're simply startled. You were made for this. Your grandparents fought the monsters, and I have, and you will. This is where you belong."

A tremor runs through my body. I jab a finger toward the screen. "I'm never going to belong with you!"

Balthazar's lips pull back from his teeth. And a bolt of pain shoots up both my arms from my wrists—from the manacles.

The burning sensation sears deep in an instant, making my lungs seize up and my knees buckle. I can't hold back a cry as I slump to the floor.

No blood pours from my wrists, but he's hurt me some other way, maybe another chemical he never told us about that the manacles hold alongside the sedative. It sears through my nerves until I'm blinking back tears.

"I haven't been there to educate you," Balthazar growls. "You'll learn."

Then he's gone, the screen gone black.

The pain fades gradually. After a couple of minutes, I manage to push myself into a sitting position. My head spins.

I don't even know how to start thinking through what our captor just told me. What he just did to me, in spite of who he claims I am.

Toni is standing on the other side of the chair I sat in, her face tight, her shoulders stiff. "I—I could help you back to your room," she offers quietly.

I flinch instinctively and shake my head. "No. I'll get there myself."

If she wants to gawk, I don't want her doing it right there beside me.

After a few more careful breaths, I swipe at my eyes and heave myself to my feet. Lingering pricks of pain travel through my nerves, but I manage to walk fairly steadily.

Down the hall. Up the stairs. Into my room. Every step feels like I'm dragging my feet through hardening cement.

I'm Balthazar's daughter. He made me in his image, for his purposes. How much of his madness is woven right into the essence of who I am?

How the hell can I help the guys I love get out of this horror show when I'm complicit in it down to my DNA?

TWENTY-SEVEN

Riva

The wind outside is biting, but it fits my mood. I roll my shoulders to pull the hood of my sweatshirt farther forward and keep my head low as I stalk around the villa.

The guys follow me, silent but a concrete presence around me. Their concerned anticipation weighs on my spirits, but not half as much as the news I need to give them.

Around the back of the building, the wind eases. The autumn air there still holds a chill, but one that's not outright snapping at us.

Part of me wants to find a bench to sit down on so I can hunch in on myself. So I can let go of the need to ensure my legs hold me up while focusing on the conversation.

But if I sit, then I know the guys will gather even

closer, tucking themselves against me, and the thought sends a pang of terror through my chest.

I was made by our greatest enemy, to an extent way beyond what any of them could guess. I have the sense of a toxin as potent as the one lacing Jacob's hidden spines winding through my veins alongside the shadows, one that might somehow seep from my skin and into my guys if I'm not careful.

One that maybe already has.

How are they going to look at me when I tell them? How is it going to shake them up, knowing that their connection to me also ties them to Balthazar in ways they'd never have wanted?

He infiltrated our group of six from my first moment of conception, well before I was even born. He's been present for every moment of our friendship and the very first glimmers of love.

And there's nothing I can do to cut him out of me, out of us, not completely. Not any more than I can erase the brutal monstrous power I've never wanted.

I turn toward the guys. They watch me, waiting, standing in a close semi-circle.

I can tell from the sway in their stances that they'd all like to draw in around me and wrap me up in love and reassurance, but they must be able to tell from my own tensed posture that I can't tolerate any attempt at comfort right now.

Not when they don't even know what they'd be reassuring me about.

Jacob motions to me with a twitch of his chin, his jaw clenched. "What's going on, Wildcat?"

The blaze in his bright blue eyes says, *Let me at whatever's bothering you so I can pulverize it.*

But he can't. Not with this.

I open my mouth and then close it again to swallow through the tightness of my throat. For a little while, as I forced myself to put together an early breakfast and then drifted through the villa while the guys ate theirs, I entertained the thought that maybe I didn't have to tell them.

Maybe it would be better for them if I didn't, if they never had to wrap their heads around the revelation like I've needed to. Maybe it wouldn't even be safe to try, when no matter what steps I try to take to conceal the conversation, our captor will realize I'm telling them.

Those are just excuses to protect myself from the fallout, though.

Balthazar has to know that I'll reveal this secret. He wouldn't have told me anything he wasn't perfectly fine getting passed on to the guys one way or another. He never even warned me *not* to tell them.

He might like the idea of their reactions to me shifting with the new knowledge. I'm not sure what exactly he was trying to accomplish by provoking Jacob a couple of days ago, but he definitely wasn't looking to encourage group harmony.

And hiding things from each other has never helped us in the long run. I'm not a great actor—the guys will be able to tell something's off. I *can't* hide my emotions from Griffin.

No, keeping this to myself and leaving them to worry

and wonder will cause more tensions than spilling the beans.

I just wish I knew how we'll pick up the pieces after I shatter their idea of who I am. I still haven't figured how to put my own sense of self back together.

I wet my lips and tuck my arms around my chest in an anxious embrace. "Balthazar called me to the drawing room to talk to me this morning."

Zian frowns. "He has a job he wants you to do alone?"

"No. Not exactly."

A hysterical bubble of laughter forms behind my clavicle. In some ways it's both not a job at all and the most immense possible job our captor could ever have laid on my shoulders.

I give myself a squeeze and yank my focus back to the conversation. "We already realized that he's part of the founding families. The third one—I guess it was Engel and the Clancys and the Balthazars."

He had said that his parents—my *grandparents*—fought the shadowkind too.

Andreas nods. His mind goes to the same place mine first did. "Is he still working with the guardians after all?"

I shake my head. "Nothing like that. He thinks they're useless, ineffective. He still wants the same things, but he figures he can only eliminate the shadowkind by taking bigger steps, stuff they'd never have agreed to."

Dominic frowns. "All of the things he's had us doing, it's somehow working toward destroying shadowkind beings?"

"Yeah. In a roundabout but incredibly ambitious way." A little of that laugh escapes me, dry and raw. "He figures he's going to take control of the whole world, or the important parts anyway, and force all kinds of countries into going to war with the 'monsters.'"

Jacob lets out a sound that's both scoff and curse. "He's even crazier than we thought."

Griffin has kept quiet until now, observing me. He takes an even gentler tone than usual. "That isn't what you're really upset about, though."

"No." My gaze drops to the ground. To my frustration, tears burn behind my eyes, threatening to spill over.

"We know that we're part human as well as part shadowkind," I force myself to say. "Obviously the human parts came from somewhere. Well, Balthazar says that for me, he swapped out whatever genetic material Engel was going to use for his and his wife's. They wanted another kid, and they couldn't get one otherwise. I'm his daughter."

The last sentence comes out strained, and then my throat closes up completely. There've been times before when admitting something I've held in felt like a release, but not this. Saying the words out loud only makes the weight in my gut expand until it's almost suffocating.

It's Dominic who speaks first, firm and calm in the startled silence. "You're not. Not really. It'd take more than donating genes to be an actual parent."

I blink hard. "But he still—whatever he is, some of that is in me too. Look at how much our monstrous sides dictate who we are and what we do!"

I hug myself tighter and drag my eyes up to meet their gazes again. That's the real problem, isn't it?

I don't have a monstrous side and a human side like they all do. Even my human side is horrifying.

Andreas steps forward and slides his arms around me, echoing my private embrace. "You're still who you've been the whole time, Tink. It doesn't change you."

It makes me rethink the person I've been, though. Would I have hurt Billy so easily if I had no biological heritage of hating shadowkind? Would I have found it easier to trust Rollick and ignore the guardians' claims?

How can I be sure that I'm really making the best choices for any of us when I have such a direct connection to the man who wants to manipulate and kill everything he decides is monstrous?

And even if my heritage hasn't had any impact on me, which seems unlikely, would he have dragged us all into his plans if he hadn't specifically wanted me? For all I know, we could have made our escape from Clancy and lived in some kind of freedom if it wasn't for this blood tie I never knew about.

Jacob shifts on his feet, his expression turned even more ominous. "Why did he tell you now? What does he want from you?"

There'd be no good in hiding that aspect either. "He was hoping I'd join the family business. Take his side instead of resisting."

Jake lets out a snort, and Andreas strokes a comforting hand up and down my arm.

Zian's forehead furrows. "What did you say?"

"No fucking way." I grimace. "But maybe I shouldn't have."

I've been wondering about that since I cooled down

enough to think clearly, although I can't say everything I mean out loud. What would have happened if I'd played along and pretended to accept Balthazar's offer?

Would I have been able to convince him I meant it? Would he have given me the chance to meet him in person? To get access to areas of the villa I could have used to help us?

It's probably too late to change my tune now. Not enough that he'd trust me.

But then, I find it hard to believe that he'd ever trust me all that much no matter how I'd reacted in the moment. Even if I'm his daughter, as far as he's concerned I'm still also a monster.

Jacob raises his chin. "That asshole is fucked up. I don't care if he hears me saying it—it's true."

"Do we even know if he was telling the truth about you being his daughter?" Dominic asks.

"He was." I can say that with total confidence, even though I don't have concrete proof. The flickers of hope I saw in Balthazar as he worked up to telling me, his anger when I rejected him… None of his reactions felt like the way he's laid out his plans or responded to our defiance before.

This was personal. *He* honestly believes I'm his daughter, in any case, and surely he would know.

Griffin sets his hand on my shoulder. "Drey is right. It doesn't change who you are—or anything else. Not if you don't want it to."

I wish it felt like I had that much of a choice in the matter.

Zian seems to gather himself, a look of protective

determination coming over his face. "Let's go inside where it's warmer and just… hang out together. Let us look after you while you're getting used to the idea. It definitely doesn't change anything about how *we* feel about you."

"Not at all," Andreas murmurs, and kisses my temple.

An ache fills my heart. I want to go along with them, to curl up within their warmth as if it can wash away everything else in the world.

But is that the right move? How will my next actions affect what Balthazar does to me—and the guys I love —after?

Can I trust any choices I make?

I rub my forehead, grappling with my conflicted thoughts—and Zian's head jerks around. He stares off toward the side garden, knitting his brow.

I tense automatically. "What?"

"I…" He pauses, his lips pressing flat as if he's realized he shouldn't say whatever he was about to. "It's nothing. I just started thinking it might be good to get a little more fresh air and exercise first."

It's not the best excuse ever, which only makes me more convinced that something else is going on. When he tips his head to beckon us, we all follow him.

Andreas stays next to me, letting one arm drop to sling around my waist. Jacob falls into step at my other side with a familiar murderous air.

I think it'd probably be best for everyone if Balthazar's employees avoid making any appearances while he's in this mood.

Zian ambles across the lawn and between the hedges and planters. By the time we're halfway to our destination,

I hear it too—a faintly cajoling voice like the one that drew me in a couple of days ago.

"Shadowbloods, over here."

Zian comes to a stop by the outer wall. After resting his hands on it for a few moments as if he's taking in the view, he bends to scoop up a rock from the ground.

It's smooth like the one I found before, but gray rather than black with a speckling of mica. I guess the exact type of stone doesn't matter for Rollick's purposes.

Zee looks down at it with a thoughtful expression and then raises his eyebrows at us. I shake my head—as soon as he picked it up, I couldn't hear anything from it.

"This should be okay," he says, and passes it to me.

The second my fingers close around the warmed surface, Rollick's voice drifts into my senses. He told me before that the magic would make the message only audible to beings with shadowkind essence. Apparently we have to be touching the source too.

"Little banshee and friends," he says in greeting. "We want you out of there fast, but we're still working out our best approach. Your new keeper built his fortress well. If you know anything that could help us get access, let us know. Otherwise we may have to resort to simply burning everything up there to the ground... and I'm sure you'd rather we didn't risk barbequing any of you shadowbloods in the process. Tap the stone five times in a row, and it'll absorb whatever you say after. Then toss it over the wall. We'll find it. I'll wait."

When his voice fades, I pass the stone to Andreas so he can listen next. As the guys take the message in one by one, my thoughts spin even faster.

Your new keeper has built his fortress well... help us get access. Rollick's people must have figured out about the protective metals built into the mountainside like Matteo mentioned.

Matteo also said there was some route shadowkind could use, but Balthazar controls that. And we have no idea what it is. What good will the information do our rescuers?

How the hell does he think they can burn everything down if they can't even get up here? I don't know how we could avoid a blaze so huge they could reach us with it from a distance.

Escape lies just beyond that wall... and I have no idea how we'll ever pull it off. We don't have an answer for Rollick yet, that's for sure.

Even if I could come up with a plan, should we trust anything that comes from my mind?

The mind of our captor's daughter.

Twenty-Eight

Griffin

While they were conditioning my emotions out of me, the guardians put me through torture I can't even describe. But even the worst of that agony doesn't hold a candle to pain that splinters through my chest as I watch Riva shuffle from the table where we've just had lunch.

I can feel her trying to hold herself together—the tangled stands of hope and doubt, conviction and uncertainty, that drag her down as she grapples with them. Every time a clearer emotion shines through, a glimpse of the woman I know, something in her shies away from it as if afraid to lean too far in any one direction.

I might be able to sense all that from the inside out, but her struggle shows on the outside too. All of my friends take in her deflated energy and tentative movements with worry hazing their eyes.

It's worse than when her anger consumed her. At least

then she was focused, determined, even if there was an unnervingly brutal quality to it.

Balthazar's news has torn a hole in her spirits like nothing else our captors have done before.

I know how hard she's found it to accept her vicious talent. Her humanity was a shield against seeing herself as totally monstrous.

But now that side of her is tainted too. There's nothing in herself that she can use as a compass to decide what's right, no part of her that's uncorrupted.

At least, that's how she sees it. To my eyes, there's nothing of Balthazar in her, nothing potent enough to dull the shine of the woman she's made herself into.

I don't get any sense that the other guys believe the association means all that much either.

But we aren't the ones having to process the revelation. I can pick up on her emotions, but I can't really understand the full extent of what she's going through.

I sure as hell can't judge her for faltering. The guardians reshaped my mind from the outside to the point that I became a willing participant in their plans. She's just found out that the enemy has been inside her, woven into the most basic essence of her existence, from before she was born.

We don't really know for sure how her heritage might have affected her all along, who she might have been if Engel had used whatever genetic material our creator originally meant to.

The thing is, I have no doubt that who Riva has been is exactly the woman we've needed regardless.

How can we get her to recognize that? Each of us has

tried talking to her here and there since she confessed to us yesterday, but nothing we've said has budged the horror all knotted up inside her.

It doesn't matter how much we trust her if she can't trust what's going on in her own mind.

With that thought passing through my head, a glimmer of inspiration sparks. I mull it over as Dominic and I move to take care of the dishes.

Yes, the approach that just occurred to me could give her the perspective she needs to boost her out of the pit she's fallen into. At the very least, I can't see any way it would hurt her.

I've got to try something. She dragged me out of my own dark cave, which I'd been lost in far longer than she has.

If I can't help her regain her balance, what the hell am I even here for?

When the dishes are clean, I slip out into the hall. Jacob's gaze follows me when I pass him, but I don't say anything to my brother or the other guys.

This is something only I can do. They love Riva, so much the feeling thrums around me from their rising in the morning to the moment they fall asleep—maybe more than I'll ever be capable of with my battered nerves. But I don't want any other factors distracting from what I'm hoping to offer her.

I follow my sense of Riva's emotional presence to the room with the cards table and the bookshelves. She's standing by the shelves, looking at the books' spines as if she's not really seeing them. Her fingers are curled into the sleeves of her hoodie.

"Hey," I say, keeping my voice soft, but she still startles before she turns to face me.

With any of the others, she'd have already known they were coming in. She's connected to them way beyond anything she shares with Balthazar.

She pushes her mouth into a smile, but I can tell it's forced. "Looking for more reading material?"

"Looking for you." I go over to her and wrap my arms around her slim frame.

I can't help noticing that she doesn't let herself lean into me the way she used to. As if she's worried she'll somehow contaminate me if we're in too close contact.

My throat constricts. That's not how I want her to be feeling at all. If she can't even let us support her—

I open my mouth to tell her what I want to do, and it occurs to me that there's another, much more uncomfortable distraction we have to worry about. The silver manacles grip both our wrists, probably projecting every word we say to Balthazar's ears or those of his employees.

He doesn't deserve a part in this conversation. And the last thing I need is Riva wondering what he's thinking about it rather than focusing on what I'm trying to convey.

Well, we found a simple enough if slightly odd solution to that problem before.

I nuzzle her hair. "I know it's chilly outside, but would you join me for a swim?"

Riva glances up at me with a question in her eyes. I'd imagine she can guess I'm not asking just so we can get a little exercise. She'll remember why we headed to the pool the last time.

For a few anxious thumps of my heart, I'm afraid she'll refuse. I have to admit I'm not sure what I'll do then.

Instead she nods, if not with all that much enthusiasm. "Sure. It might be nice to change things up a bit."

We stop at one of the bathrooms to grab a couple of towels and walk straight out to the patio that holds the pool. Balthazar didn't supply us with bathing suits along with the other clothes we've found in our bedrooms, but we made do with what we do have just fine before.

It *is* chilly, the breeze nipping at my face with hints of the coming winter. I restrain a shiver and strip down to my boxers as fast as humanly possible.

Riva moves even faster, jumping into the heated water in her bra and panties while I'm still yanking at my socks. I scramble in after her with a sigh of relief as the warmth washes away the chill.

Riva keeps her head above the water. Her braid trails behind her as she glides from one end of the pool to the other and then lingers by the wall.

As I drift over to join her, she cocks her head at me. "You wanted to talk about something."

Our manacles are well under the water, but she pitches her voice low all the same. I match her volume. "It's more that I wanted to *show* you something. But I have to explain first."

She lifts one eyebrow as if to say, *Go on.*

I can't resist tucking one arm around her bare waist. My intended goal remains at the front of my mind, but when I'm this close to her—and this close to being naked —it's impossible to totally ignore the desire clamoring inside me.

Those heady sensations are the only feelings the guardians couldn't condition out of me. The ones that helped me start to recover every other emotion I've lost.

Just by being here, by believing in me enough to let me get this close, Riva has grounded me. Brought me back at least partway to the guy I should have been.

Please, let me guide her back too.

"You're all mixed up inside," I say quietly. "Which totally makes sense. You don't know how to think about anything you've experienced. But before Balthazar told you anything, before he put those doubts in your head— that person is who you are at your core. Whether the genetic ties affected you or not, whether he had some kind of influence over you even before, it'd be wrapped into your reactions without you knowing."

Riva studies me, her damp eyelashes darkly black around her bright eyes. "Where are you going with this?"

The corner of my mouth crooks upward. "First, I just want you to confirm that you agree with what I'm saying. You couldn't have been hiding or suppressing Balthazar's influence before you had any idea it was there, right?"

She gives a slight shrug. "I guess that makes sense. But it's not like I can tell by looking back. At the time, any decisions I made seemed totally mine, totally... true. Because I had no idea I should question myself."

"Okay. And we can tell you how it looked like to us, Andreas can even let you see from the outside... but I can remind you how you actually felt inside yourself, in the moment."

Riva blinks at me, confusion giving way to a dawning understanding. "You want to project emotions into my mind—how you sensed I was feeling before."

I bow my head closer to hers. "Yeah. I—I've been incredibly aware of your inner state from the moment we were in the same building together again. And a lot of that time, I wasn't feeling *anything* myself to cloud my perception. I can show you what motivated you to stand up to Clancy, how you reacted to us and to the younger shadowbloods... All those innate reactions that weren't really under your control. Nothing could be truer than that."

Riva stays silent for a moment. She swallows audibly. "All right."

A flicker of fear reaches me alongside her acceptance. I stroke my thumb over her skin through the water. "Are you worried you'll notice something that means you *were* influenced by your connection to Balthazar somehow?"

"I mean, it's possible. Maybe there were feelings I wasn't even aware of nudging me in one direction or another." She raises her hand briefly to rub her forehead before dunking it back beneath the surface of the pool. "But I need to know either way."

That's the woman I know. The woman who'll defy even her own deepest fears to make sure she's on the right path.

The urge grips me to draw her even nearer and capture her mouth with mine, but *I* shouldn't be distracting her from our main purpose here either.

Inhaling slowly, I let my mind slip back to all the times Riva's feelings struck me most forcefully. All the pangs of emotion that I locked away in my memories like little treasures, proof that she was back with me even if I didn't know how to really reach her.

"When you were going through the facility to break out the younger shadowbloods there," I murmur, and dredge up the intrepid determination that spurred her onward. With a nudge of my mind, it flows out of me into her.

But I don't edit it to try to placate her. I leave in the tremors of anxiety and uncertainty, the resistance before she let loose her shriek.

She should have the chance to evaluate the full picture and make of it what she will. In my mind, the hesitations only make her commitment shine brighter.

Riva stands perfectly still in the water in front of me, taking it in. Her chest gives a slight hitch, but that's her only external response.

I can't pay attention to her current internal state while I'm concentrating on the past, but she's the only one who can grapple with whatever she's feeling now.

I shift to another moment, a little later. "When Clancy first explained his supposed goals to you, and you found out I was alive."

Anger and frustration, shock and confusion, and woven through it all a tiny thread of hope that gleamed brighter with her early glimpses of the island.

Moment after moment, I lead her through her inner journey. The fury and betrayal when she confronted Clancy after realizing his ulterior motives for their first mission. Her fierce protectiveness of Zian when our captor triggered his trauma. The mix of concern and pride she felt around the younger shadowbloods.

The rush of resolve when she launched into our first escape from the island. The compassion she offered me after we were recaptured. Her bittersweet farewell to the dreams Clancy claimed he was offering us and the hardening of her emotions when she killed him.

So many fragments of the past that add up to the woman I've always seen her as: strong and resilient, capable of both kindness and ferocity when they're earned, full of so much love she'll put her own life on the line again and again if it means the people she cares about get a chance to live theirs more freely.

And there are so many of us she cares about. Not just me and the other guys who grew up with her, but every one of the kids who came after us, the shadowkind who were willing to help us, the strangers she's afraid Balthazar will hurt.

Her dreams have never been anything like his.

As I run out of fragments to share, I realize that Riva has finally relaxed into my embrace. Her temple rests against my jaw, her chin against my chest near the scar from the gunshot wound that nearly killed me.

The impression I get of her now is more settled than before, like a pensive contemplation. I can't tell whether that contemplation is taking her in a good direction or a bad one—maybe she's not sure herself yet.

"You know," I add, my thoughts coming together as I put them into words, "the other thing I can say is that how you feel, how you've always felt, is so different from any of the people who've held us prisoner. And they all—the first guardians, Clancy, Balthazar... Even if they wanted somewhat different things or had different ways of getting at it, in the end they're all the same. Arrogant and resentful and rejecting any hint that they could be wrong... Even if he's your father, Balthazar is way more like Clancy or our other jailers inside than he's like you."

Riva lets out a long, shaky sigh. "I don't know how—I almost forgot what it was like, going through all that."

I stroke my hand over her back beneath the water. "We've been jerked around a lot. It's hard to hold on to a clear sense of yourself when you're constantly being treated like you're nothing but an object for other people to use."

"Yeah. But *you* always know."

A rough laugh escapes me. "I know who the rest of you are. Me—that's been trickier."

Riva lifts her head to catch my gaze. The gleam in her eyes makes my heart skip a beat. "Thank you. There's—there's been something I've been feeling like I need, but I couldn't put my finger on exactly what it was. I think I've figured it out."

An easier smile tugs at my lips. "What's that?"

She doesn't answer with words. She just bobs up on her toes to kiss me.

Twenty-Nine

Riva

Griffin's mouth sears against mine, a starker heat than the warmth of the water that surrounds us.

The certainty inside me grows. This is what I've needed, what I've sensed was missing. The last of my guys, the last of our group of six, with me in every way rather than lingering on the outside of the deeper bonds we've formed.

I don't know why the urgency has come over me so intensely, why I was already craving this connection this early morning when Griffin wasn't even in sight. But everywhere our skin touches, more need sparks.

The shadows in my veins dance with frantic anticipation.

I kiss him harder, slinging both of my arms around his neck. The water drips from my wrists, but it doesn't matter if Balthazar hears us now.

It might even be better for him to eavesdrop on our intimate moment, as much as the thought disgusts me. Let him think that our pool interlude was only about physical gratification and not about Griffin boosting my confidence to rebel against our captor.

Griffin makes a rough sound and nudges me up against the wall of the pool. My spine presses into the wet tiles, cold above the waterline and warm below.

The contrast sends a shiver through me that's far from unpleasant. I lift my legs instinctively, tucking them around his waist and drawing him closer.

We've embraced like this before, by the waterfall on the island. We had more clothes between us then, of course.

The slide of wet skin against skin sharpens my desire. That and the feel of the rigid bulge in Griffin's boxers, lining up against my panties.

I whimper into his mouth, and he exhales raggedly. One hand comes to rest on my thigh while the other delves into my hair, loosening my braid.

He rocks against me, sending pulses of bliss through my core. I can't restrain myself from grinding my pussy into his erection in return, but I can't see why I'd want to stop.

The friction of our movements brings a gasp to my lips and earns me a groan from Griffin. His head dips next to mine, his lips branding the crook of my neck.

It isn't enough. I'm not looking for another hasty release through our clothes.

I want to feel all of him; feel him becoming a part of me and me a part of him.

I *need* it, right down to the center of my being, with a wrenching longing I can't explain.

But when I lower one hand and hook my fingers around the waist of his boxers, Griffin tenses. It's a tiny shift, only noticeable because I'm pressed so tight against his body, but it echoes through his muscles into mine.

I can't hide my flicker of surprise and disappointment, not from him. Griffin goes still. "I'm sorry. I—"

"It's okay," I say, even though accepting his rejection sets my eyes burning. I close them, willing my emotions to settle so I won't make him feel guilty. "If you're not ready—"

He shakes his head before I can finish that sentence. "I'm ready. I think I've been ready for you my whole life, Moonbeam. I just don't know if I can be what *you* need now."

I frown and cup his cheek, startled enough that I can meet his gaze again. "What are you talking about? I love you—you know that. I trust you. I don't hold anything that happened before against you. None of that matters."

"It matters to me," Griffin says softly. "I'm still not back to normal—I still have the nightmares. Almost everything I feel comes with a jab of pain, and I don't know if that's ever going to completely fade. I love you so much, but I can't love you the same way the other guys can, with nothing else getting in the way."

"Griffin…" The ache expands up to my heart, with a bittersweet poignancy that has nothing to do with lust.

This man just reminded me in the most vivid possible way of who I am. Rebuilt my foundations of confidence from the ground up like no one else could have.

How can he think he isn't worthy of me?

The greatest truth he reminded me of had nothing to do with my emotions from the past several weeks and everything to do with our deeper history.

I tamp down on my impatient desires and hold his sky-blue gaze. "You could never not be enough for me. We're blood. No matter what happens, no matter how buried we get in the shit that's thrown at us, we'll find each other. I wouldn't even know how to ask for more love than that."

There was one massive truth I'd almost forgotten in the wake of Balthazar's horrible revelation: I already have a family. The five guys I grew up with are closer to me than genetics, more a part of me than any shared DNA.

We share something Balthazar could never understand, both in the training we endured and the supernatural essence flowing through our veins. Nothing could bind me tighter to anyone.

Not only do I have a family, I have a huge one. These five guys I grew up with, who own my heart, but all the younger shadowbloods too. There's no impact Balthazar could have on me, aware or unconscious, that could come close to my kinship with them.

The very fact that he doesn't recognize those ties only proves how little he knows me.

I'm not sure how much of my thoughts Griffin can discern from my emotions. Enough that between whatever he senses and my words, a bright smile crosses his face.

"You should always ask for more," he says. "And we'll all give you everything we possibly can."

I smile back, a strange shyness gripping me. "You

could show me *you*. All that love you have in you already. Then you'll know for sure that I'm more than satisfied with what you can offer."

Griffin stares at me for a moment. Has he ever projected his true feelings to someone else, shown them what it's like inside him the way he can absorb everyone else's emotions?

Then the sensations reach me. A potent, joyful warmth rises up through my chest, tentative at first but unfurling until it's flooded every cell.

A few sharp pricks of resistance that I know aren't really him, only his lingering conditioning, tarnish the happiness. But there's so much more as well—hope and gratitude and determination, and twined through it all a longing so heady my heart starts thumping faster.

I tug him toward me, and he comes, his mouth crashing into mine. We kiss roughly, like we're running out of time.

Which maybe we are.

As my body strains toward his, Griffin keeps casting wave after wave of emotion into me. The tang of our matching desire twines together like our tongues.

His love fills me with so much light I can't separate his devotion from my own. It's all merged together into a blissful tsunami.

The clamoring of my shadows peals through everything else. The same urgency quivers through the feelings I'm absorbing from Griffin.

This time when I yank at his boxers, he helps me shove them down his hips. Beneath the water, he peels off my soaked panties in turn.

I curl my fingers around his hardened cock, and his groan reverberates through me with an internal keening of need. An answering whimper spills from my lips.

The first time I've slept with each of my guys, there's been a magnetic power to it, a point when it's hard to imagine we could possibly resist the compulsion driving our bodies toward each other.

This—this sensation is even more potent than that. The marks on my collarbone sing, my blood thrums through my veins alongside the drumming of my pulse in my ears, and I'd swear the entire world is propelling us together, waiting to witness the power of our joining.

Griffin was my first kiss. He'll be my last lover.

Somehow this moment between us encircles everything I've found and formed with all five of my men.

His fingers dig into my ass with a jolt of pain that only heightens the pleasure racing through my limbs. Then he's thrusting into me, and the rest of the world might as well not exist at all.

This act has been so long coming and so long wanted. My shadows cry for more, and I buck with Griffin, barely feeling the splash of the water across my shoulders.

There's only the bliss expanding in forceful pulses inside me and the heat of his body encompassing me, as if we really will meld together beyond the possibility of separation.

We will, though, won't we? I can never truly be torn away from any of my men while the connection of our marks shines between us as clearly as a homing beacon.

I run my hands over his scarred chest and then grip

the back of his neck. My body sways frantically, crashing into his.

Griffin's breath fractures. He pushes deeper, faster.

His heady delight swells through me, resonating through my nerves and sending my own bliss spiking higher. I'm whirling toward the edge, careening beyond self-control.

My head tips back with the rush of my coming release. I can't rein it in.

My climax sweeps through me so scorchingly bright it whites out my vision and tingles across every inch of my skin. As I cry out with the burst of pleasure, the sizzling shadows seem to explode right out of me.

A vision crackles through my skull of the dark power beaming from my chest as if I'm a shadowblood sun, blazing rays streaking from me not just to Griffin but my other four men as well.

Jacob told me once that I'm the sun they all orbit around. I've never felt it so solidly before.

Like everything we are radiates between the six of us through me at the center.

Griffin lets out a choked sound as he follows me over the edge. I splay my fingers so the claws that've shot from the tips don't cut into his skin.

Another surge of his emotion washes over me to mingle with my own. Joy and pleasure and the deepest sense of fulfillment I can imagine.

His thrusts slow, his chest heaving. He lowers his head to claim another, sweeter kiss.

A faint prickle quivers from the spot right in the middle of my chest, between my collarbones, where his mark has formed. It finishes the necklace of splotches dappled across my skin.

But unlike with the other guys, the sense of our merged shadows doesn't fade away. The intensity of it ebbs, falling into more of a whisper than a blaze, but I can't shake the impression that we're still totally intertwined from the inside out. That I could tug and draw something of Griffin back into me if I tried.

So I do. I grasp hold and pull instinctively, absorbing in the shadows humming between us—

Griffin's head jerks up. I feel his flash of panic—but not because he's projected it into me.

No, I can feel so much more. I can taste the restless frustration emanating from a presence I recognize as Jacob, off within the villa. The uneasy boredom Dominic and Andreas are trying to fend off with a card game. The worries Zian has hovering over him like a cloud.

And more. Glimmers and twinges from elsewhere in the villa, from more distant sources that graze my senses like tendrils of mist.

There's so much of it—it swells inside me, overwhelming my thoughts—

I heave the essence I grabbed hold of back toward Griffin. All the broadened awareness rushes out of me, and he inhales with a hitch of relief.

I come back to myself, clinging to him amid the rippling water of the pool, staring at him like he's gaping at me.

"What did you do?" he murmurs.

"I—I don't know."

That's not totally true. An inkling of an idea is tickling up from the back of my mind.

If what I just experienced means what I think it does… our connection is so much more than even Clancy ever suspected.

So much more than Balthazar can possibly be prepared for.

I pull Griffin to me for one last kiss and then hook my elbow over the side of the pool. "We need to get the other guys."

THIRTY

Riva

When all six of us are standing in the back garden, as far from the villa as we can get, the guys look at me with an unspoken question. They know better than to ask out loud when Balthazar could hear us, but I've got to give some kind of explanation for dragging them over here.

"I had an idea—it might sound kind of strange," I say with the improvised excuse I came up with while Griffin and I gathered everyone. "We should meditate, all of us together, and maybe the right idea will come to us that way."

It's an excuse for our silence while we work out the rest. Jacob gives a bemused snort, but they all nod.

"Sure," Andreas says, with a sparkle in his eyes that tells me he knows perfectly well I'm up to something else. "Can't hurt to give it a shot."

The new awareness of the shadowy bonds between us

remains, the whispers of energy tickling my senses. Are they picking up on the change too?

I think they must have. I don't have the vivid understanding of their emotions that hit me in that moment in the pool, but quivers of curiosity and anticipation have filtered through the connection between us from the first moment Griffin and I went to talk to them.

I suspect they also know what must have happened to cause that shift. When Jacob saw Griffin and me together, his lips twitched with a knowing smirk that erased my worries about how he'd react to our new closeness.

We're all together, all meant for each other. No need for competition or jealousy.

And that might be true now beyond what any of us could have predicted.

I sink down onto the grass below the level of the nearby hedges, folding my legs. No one will be able to see what we're doing from inside the house, and Zian will hear footsteps before any intruder gets close enough to spy.

After what I experienced with Griffin, I thought I might feel the need to sit at the center of our circle, the hub to the wheel. But now that the guys are here with me, we settle naturally into a simple ring with me alongside them.

The deeper connection might have blazed forth from my body, but it tingles between us now not like spokes but a more intricate web, tying all of us together. The guys' essence reaches out to one another just as it does to mine.

Good. If I'm right, then that means our advantage is even bigger than I'd hoped.

While we were assembling our group, my mind was whirling through the possibilities of how I'd begin my demonstration. I need something that'll be clear—and clearly not from me.

I wet my lips and extend my hand toward Andreas at the opposite end of the circle.

He starts to shift toward me as if he thinks I want to grasp his hand, but I shake my head. I suspect we can do this without physical contact.

It'd be useful to know for sure.

If you asked me to describe it, I'd have to say the impression of shadowy energy that winds through each of us is pretty much the same, in every way I have concrete words for. But there's a vibe to each of the guys that's distinctly *them*.

Just as I always know where each of them is through my marks, never confusing one tug of sensation with another, I'd feel that it's Andreas's essence I'm reaching toward even with my eyes closed.

I do close my eyes then, concentrating hard on the whisper of energy he gives off. It's not all one sound but two separate murmurs. I can taste the idea of what they offer on a level below conscious understanding.

I grasp hold of the one I want and yank it into me.

The power flows into me without resistance. It coils through my own essence, etching the patterns of its function inside my skull.

It tells my body how to use it. All I need to do is hold that thrum of energy tightly and contract in on myself, peeling my presence out of view.

Zian lets out a startled grunt. My eyes pop open to find all five of the guys staring at me.

Or not really at me. At the spot where they saw me a moment ago, before I appeared to vanish.

Dominic's head swings around toward Andreas, but Drey gives a sharp shake of his head to indicate that he didn't have anything to do with my vanishing. His eyes have widened.

Zian cranes his neck around as if searching to see if I've simply slipped away. Jacob studies the spot where I'm sitting with a calculating air.

Griffin knows I'm still there. I must show up to his empathic sense as clearly as ever.

He lifts his hand and sets it on my shoulder. Showing the others that I haven't moved.

Did he already know what I did back in the pool, when I stole his talent from him just for a moment? Or did he only figure it out now, seeing this?

I push myself back into visibility—and nudge the thread of essence I grasped back into Andreas. He looks down at his hands and then back at me, speechless.

We can't say anything about this out loud. If Balthazar finds out we can trade talents…

Before I can follow that unnerving line of thought any farther, Jacob shoves his hand toward me. Offering himself, watching avidly to see the results.

I might as well confirm this part for them before we try anything else. I focus on his energies and tease out the more potent one to wrap through my limbs.

Oh, that's a power all right. It vibrates through nerves almost as insistently as my urge to shriek.

I glance around for a suitable test object. My gaze locks on to a planter that's a few feet long, set in front of one of the hedges, its flowers wilting.

At a motion of my hand and a heave of the borrowed power, it lifts several inches off the ground.

The weight radiates into my body, but I can feel even without any further practice that I've taken in the strength to lift and shake so much more than this one object.

Discomfort twists in my chest at the thought of stealing so much of Jacob's power, though. I release it and let it stream back into him.

Shocked silence has descended over our group. None of us could have expected this.

I have no idea how to explain it. I doubt even Engel suspected that raising us so closely, allowing us to bond so deeply on every level, would mean we'd find ourselves able to exchange our powers as well.

I glance at Dominic, whose forehead has furrowed with a pensive line. I know he'll handle any experiment I offer him cautiously.

Catching his gaze, I touch my chest and move my hand toward him—but not as if I'm asking for something from him. As if I'm trying to pass something over.

Startled comprehension lights in his hazel eyes. They become both more intent and more distant as he focuses on me.

The whisper ripples through my veins, as if I've shed a layer of fabric as filmy as gauze. Dominic stares down at his hands and flexes his fingers.

Claws spring from the tips.

An awed laugh sputters from his lips before he catches

himself. As he tests the supernatural speed that came with my bodily powers, swiping at a nearby hedge, Griffin turns to Zian at his other side.

At Griffin's gesture, Zee blinks in confusion. Then, with a lift of his eyebrows, he nods.

Griffin hovers his palm next to Zian's arm, his face tensing with concentration. Then he lowers his head.

His body twitches, and muscles bulge across his arms. Dark fur sprouts from his neck. His face warps with the start of a wolf-man muzzle before he reverses the shift.

Throughout our ring, bewilderment falls away in the wake of exhilaration. For several eager minutes, we don't do anything except borrow one power and then another: Jacob burning a few tufts of grass with Zian's X-ray vision, Andreas bringing the blades back to green life with Dominic's healing touch, Zee adding Jake's toxic spines to his arsenal, and on and on.

As the thrill tapers off, we sort ourselves back into the powers that belong to us. Using the others' talents doesn't feel quite as natural and innate as my own—I don't think I'd ever feel comfortable trying to keep any of theirs for an extended period of time.

But in the short-term? The possibilities are endless.

Dominic pulls out a paper and a pencil, because of course he'd have thought about alternate methods of communication when I indicated I wanted this meeting. He scrawls a hasty question at the top.

How can we use this in the escape plan?

I wet my lips. That is the big concern, the reason I wanted us to see what we could do.

Unfortunately, I haven't come up with a definite answer on my own.

Jacob takes the paper from him and adds a comment. *Whatever we do, they'll try to stop us. We can swap powers in the middle of a fight to take them by surprise.*

At Zian's motion, he passes the paper over. The larger guy scrawls a question. *The real problem is how to get Rollick's people up here to start the fight, right? If we do anything on our own, someone will knock us out before we get very far.*

We sit for a moment in grim silence. He's right, and exchanging our abilities doesn't get us any closer to discovering the secret route up the mountain or opening it to the shadowkind we want to bring in.

I reach for the page next. *We can't leave the grounds while we have the manacles on. But if Rollick can burn everything up, that could destroy the security systems too. Or at least we'd be able to work on the problem without anyone left to trigger them on purpose.*

Griffin nods and makes a follow-up note. *We just have to not get burned up too. Maybe combining our talents in a new way could make that easier?*

Andreas cocks his head and beckons for the paper. I pass it over.

Do you think your power could shield against the heat of a fire like it has against bullets? he writes, with a pointed look at Jacob.

Jake frowns and lifts his shoulders in an uncertain motion. I don't know if we want to gamble on a use of his power he's never attempted before, especially not with a supernatural fire that might be more potent than anything we've encountered in the past.

Griffin perks up, his gaze traveling across the grounds before coming back to us. He slips his fingers around my still-damp braid and squeezes a few drops of water from it, pointing it out emphatically to the other guys.

My heart lifts. Yes, if we were in the pool, the water would protect us from the flames. Other than we'd still need to breathe. Our heads could end up scalded by the wafting heat.

Dominic's expression has gone even more solemn. He takes the paper again, flipping it over for more room.

What if I borrowed Jake's power? If I drew strength from the plants nearby, I could make an even more effective shield and hold it for a long time. And with my healing energy working in combination, I could keep burns at bay even if too much heat seeps through. If we were mostly protected by the pool, I think I could handle it.

He motions toward the nearby garden. There's plenty of vegetation he could siphon energy from around the pool.

Jacob's mouth tightens, but he dips his head in acceptance. It makes more sense for him to pass one of his powers to Dominic than for Dominic to give up both of his.

Andreas takes the paper again. *Griffin and I can confuse Balthazar's people. Maybe Griffin could make him panic, keep him focused on his own life rather than doing anything to us, so he doesn't have a chance to suspect that the attack is meant to help us?*

Griffin smiles, and my own lips curl hesitantly. The fire

will provide plenty of chaos, and the two of them can add even more.

I can contribute to keeping everyone's attention off us too. In the confusion Rollick's fire causes, I could use my mental scream to take down Balthazar's people as need be without it being obvious that I caught them rather than the flames. That'd give us an additional layer of protection.

From the outside, it'd look like we ran to the pool to save our lives, a totally natural instinct and not at all mutinous. If anything goes even more wrong than we're anticipating, we can hope that a swift exchange of powers could tip the odds in our favor.

And when the place is ashes and Balthazar hopefully charbroiled too, there'll be no one and no equipment left to set off the worst effects of the manacles. We'll have time to figure out whether the knock-out boundary is still in effect and how to destroy that too.

I don't think I've ever hated anyone as much as I do our current captor, but somehow the thought of him being gone sends a twinge of loss through me too. Balthazar might not be my family in any way that matters, but he is a connection to a part of me I didn't know.

I don't want anything to do with *him*, but I'd have liked to know more about the woman who's technically my mother. What I might have gotten from her.

She didn't look horrifying in the photos I saw of her. The love she had for her son was obvious.

Maybe even Balthazar wasn't so horrifying until he lost them.

But if I have to pick between understanding my history better and saving myself and the guys I love, it isn't even a question. The way he's treated us is *forcing* me to destroy him, even the bits of his existence I might have wanted him to share.

I fish the stone Rollick left for us out of my pocket, where I've been carrying it with me ever since. The guys go still with anticipation, other than Griffin taking the paper.

We'll need them to give some kind of warning that the fire is coming, so we have time to get to the pool.

And I need to convey our entire message to the stone in my hands without Balthazar realizing what we're really talking about.

I inhale slowly. I can't talk to Rollick about the future openly, so all that's left is the past. The pieces of our history he was a part of.

Andreas motions to catch my attention. He meets my gaze and sends a memory flitting through my head.

The underground parking garage—the guardians attacking, the shadowkind tearing through them after my plea for help.

It isn't a happy memory. That was the first time we saw the full violence the shadowkind are capable of, and one of the younger shadowbloods got caught up in it.

We don't have to worry about that part this time, though. There's no one left here that we'd want to protect except ourselves.

I cup the stone between my hands and tap it with my thumb. Then I start talking as if I'm simply having a conversation with the guys.

"You remember that time we got ambushed in the parking garage? I was just thinking it was a good thing the light fixture fell when it did, so we knew to get out of the way before the attack really got started."

Zian's lips twitch with a hesitant smile as he plays along. "The guardians might have hurt us pretty bad if we hadn't had the chance to get to shelter, for sure."

"I was all worried about who else might get hurt," I go on, aiming for a casual tone. "But I guess sometimes you've got to fight fire with fire. Now I'd say, 'Just take them all out, whatever you have to do. We'll look after ourselves.'"

Griffin leans closer to me so his voice can reach the stone too. "Priorities shift, huh? Like the shadowkind man Balthazar has working for him—hard to figure that. And who'd have thought Balthazar would build this place with a secret route for the 'monsters' to get up here."

"He's an interesting guy," Andreas says dryly.

I scan the others to confirm no one else has anything they feel we need to pass on to Rollick. Then I tap the stone again, hoping whatever magic it contains was able to catch everything we said.

We all get up. Dominic brushes Zian's arm and points to the paper he left on a patio stone.

As Zian crouches down to burn it into cinders with his searing sight, I amble over to the wall. There's a section nearby where the cliff is totally sheer beneath it.

I lean my arms onto the top of the wall as if I'm admiring the view and roll the stone between fingers, concealing it from the house with my body. After a moment, I fling it down the mountainside with a swift flick of my hand.

Now all we have to do is wait for Rollick's warning...
and hope we're ready for what's to come.

We meander through the gardens for a while before
heading back to the house, to fully sell the story that we
simply wanted to stretch our legs in the fresh air. As we
come up on the side door, it opens for us.

Toni stops on the threshold, and we jar to a halt too.
For a long moment, we simply eye each other.

I expect her to summon us to another conversation
with Balthazar. Oh, God, what if he insists on sending us
off on another job and Rollick strikes while we're away?

No, that might actually be even better. Whoever's
away from the villa will be safe. And he isn't likely to send
Dominic if it's only some of us—he saw Dom as so
unnecessary to his plans that he left him unconscious for
ages.

Whoever's still here will be protected.

As all that runs through my head, I brace myself. I'm
not prepared for Toni to swipe her hand across her mouth
in an uncharacteristically anxious gesture and hold up her
phone in front of her chest for us to see the screen.

The typed words show starkly against the white
background of the Notes app. *I'm sorry. He isn't the one I
should have been helping. She wouldn't have wanted this.*

My gaze jerks to Toni's face. She offers me a pained
smile that matches her apology, the whiff of pheromones
she gives off tasting of fear... and sadness.

My stomach knots as I think of the instructions I just
sent to Rollick. I can't tell her about our plan—even if I
trusted her enough to want to.

I just told our shadowkind allies to kill her along with everyone else.

But if she means it, if she does help us, we could protect her too. There is one thing she might be able to do that we couldn't figure out for sure.

I lift my arms and touch one of my manacles. Toni's mouth twists tighter, but she swivels her phone to tap on it before showing us her answer.

I'll see what I can do.

THIRTY-ONE

Dominic

Tucked into an armchair by the sitting room window, I let my gaze drift toward the glass again. And then jerk it back to the pages of my book to make sure I don't look like I'm watching for something outside.

I've never been the type to leap into action quickly. Andreas used to tease me about always needing to think through every angle of a problem before I was confident tackling it.

But I've got to say that waiting on someone else to launch a plan you've already decided to go ahead with makes my top ten list of things I'd rather not experience again.

I know what I'm going to need to do. I'm the cornerstone in this plan.

I just have no idea *when* I'm going to need to do it—

and I won't know until minutes if not mere seconds beforehand.

Across the room, Riva stirs in her own chair with what I recognize as suppressed restlessness. I can only imagine how impatient she's getting when Balthazar might try to rope her further into the family business at any point.

We don't know how long it'll take Rollick to find our answering message. Or how much time it'll take after that for him to rally whatever forces he's bringing.

The fire he promised could arrive by daylight or in the middle of the night. His warning signal could be anything at all.

From what I've seen of the demon, I trust him to mean his offer of help honestly, but I'm also aware that fully "monstrous" minds operate on somewhat different terms from our partly human perspective as shadowbloods.

It's only been two days. Two days of constant anticipation churning in my stomach and furtive glances between the six of us.

Footsteps in the hall draw my attention to the doorway with a hiccup of my pulse, but it's just one of the members of the discreet household staff passing by. The woman doesn't even look our way.

The sight of her reminds me of the other unknown variable in our plans.

Toni indicated that she'd help us with the problem of the manacles. She doesn't know that there's any deadline by which we'll need that done, but then, we couldn't tell her the exact timing even if we wanted to risk revealing more.

She has to realize that we'd want to leave as soon as possible. Every day, every hour we spend under the villa's roof puts us in more danger.

Riva's rejection upset Balthazar. There's no telling what he'll do next.

And we all know he has no qualms about spilling our blood.

Should we have made the urgency of our situation even more clear in our message to Rollick? Will the demon understand how important it is that he gets here as soon as possible?

We're so restricted in this beautiful cage that it was hard to plan out our whole strategy thoroughly.

I realize that I've been staring at the same page for a couple of minutes without absorbing any of the words. I turn to the next just to put on a show of actually reading.

I lost track of the plot a few chapters ago. I can't say I really care.

Movement beyond the window catches my eye with another lurch of my heart. But it's nothing supernatural.

A couple of men in the blue uniforms Balthazar appears to have given all his staff are tramping across the grounds with a purposeful air. One of them holds what looks like… a very large aquarium net.

They're walking in the direction of the pool.

I guess they're going to clean it? But something about their demeanor sends a prickle of alarm through my nerves.

I set my book on the side table, stretch my arms and the tentacles I've kept coiled out of the way, and amble over to the door. There's nothing unusual about one of us taking a stroll through the garden in the early afternoon.

Or more than one of us. Riva follows me, shooting me a quick smile as she catches up. "I could use a walk too, if you don't mind the company."

I take her hand in mine and sling one of my tentacles around her waist. "Of course not."

There's something amazing about the quiver of energy that unfurls between us now when she's close—when I'm within a few feet of any of my friends too. The threads of essence connecting us on a level beyond sight.

We're blood now in a way none of us ever imagined. So attuned to each other that in some ways we might as well be one joint being.

Balthazar can't be prepared for our newfound unity. The knowledge brings a faint smile of my own to my lips despite my uneasiness.

We meander out the side door into the grayish sunlight beneath a thinly clouded sky. The breeze whips through the strands of my hair that've fallen loose from my short ponytail, licking a sharp chill across my skin and making me wish I'd stopped to grab my jacket from my bedroom.

I might have gone back inside to get it if the scene in front of me didn't freeze my legs under me a moment later, for reasons that have nothing to do with the cold air.

The two workers have gone over to the pool, yes. One of them is dipping the giant net into the water to scoop out stray leaves and twigs that have blown in.

The other has opened a panel in the tiles around the pool's edge and is twisting something beneath it.

A faint gurgle reaches my ears. It fades away a moment later, but a sickly sensation remains in my gut.

The man straightens up and brushes his hands together. "Make sure you get all of it," he says to his companion. "Boss doesn't want any crud left in the bottom."

Left in the bottom… after the water's gone?

Riva stays silent, but her hand tightens around mine. How the hell are we going to carry out our plan if we haven't got the pool to shelter in?

I can't tell yet if the waterline is descending, but it seems unwise to simply stand there and stare. We wander toward the wall along the edge of the grounds.

Worries whirl through my head. We'll have to readjust our entire plan. We can't even talk about it if we don't have the water to cover our voices.

Can I get away with the trick of writing it out again? Even the first time was risky, knowing we could be interrupted and caught.

My distress must be loud enough for Griffin to not only pick up on it but get concerned himself. We're just circling back toward the villa when the other four guys emerge, Griffin's expression shadowed with concern and the others looking uncertain.

He won't have wanted to tell them why he was suggesting they come out here, but they'll have been able to tell it wasn't to celebrate a victory.

Andreas cocks his head at me and Riva with one of his wry smiles. "Decided to have a party out here without the rest of us?"

Riva rubs her arm through her hoodie. "Not much of

a party. We just got tired of being cooped up in there, you know."

I'm debating whether I should overtly point out the pool, but Zian has already glanced in that direction. His stance stiffens. "What are they doing over there?"

It's now obvious to me that the water is sinking. It looks at least a foot lower than it was when we first came out.

Fucking hell.

Jacob's shoulders tense too, but I don't hear anything breaking nearby, so maybe he's gotten his telekinesis a little better under control.

Griffin's lips purse in a grimace. "It looks like they're emptying the pool."

The man who opened the drain has replaced the panel that conceals the controls. The guy with the net appears to have finished his cleanup. They stride away without any sign that they're aware they may have signed our death sentence.

We let ourselves meander toward the pool. I watch the level of the water dip slowly but surely lower.

"So much for swim time," Jacob mutters before lapsing into a moody silence.

None of the rest of us knows what to add. We stand there like mourners at a funeral.

That image is a little more accurate than I'd like. It *could* be our funeral, literally.

Can I shield us against a fire strong enough that Rollick expects it to wipe out all our enemies without the extra help of all that water? The thought of protecting just our wet heads seemed a lot less intimidating than cloaking our entire, totally flammable bodies.

I wasn't even sure I could do the easier version without having to heal up injuries while I did.

The water keeps sinking. When it's around knee-level, Riva sighs and turns around.

She halts, going still, and we all jerk around to see what's caused her reaction.

Toni is walking over to join us, her arms crossed loosely over her chest. *She* had the sense to wear a jacket— a trim wool one that seems to emphasize her professional air.

She peers past us. "Mr. Balthazar ordered it drained."

Jacob glowers at her. "We can see that."

But she isn't here to rub in the loss. The corner of her mouth turns down as she contemplates the pool. "He said it was time to close it up for the season. It wouldn't be safe to use anymore."

She flicks her gaze toward us, and I understand. He realized that we've been using the pool to obscure conversations we didn't want him overhearing.

So he's taking that option away for us.

He doesn't even know just how badly he's screwing us over.

"That's too bad," Andreas says carefully. "We were really hoping to get at least one more swim in before it's too cold outside."

Toni studies him. Her expression stays apologetic even if her tone is curt. "There's nothing I can do about it. You're lucky you had the use of it for as long as you did."

Well, I guess we can't argue with her on that point.

But how are we going to protect ourselves from the shadowkind's fire now?

How am *I* going to protect everyone else?

Somehow I don't think filling up the few bathtubs and soaking in them is going to do the trick.

Of course, none of that will matter if Toni can deactivate the manacles. Then we can simply get the hell out of here when the warning comes.

But if she'd managed to disable them already, she wouldn't be so cautious in how she's talking to us.

Riva's mouth twitches as if she's grappling with what to say. She draws herself up a little straighter. "That thing you said is going to happen—soon it isn't even going to matter."

Her words could be taken as a mild, vague threat to someone who doesn't know what Toni recently offered us.

The older woman stares at Riva for a second before dropping her gaze. "We all have our limitations." Then she tilts her head toward the villa. "Come on. Balthazar wants to talk to all of you about something."

As we trudge after her toward the doorway, my stomach sinks. Has our captor figured out even more about our covert activities?

Or maybe he's simply going to throw as many wrenches at us as he can and hope at least one of them jams up anything we have in the works. He wants to rattle us—that's obvious from the way he needled Jacob the other day and his decision to reveal Riva's genetic heritage to her.

But what—

Zian pauses a few steps from the door with a flick of

his gaze toward the far end of the garden. The rest of us hesitate too.

He motions to his ear, indicating that he heard something.

Before the rest of us can respond, Rollick's dry voice blares through the quiet of the grounds. "Ready or not, shadowbloods—here we come!"

My pulse stutters. I drag my gaze across the landscape, searching for any sign of an immediate attack, and yank it back to Toni… who's blinking at the rest of us with an air of mild confusion.

She couldn't hear the message. Of course not— Rollick's been using some magic that means only we shadowbloods can make out his words.

Then the horror of the situation hits me like a punch to the gut.

The shadowkind assault is happening right this minute. And we're not prepared after all.

Riva swivels, probably scrambling for a solution. "It really doesn't matter now," she murmurs.

She looks toward the pool, but there can't be more than a few inches of water left in it. We'd be better off with bathtubs.

Instinctively, I take a step toward the pool. Maybe if we can pry open the panel and start the water running again—if Balthazar somehow doesn't find out what we're up to until it's full enough to protect us—if we can even accomplish that much before the attack starts—

A crackling bolt of flame sears from the sky and smacks into the roof of the villa. In an instant, the fire surges across the undulating terracotta as if the clay is as flammable as paper.

"Shit!" Toni stumbles to the side, her eyes widening. She stares at the fire and then at us with dawning understanding.

She fumbles with her phone and jabs her thumbs at the screen to compose a hasty message. As she holds it up to us, she flings her hand to point to the northeast corner of the grounds.

"Get away from the house!" she shouts. "Mr. Balthazar won't want you hurt."

Her phone's screen tells us the rest: *Move the solo granite vase. 5-3-9-7. Go down. I'll try.*

I've barely had time to read all of it before she's dashing away into the house. Another fiery bolt warbles from some source I haven't spotted and crashes against the front of the building.

I push the others toward the spot Toni indicated. "Come on! The whole thing's going up."

My heart thuds as we sprint across the courtyard and between the hedges. We have to keep up the charade that we're only trying to stay clear of harm, not complicit in this attack, for as long as possible.

Long enough for Toni to sever Balthazar's connection to our manacles… or for the man and anyone else who'd carry out his intentions to die.

Heat wafts against our backs. The fire hisses and roars, billowing across the villa in sizzling waves of flame.

I spot the "vase" Toni must have meant—a three-foot flowerpot of solid stone holding a shrub that's browned with the colder weather. But as I push myself forward with a fresh burst of speed, voices ring out behind us.

"Hey, where do you think you bunch are going?"

"Stay where you are!"

Jacob whips around. The two guards charging after us trip at the same moment.

Their skulls collide hard enough to smash the bone.

Okay, there's no coming back from that. We just have to hope that if Balthazar still has control over the metal around our wrists, any surveillance cameras pointed this way have already melted.

The whole side of the villa has been swallowed by flames. They're streaming down to the garden now, gorging on the grass, sizzling madly. Smoke hazes the air.

Zian slams into the flowerpot. It topples over to reveal a manhole cover that's about two feet in diameter, with a keypad lock in the middle of it.

Through the pounding of my heartbeat, it clicks in my head that Riva said she and Zian saw the shadowkind man hanging around in this part of the grounds the first time. Does this hole lead to the secret route through the hill?

The numbers from Toni's screen flit through my memory. I dive between Griffin and Andreas to tap the four digits in.

The lock rasps over. As Zian drops down to wrench open the cover, my gaze darts around us.

I don't know what we'll find down there, but there might not be anything *alive* other than us. If I'm going to be much help in whatever we face next, I'll need fuel for my—and the others'—powers.

My hand swipes past Riva, focusing on that new,

sharper quiver of energy that runs between us. With a mental tug, I borrow her supernatural strength.

Then I wrap my tentacles around two nearby saplings and wrench them out of the soil roots and all.

Andreas gapes at me and lets out a rasp of a laugh. I push Riva's power back into her, and she leaps through the hole into the darkness below.

I jump down last, tossing my saplings ahead of me. By the time I'm sliding over the lip into the unknown space below, the flames are already crackling through the hedge that stands just a few feet from where I was poised. My nose prickles with the smoke billowing on the breeze.

A cough sputters out of me. As I plummet, I wrap the end of one of my tentacles around a handle on the inside of the cover and slam it shut above me.

My feet thump to the ground a little sooner than I dared to hope. Zian catches my elbow to steady me.

"I'm going to borrow this," he tells me. There's a crack as he snaps a branch off one of the saplings.

With a flick of his gaze, he lights up the jutting twigs with a fire much less intimidating than the one raging overhead. The wavering glow washes over the room we've found ourselves in.

The floor, walls, and ceiling all appear to be stone—other than the manhole we just dropped through and three doors around us. There's one to my right, where the floor slopes slightly upward, and two to our left, side by side.

They gleam with the sheen of steel. The one at the right and the second door at the left have keypad locks like the manhole cover.

The first door on the left is just a solid slab of metal, not even a handle protruding from its smooth surface.

"Where do we go?" Riva asks into the sudden silence.

"Not up," Jacob says grimly, turning toward the pair of doors. He motions to me. "Try the code."

I hustle over and tap the same sequence of numbers into the keypad on the second door. It gives a hostile beep and a flash of orange light.

Andreas swears under his breath. "I doubt it's safe to stay right here."

Zian peers around us. "But as long as we're *in* the hill, not going past the line of the walls, our manacles shouldn't knock us out, right?"

Riva glances back toward the upper door and exhales roughly. "As long as no one activates them manually."

We can't afford to wait around and find out if that'll happen.

I motion toward the lower doors. "We'll have to break one open." My mind whips through the possibilities. "The one without the extra lock. We just want to put some distance between us and the house—no point in messing with anything especially defended that might set off the security system."

Really, anything down here could be dangerous, but we might as well do our best not to trigger our doom.

Zian shoves at the smooth door, but it doesn't budge. Then he narrows his eyes at the shiny surface.

A searing red line traces across the top of the metal. But after a moment, he shakes his head. "It's really thick. I don't know if I can cut all the way through. I can't even see the other side—it's all dark."

My pulse kicks up a notch. "You'll be able to if you power up. I could—"

I stop myself, realizing there's a simpler solution. One that means handing over my talent rather than playing the hero myself.

But then, that's always been my main role in our group anyway—a supporting one. I've gotten us through an awful lot that way.

I reach toward Zian. "Take my energy-absorbing power!"

It's as if he pulls it and I push it toward him at the same moment. With an unnerving tingle, my frame feels somehow lighter.

Zian hesitates, then grasps one of the saplings I brought along. His hand clenches around the narrow trunk, and his eyes flare.

The young tree withers in his grasp, and the metal whines with the slice of his brutal vision.

As I watch him, a different sort of lightness rises up inside me. He's taking the supernatural skill I've loathed, the one that made me feel like a monster, and using it to save our skins.

The tree dies, but the rest of us live. Can I really say that's a bad trade-off?

The steel warps and bends. The chunk Zian is cutting out of it sags open.

He flings my power back into me, and we scramble through the opening.

I remain at the back of the pack, dragging the second sapling. I'm just heaving it through the rough hole when the door at the upper end of the room flies open.

"There they are!" a figure in a military-style helmet shouts, his gun pointing straight at me.

There's no room for the others to maneuver. Instinctively, I snatch through the energies around me to grab at Jacob's and then wrench my arm upward.

Half a dozen purple spines fly from my forearm like porcupine quills... only deadly. They sink into our attacker's throat and chest before he can pull the trigger.

Then Riva is beside me, her hand on my waist, her gaze searching the room. Three more armed men thump through the doorway toward us—and topple one after the next with a spasm of their limbs before they hit the ground.

She cut them down in the space of a few thuds of my pulse, her eyes narrowed but no sound leaving her lips.

Am I supposed to be horrified by how quiet her vicious skill has become? All I'm filled with in that moment is awe.

"Let's go!" she says, urging me ahead of her with a tight grin, and hefts the other end of the sapling to help me carry it.

Andreas's voice carries from up ahead. "We're all still conscious and wrists intact. Something must have stopped the manacles from working."

Or someone. I glance toward the room we just left, which is falling into darkness as we hustle down the steeply sloping tunnel on the other side with Zian's torch.

Is Toni going to be able to get out of the villa alive? I can't say I feel exactly *friendly* toward her, but she did help us at least a little in the end.

We might be dead already if she hadn't directed us to this passage.

As the floor veers even more steeply downward, I run my free hand along the lumpy wall to help keep my balance. "I guess this is taking us right down the hill?"

"I hope so," Riva says. "This has got to be the secret route for the shadowkind, and they could climb partway up the cliff through the shadows. But somehow I don't think Balthazar would leave the very bottom unprotected."

No, that doesn't fit his typical M.O.

The tunnel swerves sharply to the right. We hurry along the turn, our footsteps rasping over the stone.

And then the ceiling crumbles with an unearthly groan.

Rocks pelt down on us. Riva tackles me to the ground, sheltering me as well as she can with her smaller but tougher body.

There's an oof and a dwindling of the light as Zian must drop his torch while he shields the others.

Griffin's voice breaks through the clatter of falling stone. "Jake!"

I wrench around on the rough floor. A few feet from the guttering flames licking along the broken branch, Jacob lies slumped, his forehead streaming blood and smoky essence where a particularly large rock bashed him.

There's another rumble, and the ground shudders beneath me. Panic shoots through my chest alongside an unnervingly cool sense of certainty.

I have to be a hero here after all.

Jacob's knocked out, but he isn't dead. The energy of his powers still hums when I reach toward him.

My fingers curl around the sapling alongside one of my tentacles. I thrust my other hand upward just as another shower of rocks rains down on us.

They bounce off the invisible wall I just cast around us, pushing the air into a barrier with the telekinetic power I borrowed from Jacob.

I need to heal him too, but not until I'm sure the rest of us aren't going to get our heads smashed open.

My nerves wobble with the striking of the jagged rocks —all of them bigger now. The effort of holding the shield in place is already wearing at my own energy.

So I'll just have to draw what I can out of the sapling. Killing so that we can live.

A faint twinge flutters through my strange appendages, and I know that means they're creeping a little longer from my flesh. But the flash of revulsion that comes with the thought isn't the only thing I feel.

It's kind of incredible, isn't it—the way I can boost myself or any of the others when *I* choose how I use my powers? I have to remember that.

As a thrilling stream of renewed energy courses up through my tentacle into the rest of my body, the last voice I'd want to hear reverberates from an unseen speaker.

"Did you really think I wouldn't have other fail safes in place?" Balthazar says, his voice taut with derision and maybe anger as well. "I'll bury you all, you traitors."

A chill lances up my spine. I don't know how long I can maintain this shield before I've sucked all the energy out of my one source.

And if he collapses the entire tunnel, it won't matter. We won't have any way to get out.

I suck in a shaky breath, my mind scrambling for a solution—and Riva pushes herself away from us, scrambling over some of the stones that've fallen farther up the path. Her voice peals out into the dimness.

"Dad—wait!"

THIRTY-TWO

Riva

"**D**ad—wait!"

The words make me want to vomit even as I force them from my throat. But it's the only thing I can think to say that might get Balthazar's attention and divert him from his murderous goal.

I've never called anyone "Dad" before. And he—he won't have heard that name addressed to him since his son died.

In the momentary silence, I catch Griffin's empathic talent from him. Just for a few seconds, long enough to extend my awareness and trace the churn of emotions that matches the tone of Balthazar's voice to some point I can't distinctly define but can tell isn't far away.

He's here. Below the hill's plateau with us. Maybe behind the other door we saw—the one that was locked?

I push a whiff of sentimentality toward the man before I release the ability back to Griffin. If I'm lucky, if Griffin understands what I'm aiming for, he'll keep up the same strategy on my behalf.

No more rocks careen toward our heads. From the corner of my eye, I see Dominic relax slightly, getting a momentary reprieve from the need to project a telekinetic shield.

How long will that reprieve last?

Finally, Balthazar's voice returns, warier but also less arrogant than before. "Do you have something to say to me, Riva?"

I pitch my voice to carry, not sure exactly how he's hearing my response. Not letting myself care that the guys will all hear it perfectly clearly too.

"Please, let me come back. I was surprised before, and scared, but I don't want to die like this. I never even got to really know you. Can you give me another chance?"

My voice wavers of its own accord. I'm genuinely scared—scared and desperate and not sure this attempt will even work… and hating that I'm trying out the tactic at all.

But I have to. I have to use every card in my hand.

Play along until we can escape. That was always the plan.

I just didn't know how hard it'd be to take on the final role our captor could ask from me. The one he almost begged me to step into the last time we spoke.

You can stand beside me. We'll work together and set things right. Don't you see it?

"You said 'me,' not 'we,'" Balthazar says in the present. "Are you asking only for yourself, then?"

"Would you let any of the guys come back with me?" I ask, already knowing the answer.

He chuckles. "I can't trust any of them near me. I can't even trust *you*."

But I'm the only one with his DNA woven into my body. His and his wife's. The last living reminder of the woman I suppose he loved, in whatever warped way this psychopath is capable of.

I make my tone meek. "I know. I'll do whatever you ask me to. Before... I didn't know how to wrap my head around the idea of having a real family. I'm sorry I ran away from you."

The man who'd call himself my father doesn't really know me. If he did, he'd realize that I'd never really abandon my guys, not even to save my life.

My stomach churns around the lie. Oh please, let the guys remember my devotion to them like they didn't when I was forced to leave them before.

Traces of wrenching fear waver through our bonds, but I don't know if it's for me or for themselves.

"What are you doing, Tink?" Andreas croaks, but I think I catch a flicker of a smile from him in the fading firelight. I want to believe he already knows the real answer to that question.

I pretend to ignore him. And also Griffin's pleading, "Moonbeam?" which cuts me to the core even though if any of the guys can tell what's going on inside me, it's him.

Balthazar finally speaks. "Come along then. But don't think I'll be careless enough to give you an opening to hurt me."

"Thank you—thank you so much!"

I turn my back on my guys—and grope through their mingling energies for the one power that could save us all.

Dominic's voice rasps out. "You don't have to do this, Riva."

He might even mean that, not just be helping to sell my story. But I do have to.

I do, or we all die here while Balthazar sneers at our downfall.

I say nothing, just trudge up the tunnel.

Most of the rocks fell directly on the section where Balthazar caught us, but a few stray stones lie on the increasingly darkened path. As I push myself up the steep slant, my calves burning, I nearly trip over one I didn't see.

"I'm coming, Dad," I call out to keep him focused on me. "Just can't see much in here."

He won't shake loose any more projectiles with that "fail safe" of his until I'm out of the passage, right? He wouldn't want to risk cracking open *my* head—not his daughter's, not when she's finally accepting his mercy.

Once I'm out, he'll bury the guys like he's promised.

So I need to take care of this problem before I leave the tunnel.

The light behind me fades completely with a curve in the passage. I run my fingers along the walls, feeling my way.

And aim the penetrating sight I stole from Zian through the layer of stone at my left.

I'm not attempting to burn through anything right now, only to use the incisive vision that lets him see through solid surfaces. After a few attempts, I catch a glimmer of light a few feet through the rock.

There's another passage parallel to this one. I glimpse it in brief flashes—carved stairs in contrast with the uneven floor I'm stumbling along, occasional light fixtures mounted on the ceiling.

An escape route rather than a secret passage, meant for a man with higher standards than he offered his shadowkind collaborators.

And somewhere along that passage, I'll find the madman himself.

It's so dark in my tunnel that I don't see the door Zian tore through, only feel a slightly more forceful draught of air when I get near it. I cast my gaze toward the wall again and have to clamp down on my jolt of surprise.

There's a whole control room of sorts at the start of the other tunnel, presumably behind the locked door we saw. Screens and electronic consoles gleam along the stone walls.

And by one of those consoles, peering at a screen I can't make out, stands Balthazar, intent as the grizzled lion he's always reminded me of. His hands are braced over a keypad.

The vision flickers away in my surprise and my lack of practice with the X-ray vision. I pause as if to briefly catch my breath.

Leaning one hand against the stone surface, I pull my scream into the back of my head. I have to launch my attack fast, before Balthazar catches on that I can use my power on him even while he's theoretically beyond my view—

But as I lift my gaze to the wall to focus it on the man

who's my father and my tormenter, a tickle of frantic, aggressive pheromones reaches my nose.

Two facts click into place in my head in the split-second I register the tang.

They can't be coming from Balthazar, because the chemicals his body gives off could never penetrate this stone. Someone must be just beyond the broken door to this tunnel.

And that someone has nothing good in mind for the person they must be waiting to ambush...

Me.

My head jerks around just as a gaunt body hurtles through the ragged opening.

Matteo still has the benefit of a little surprise. I might have started to catch on, but I had no time to really brace myself.

"She's doing something!" he calls out in a thin voice as he jams a gun to the underside of my chin. He's got a plastic contraption fixed over his eyes—some kind of goggles to help him see in the dark? "She's got a trick—"

Fury and anguish flood me as swift and scorching as the fire that consumed the villa. In that instant, any revulsion I still held about using the most vicious part of my powers fades away.

This man reveled in how far he could stretch my talents, how much pain he could force me to deal out. He should be happy to experience firsthand what he celebrated so avidly.

The shriek peals from my mind in a torrent so scathing my nerves rattle with it. But even as my rage of retribution pours out of me, my thoughts are still down the passage with my guys, knowing I'm here for them as much as myself.

Matteo warned Balthazar that I'm going to attack— that I can. I have no idea what our captor will do with that information.

I'm going to carve every scrap of pain I can out of Matteo to bolster my strength—but I have to do it quickly.

Just this once, I'm grateful for this asshole's "procedures," all the exercises and tests he pushed on me. My mental shriek hits him and starts at precisely the perfect spot, shattering every bone in the hand holding his gun.

As the pistol slips from his suddenly flimsy fingers, Matteo cries out. I slam my silent scream into his throat next, smashing his vocal cords but not cutting off his breath.

I'm not letting him die just yet.

My power rips through him with brutal efficiency. Crack his kneecaps. Slice the skin between his toes and along the arch of his foot. Carve a path from his stomach up to his ribs.

Everywhere it'll hurt the most. All that agony streaming into me, fueling the power I'm inflicting on him.

The rush of exhilaration sweeps me through a few ragged breaths. I might have kept going a little longer, taken in even more strength from his pain, but the ground beneath me trembles with a distant thunder.

Fuck. Balthazar is done waiting—he's set off the rockslide again.

My final silent shriek blasts apart Matteo's heart. I shove his disjointed body off me, letting it thud lifelessly to the ground.

The agony I absorbed thrums through my limbs. I spring to my feet and dash through the broken door into the entry room.

As I spin toward the door with the lock, my renewed strength propels the X-ray vision I borrowed from Zian through the thick steel. I have to find Balthazar—I have to shatter his heart too before he can do any more damage—

I can't see him. I make out the hazy screens and the lights blinking on the consoles, but he's ducked out of view.

He must be somewhere near the controls. His voice resonates through the underground chamber. "Whatever you think you're going to do, you don't need *them* anymore."

No.

Panic spikes through my veins, and I do the only other thing I can think of that might stop him. I flick my gaze toward the ceiling over his control room instead.

The searing power of Zian's vision slices through stone much more easily than steel. A massive chunk of rock crashes down on a few of the screens, sending sparks flying.

Then another and another, hitting the floor or the consoles in a pounding thunder.

If I can cut through enough, if I can hurl enough boulders at Balthazar, I can kill him that way, I can pulverize him right out of existence…

The other tunnel goes quiet, the rumbling sensation ebbing. An ache spreads through my skull.

I scan the room beyond the locked door as intently as I can, ignoring the strain stabbing through the middle of my brain, and catch a flash of movement deeper inside. A blur of fabric—someone stumbling away—

And then my sight fades to a hazy gray. The headache jabs deeper, forming spots behind my eyes.

Every particle in my body is shouting at me to race after Balthazar, if that was him. To rip through these passages until his lifeless, bloody body slumps before me.

But I don't have the strength. I've worn myself ragged with what I've already done.

And the guys—the guys still need me. I don't know how much rubble he poured down on them.

Another hitch of fear propels me down the first tunnel. I sway and stagger, shoving myself onward, my clawed fingers scrabbling over the walls.

The faintest flickering glow comes into view up ahead. It trembles through a crack in a heap of massive stones that cuts off the passage.

A groan sounds from somewhere within that pile.

Oh, God, no. I can't stop a wordless cry from spilling from my lips.

They're all still there, still right in front of me, hidden by the deluge of stone. Quivers of pain and desperation flicker through our connection, blurring together so I can't tell what's from who.

I still haven't been forced to find out whether I'd still be able to sense my guys' presence through my marks if one or more of them died. I can't say for sure whether all of them are still alive.

Blinking back searing tears, I grasp one of the stones and find that I haven't drained all of my bodily strength even if my sensory talents have frayed. I manage to heave a couple of rocks about as big as my torso farther up the path.

"Zee!" I call out. "I'm giving your sight back, if you can use it. If anyone needs my strength, you can take it. I don't know how much else I can do from out here."

I push the stolen vision back toward Zian. If he's pinned so that he can't easily lift the boulders, maybe he can crack them open to make them easier to handle.

Grasping hold of a bigger rock, I dig in my claws and drag it, tug after tug, out of the way. Just as I'm reaching for the next one, it lurches toward me as if of its own accord.

I yelp and dodge, and it rolls farther up the passage.

A raw but audible voice reaches me through the gap that's opened up. "Good to see you, Wildcat."

"Jacob!" Desperate joy sweeps through me. I drop to my knees by the crevice. "You're okay?"

Dominic's voice carries through next. "I had a moment to patch him up, thanks to you. We've still got plenty of cuts and bruises to go around, but as long as we can actually get out of this hill back to the outside world, I think we'll survive."

"Let's upgrade that to an 'I know,'" I mutter, and heft another stone out of the way.

Once I've cleared a large enough gap that I can squeeze through to the pocket of space where Jacob and Dom are hunched, they turn their attention to the other end of the tunnel. Zian has, in fact, been slicing and dicing some of the larger rocks.

He punches the reduced chunks farther down the tunnel while Andreas shoves at the bits he can handle despite the blood streaking down from his shoulder. As I squeeze over to reach them, they've just opened a gap big enough for my tiny frame to squirm through.

"Don't go leaving us behind," Andreas teases hoarsely as I push into the opening.

I freeze. "I never would have—"

He rests his hand on my calf. "I know. I know, Tink. You did fucking amazing."

All at once, I'm choked up again. I blink hard and push onward.

Working from the opposite side of the cave-in, I help the guys dig out a wide enough path that Zian can shimmy even his bulky body through. The second the five of them have pushed through, I find myself wrapped in their joint embrace.

I sag into their encircling arms just for a few ragged breaths. Griffin presses a kiss to the back of my head.

"We've got you, Moonbeam. We've got you—just like you looked after us."

I swallow hard. "I don't think I took him out. I tried— Matteo got in the way, and then—"

Jacob interrupts with a dismissive sound. "It's okay. We're getting the hell out of here. That's what really matters."

"His whole fucking house is ashes now," Dominic says

darkly. "Any equipment he had in there, any plans he'd made... We'll deal with the rest later."

I turned one of Balthazar's key underlings against him —and slaughtered the other. I destroyed even his hidden control system.

I sent the madman running. Finally, he was the one who had to flee *my* wrath instead of us quaking in fear of his.

Despite all his money and technology, all the power he wielded over us, we beat him in the end. He couldn't stop us from making our escape.

If it's a shame he got to escape too, well, Dom is right. We'll hit him again.

A grin of victory tugs at my lips with a rush of exhilaration.

Next time it'll be easier. We'll hunt him down and finish him for good.

The lingering flames finally sputter out completely. Darkness closes in around us, but it's not so suffocating now.

We venture on down the sloping tunnel, around another bend, and jolt to a stop at a sudden flare of light right in front of us.

A familiar suave face gleams into view in the conjured glow.

"Oh, excellent," Rollick says with a warm grin. "You saved me having to climb up the whole damned mountain."

THIRTY-THREE

Riva

As we follow Rollick the rest of the way down the tunnel, questions tumble from my lips. "How did you find the secret route?" comes out first.

Rollick opens his mouth, but before he can answer, another shadowkind glimmers into being next to him. With a bounce of her glossy blond curls, Pearl beams at me.

"The people from that high house had to come down to civilization sometimes," she says. "So I worked a little of my succubus charm…"

She sways her rounded hips suggestively and giggles. Even her laugh is pretty.

I cringe at the thought of Pearl having to get up close and personal with any of Balthazar's men. "I'm sorry it came to that."

She shrugs. "Hey, I've got to feed one way or another. I enjoy it more if it's helping a friend at the same time!"

Her cheerful attitude seems to brighten the rocky passage more than the supernaturally conjured ball of light hovering alongside us does. Hearing her call me a friend sends a bittersweet pang through my gut.

I wasn't that great a friend in the last few days she knew me. I nearly killed a shadowkind who'd been a much better friend of hers—and nothing but kind to me too.

But she came to our rescue anyway.

It's hard to phrase my next question without it sounding like a criticism. "The fire started a while ago… You were only just coming up this way now?"

Rollick's chuckle rolls through the narrow space. "Why didn't we get our asses up there sooner, you mean? Pearl's little foray gave us the location of the entrance and the code to open it, but failed to uncover the fact that the hidden door was made out of layers of steel and iron so thick *I* couldn't even handle it long enough to haul it open. We had a little delay tracking down a nearby mortal who could do the job for us."

I sense Jacob's frown in his voice, traveling from behind me. "*Someone* was up there already, right? Sending out the fire?"

Pearl claps her hands together. "Oh, you'll meet her soon. She's great. *She* could have opened the door for us, but of course she was busy by the time we realized."

"She" not "They." My eyebrows rise. "Was it just three of you on this rescue mission?"

Rollick shoots me a sideways glance tinged with obvious amusement. "Still can't make out your sort-of brethren when they're in the shadows, hmm?"

Oh. My gaze darts to the dark patches filling the

cracks and crevices in the rocky surfaces, my pulse wobbling.

Who knows how large a force he brought along if most of his shadowkind companions are sticking to the shadows?

Not that I'd want them all to emerge right here. The tunnel feels claustrophobic enough without a bunch more bodies crammed into the tight space.

The thought of the unknown beings who've come with the demon brings up one more uncertainty I'm even less comfortable voicing. I grapple with it for a minute before finding an approach that doesn't make me wince.

"What happened to the six younger shadowbloods we broke out of the facility the last time we saw you, before the guardians captured us again?"

We sent those kids off to the waiting shadowkind Rollick was leading, intending to follow them and regroup. Intending to save them.

Clancy showed us photographs of the kids sprawled in the forest as mangled corpses. But he lied to us about so many other things.

He'd have wanted to lie about that.

Rollick shows no sign that it's even occurred to him I might think the escapees were harmed. "Oh, I ended up bringing them back to the hotel, since it's as good a place as any to stash people who have nowhere else to go. They've been enjoying a lot of room service. I'm not sure how much the free food and the beach life has been helping them recover from their former captivity, but I'm reasonably sure it hasn't traumatized them further."

My breath rushes out of me. "So they're all okay."

The demon glances over at me more directly, a faint furrow of confusion marring his brow. "Of course. The hard part was you getting them out of that underground bunker slash lab slash whatever else it was."

If I never have to tell him that there were a few weeks when I believed that the shadowkind under his watch murdered those kids, I'll be ecstatic.

"What *happened* to you?" Pearl asks me with typical awed dramatics. "You went back in and then you just... never came out again. We waited as long as we could—I didn't want to leave."

Andreas answers for me. "The guardians had set a sort of trap for us and knocked us out. I'm not sure how they moved us out of the facility, but when we woke up, we were in a totally different part of the world."

He's tactfully left out Griffin's role in that trap, which is probably the right call, seeing as the shadowkind haven't met Jacob's twin before. I'd rather not sour their first impression of him when we all understand the choices he made and his regrets about them now.

"Did you see anyone coming out at the bottom of the hill?" Zian breaks in with a hint of a growl. "The maniac who had us trapped up there got away from the fire."

"I could feel him heading down a different path for a while," Griffin adds. "I've lost my sense of him now... I never had a very strong grip on it."

Rollick shakes his head. "We didn't see another entrance near this one. But we didn't look very hard. Some of my people waited at the base of the hill as backup—if anyone they weren't expecting came barging out, they'll have caught him."

Pearl bounds ahead faster. "There's the door! Phew, I can't wait to get out of this place."

She has no idea how much I share that sentiment.

We pour out into cool, fresh air on rocky terrain spotted with straggly grass and hunched shrubs. Most of Rollick's "backup" shadowkind must remain in the shadows keeping watch, but one familiar figure wavers into view with a smile already springing to his lips. "You found all of them! And one more."

Billy the faun pauses and blinks at Griffin, tilting his head with its dark waves of hair and spiral horns at a curious angle.

My feet jar to a halt. As I stare, my throat constricts around my voice.

The last time I saw Billy, he was a huddle of broken limbs streaming smoky essence. Because I'd caught him in my shriek, mistaking him for an enemy in the midst of a larger attack.

I can't see any sign of the injuries I dealt to him. His light brown skin is perfectly smooth, his youthful face still full of eager excitement.

He notices me staring, and his smile turns a little tight, as if he's afraid of what I'd have to say to him. "I'm glad you're okay, Riva."

I can't help sputtering a ragged laugh. "I'm glad *you're* okay. I—I'm so sorry. What happened before—I wouldn't have meant to—"

Rollick interrupts my stumbling apology with a brisk wave of his hand. "We can talk about our past mistakes later. Come on—you should see what we've made of your prison."

He sets off toward a low hill dotted with a few leafless trees. As we hurry after him, Billy shoots me another smile, this one more shy than anything. "I know," he says quietly, as if those two words can absolve me of every way I screwed up.

I'm not sure I deserve his forgiveness that easily, but now obviously isn't the time to start flagellating myself.

Rollick stops at the top of the rise and turns to face the towering hill. The rest of us gather around him.

When my gaze lifts to the top of the sheer cliff the villa's grounds were perched on, my jaw goes slack.

The jutting stone precipice looks like a gigantic candle, the entire plateau at its top ablaze. The flames surge up toward the sky all across the hilltop and even partway along the drawbridge that was lowered as some of Balthazar's people must have aimed to escape by the road.

I can't believe anyone still up there could possibly be alive.

Zian lets out an awed whistle, and Jacob gives a crow of delight.

A fresh wave of triumph surges up inside me. *Take* that, *you fucking psychopath!* How the tables have turned.

My satisfaction dims slightly at the thought of Toni. Was she able to make it out?

We might not have if it wasn't for her help.

Then a glowing form materializes right overtop of us with a warble of fire and moving air.

The woman drifts down to the ground across from us, her scarlet hair streaming from its loose ponytail and the massive wings that stretch from her back flapping lazily in the breeze. Every "feather" on those wings is a lick of flame.

As her feet touch the earth, her wings contract and vanish. In the space of a heartbeat, she looks like a mostly normal if striking human being.

She folds her toned arms over her chest and glances back at the hill. "I think I did a pretty thorough job of it. There's nothing up there but cinders now."

When she returns her gaze to us, a glint dances in her copper-brown eyes as if they hold their own flames. "And this bunch must be the shadowbloods I've been hearing so much about. I guess I'm not so special anymore."

I stare at her, momentarily struck dumb.

Rollick steps between us and the fiery woman with a wry grin. "Sorsha, these are the shadowbloods. At least, the oldest of them. Shadowbloods, this is Sorsha—the one other hybrid being I'm aware of in existence."

I manage to reel my jaw back in. "You said you couldn't get in contact with her."

The demon arches his eyebrows. "You've been gone a while. I kept trying."

He tips his head toward her. "Like all of you, she isn't bothered by inconveniences like iron and silver protections. That's why we went with fire as our weapon of choice."

Sorsha laughs. "That's me, phoenix for hire. Not that I've ever bothered to charge you for these epic battles you keep roping me into." She taps her lips. "Come to think of it, I probably should. You've got plenty of dough to cough up."

Rollick rolls his eyes at her. "If you find yourself low on funds, I definitely owe you a few favors."

"Oh, where would the fun be in cashing those in just yet?"

She ambles closer to us, scanning us with open curiosity. "So much for hybrids being the rarest beings in existence. How many of you *are* there altogether? Rollick said there were younger ones too. What—"

The demon clears his throat. "I think we should probably get these kids all the way to safety before we get into any long interrogations."

I would bristle at being called a "kid" if Rollick hadn't mentioned at some point that he's thousands of years old. It's hard to take the label as an insult in that context.

Sorsha bobs her head apologetically. "Right, right. To the Everymobile we go!"

Before I can wonder what the heck an Everymobile is, Dominic gestures to Rollick. "I'm not sure how much farther we should go without getting rid of these." He taps one of his manacles. "The man who trapped us was using them to control us. It's possible he has a way to reactivate the system somewhere else. There's some kind of trigger in them that's supposed to hurt us if we try to break them—"

Sorsha is already reaching for his wrist. "I bet I can take care of that lickety-split."

It actually takes her a few minutes of studying the metal band before her expression firms with certainty. Then there's a flare in her eyes and a faint hiss, and a pleased smirk crosses her lips.

She lets loose another, slightly larger surge of her phoenix fire, and the band completely disintegrates. The dust falls from Dominic's wrist, leaving only a smudge where it used to be—and him completely unharmed.

Once Sorsha knows the part she has to destroy before removing the rest of the manacle, she makes short work of the rest of ours. I'd gotten so used to having them clamped against my skin that I'd barely registered their slim weight unless I was thinking about it. But rubbing my wrists after they're gone, I feel as if someone has lifted an anvil off my heart.

With her on our side, we shouldn't have any trouble finishing the battle we've started today.

Wrists freed, we tramp across the hill and find ourselves faced with a parked RV.

It isn't like the fancy ride Rollick hooked us up with back in Miami. The siding is dented and smudged, the fixtures look like they're from some decade past, and weird protrusions poke from its sides and top: a crooked satellite dish, a propeller, and an assortment of streamers that flutter even while the RV is stopped.

But Sorsha pats the side of the vehicle like you might a horse and beckons us toward the doorway. "Everyone on board!"

I guess a lot of the shadowkind still lurking in the darkness will slip onto the vehicle too. Who knows how many it can hold when they aren't taking physical form?

Rollick, Pearl, Billy, Sorsha, and us six shadowbloods clamber into the cramped retro interior. Zian immediately eyeballs the motor area, maybe using his X-ray vision to compare it to the posh luxury RV we had before.

"We've been getting organized in a rented villa not too far from here," Rollick says, sprawling on the worn but comfy-looking leather seats of the C-like seating area. The layout is pretty similar to his RV even if the styling doesn't match. "We can stop there briefly to get you all patched up and decide on our next steps."

My thoughts dart off into the future. "Balthazar grabbed all the younger shadowbloods too, but he sent them someplace else. We have to get them away from him." My stomach lurches. "Any of them that he hasn't—"

Sorsha interrupts with an urgent sound from the driver's seat. "Thorn and Crag grabbed someone."

We all rush to the front of the RV to peer through the windshield alongside her.

There's no way I could have anticipated the sight that meets my eyes. Two huge, winged men, both even bigger and brawnier than Zian, are soaring toward us, restraining a woman between them.

The shadowkind on the left flaps broad, black-feathered wings, his silver-blond hair streaming behind him like he's some kind of dark angel. He's clamped one hand, the knuckles glinting like crystals, around the woman's wrists, the other arm slung around her shoulders to hold her steady.

His companion appears to be made out of stone, all sharp-edged gray planes. His batlike wings sweep through the air as he holds the woman's lower legs secure.

The woman herself looks absolutely terrified, skin sallow and lips pressed tight. Her black bob has been rumpled by the wind and whatever tussle led to her capture.

But I can easily recognize her all the same.

"That's Toni," I burst out. "She helped us escape—she

was working with Balthazar, but she took our side in the end."

Rollick hums to himself. We hustle back out of the RV to meet the arriving shadowkind.

Sorsha calls to the winged men. "You can put her down. It sounds like she's one of the good guys."

The man with the feathered wings gives her a sternly skeptical look but loosens his grip as he and the living gargoyle touch down. The gargoyle frowns as he lowers Toni's legs so she can stand on her own feet.

She wobbles in her low heels, her jacket askew over her blouse and her stance tensed. Her gaze flicks between the shadowkind arrayed around her before settling on us in their midst.

She's thought of these beings as monsters for at least as long as she's been working for Balthazar. Getting kidnapped by two of them is not how I'd have wanted her introduction to the reality of shadowkind to go.

"I told you I *wanted* to talk to the shadowbloods," she says, managing to keep her voice typically brisk if slightly shaky. "You could have asked them and they'd have confirmed."

The stony guy grunts. "Better to be careful. We're not going to risk getting tricked."

The maybe-angel appears to be a little more courteous. He lowers his head in a brief bow. "I apologize for the unnecessarily unpleasant trip."

"I'm sorry," I say to Toni. "We only just got out—we haven't had the chance to fill them in on all the details."

She exhales with a sigh and gathers herself. "It's been… a chaotic day."

She tucks one arm under the other, and I notice the sleeve is charred. Did her arm get burned?

Dominic can heal her up if so. We owe her that much.

He steps up beside me, possibly thinking the same thing, but before either of us can suggest it, Toni draws her tall frame up even straighter with an air of determination. "I don't know what I'm going to do now. It's not as if I'm equipped to be much of a fighter. But there are things you need to know if you're going to try to free the others like you."

Her gaze rests on me for a second, and something in her expression softens. "I assume that's what you were planning on doing."

I smile crookedly. "I guess you did pay attention to what matters to me even if it took a while for everything to sink in."

Toni grimaces. "I'm sorry. I couldn't say it properly before, but I am. There's so much—"

She stops herself with a press of her hand to her forehead. "We can get into that later. What's important is —he made it out. Balthazar."

We already assumed as much, but I can't help grimacing at the confirmation. "How do you know?"

She pats her jacket pocket, which must hold her phone. "He texted me. I haven't answered yet… Maybe it's better if he thinks I didn't survive. But that's why I knew I had to talk to you."

Dominic studies her. "About what exactly?"

Toni inhales sharply. "That monster, whatever it is you call them, who you turned to before? Rollick?"

Rollick props himself against the front of the RV with

a bemused expression. "That would be me. The preferred term is 'shadowkind,' if it matters to you."

"Right." Toni's throat bobs with a swallow. "You had a theft at your hotel after you left Miami."

The demon's eyes narrow. "I haven't heard any reports of that."

"You wouldn't have," she says. "The mons—the shadowkind Balthazar sent, one he can control, wasn't caught. He didn't take much. And he waited until Balthazar expected you'd be distracted by Riva's message."

My posture goes rigid. "Wait—Balthazar *knew* I'd contacted—then why did he—"

Toni hugs herself. "He wanted you to. That's part of the reason he agreed to your little trip. He figured you'd try something like that, and it would give him an opening. He assumed the villa had enough protections against shadowkind that there was no way they'd actually succeed in making an attack."

He hadn't counted on them having a hybrid they could call on for help—or on Toni turning against him. But…

I knit my brow. "What would he need an opening *for*? What did Rollick have that—"

The answer hits me with an icy smack. Oh, shit.

My voice weakens. "Engel's laptop. I told him that I left it with Rollick. I figured that put it out of his reach anyway, that it couldn't hurt to say it…"

Jacob glances between us, his shoulders flexing with restrained tension. "What the fuck does it matter? What could he get out of Engel's laptop? It didn't do much for us."

"It had all of her notes on it," Dominic puts in. "There were lots we couldn't understand because they were in code."

Andreas makes a face. "He worked closely with her. He might have known how to break it."

Toni nods. "He did. He has her documentation of the original processes she used to create the six of you. Which means he can replicate them."

Zian cocks his head. "But that's not a big problem right away, is it? I mean, any shadowbloods he creates are going to start as *babies*. We can stop him before he could make them hurt anyone."

It's a moment before Toni can seem to find the words. She inhales with a rasp.

"He already had Matteo working on other sorts of procedures. You experienced some variations on those. But he was missing the key…"

The chill that hit me before digs its claws right through my ribs. "What are you saying?"

Toni drags her gaze to meet mine again. "Balthazar has a method for turning fully-grown adults into shadowbloods. I met his first attempt last night—the first soldier in his new army."

About the Author

Eva Chase lives in Canada with her family. She loves stories both swoony and supernatural, and strong women and the men who appreciate them. Along with the Shadowblood Souls series, she is the author of the Heart of a Monster series, the Gang of Ghouls series, the Bound to the Fae series, the Flirting with Monsters series, the Cursed Studies trilogy, the Royals of Villain Academy series, the Moriarty's Men series, the Looking Glass Curse trilogy, the Their Dark Valkyrie series, the Witch's Consorts series, the Dragon Shifter's Mates series, the Demons of Fame series, and the Legends Reborn trilogy.

Connect with Eva online:
www.evachase.com
eva@evachase.com

Manufactured by Amazon.ca
Bolton, ON

33508214R00219